'I must be looking worse than I had thought.'

A little smile hovered at the corners of his lips, and Cecilia thought for a moment that she had never seen so handsome a man.

'I had scarcely seen you,' she excused herself, 'and then there was the lightning. It lit you up. . .' She saw again the tall figure rimmed with that unearthly glow. Her face was more expressive than she knew, and for the first time he smiled a genuine smile.

Dear Reader

We have a Regency treat from Petra Nash this month, when ALL OF HEAVEN follows the tribulations of Miss Cecilia Avening. Lord Marcus Inglesham doesn't know what he holds, but the children make sure he finds out! We welcome back Sarah Westleigh, as she moves from medieval to the Devon of 1866, when eighteen-year-old Charlotte Falconer discovers her real father is Sir George Bradgate. We think you will enjoy HERITAGE OF LOVE. Have fun!

The Editor

Recent titles by the same author:

HEIR APPARENT
MR RAVENSWORTH'S WARD
BRIGHTON MASQUERADE

ALL OF HEAVEN

Petra Nash

First published in Great Britain 1993
by Mills & Boon Limited

© Petra Nash 1993

Australian copyright 1993
Philippine copyright 1993
This edition 1993

ISBN 0 263 78052 X

Masquerade is a trademark published by
Mills & Boon Limited, Eton House,
18–24 Paradise Road, Richmond, Surrey, TW9 1SR.

Set in 10 on 12 pt Linotron Baskerville
04-9305-77263

Typeset in Great Britain by Centracet, Cambridge
Made and printed in Great Britain

CHAPTER ONE

THE stage-coach to London started its journey at the White Lion Inn, Bath. The young woman who took her place on it paid no attention at all to her fellow passengers for the first few miles, but sat with her eyes fixed resolutely on her lap, where her fingers in their neatly darned kid gloves were gripping her reticule with a rather desperate tightness. It was hard, but she had promised herself that she would not give way to emotion, and, although the tears did well up once or twice when her disobedient memory strayed back to the farewells she had just made, she bit her lip and managed to prevent them from falling.

Her companions eyed her and each other, exchanged such greetings as seemed proper to each, and were themselves preoccupied with arranging themselves and their belongings in as comfortable a fashion as might be achieved, and in the usual last-minute worries of most travellers about the locking — or otherwise — of doors and windows, the sending of messages, and the whereabouts of such indispensable items of travel as flasks, smelling salts, and sundry squashy parcels of an edible nature.

The first part of the road was so familiar that Cecilia had no need to glance out of the window by which she sat, but allowed the well-known landmarks to pass by her, seeing them in her mind's eye gilded with the seemingly eternal sunshine of childhood picnics and treats. After a while, however, she risked a glance outside, and saw that she had already passed beyond the limits of the world which, for the last fourteen years, had been her only home since she had arrived, a bewildered and unhappy five-year-old, at the school in Bath that she had just quitted.

Now, at last, she felt her spirits rise. However sad she might feel at saying goodbye to Miss Herring, it was impossible not to feel a lift of excitement at the prospect of going out into the world. And into a world, moreover, that seemed to have decked itself for her particular delight, the April sunshine streaming so brightly from a sky that was almost midsummer-blue, its colour made yet more intense by the puffs of white cloud that raced across it with almost the same abandon as the lambs in the newly verdant fields. After a winter that was the hardest in living memory, with the land held in the grip of ice and snow for more than two months, spring was at last making a delayed, tentative appearance. The first silver-white blossom shivered on cherry and pear trees, and in cottage gardens the daffodil buds were bursting yellow.

To be nineteen, and going to a London where the abdication of the Monster, Napoleon Bonaparte, was already being celebrated with all the abandon that the city could show, was cause enough to set little bubbles of pleasure fizzing in her blood. She would not think of the reception that might await her at the end of her journey, but fixed her imaginings on the promise of the parades, fêtes, fireworks and fairs that the Regent, with his love of display, would be sure to provide.

Some children playing in the roadway waved and shouted as the coach went by, and Cecilia smiled at them, aware as she did so that the stout woman opposite her was leaning forward to wave back, her momentarily unregarded basket sliding forward and threatening to tip altogether from her ample lap. Cecilia put out her hands and steadied it, earning a beam of approval as the woman abandoned her waving and leaned back in her place. The dyspeptic-looking man sitting next to the stout woman looked disparaging.

'Ragamuffins!' he muttered. 'Scandalous, that these children should be playing on the roads! A danger to themselves and to others! They should be at their books, or pursuing some useful activity in the fields, or at home. The parents are much to blame. Don't know what the world's coming to. Never happened in my day.'

The stout woman bridled.

'I would have you know,' she responded, turning her formidable bulk sideways so as to face him fully and allow him to receive the full battery of her displeasure, 'that those are my own niece's children, the pretty dears! Come out a-purpose to wave to me, being as I goes this way every month to visit my sister in Newbury, as is their own dear grandmother. And,' she continued in withering tones, 'no child in my family is sent out to chase crows, or pick stones in the field! The very idea!'

Though momentarily quelled, the thin man made a valiant recovery. He made a jerky little bow, indicative of apology, but the corners of his mouth continued to turn down.

'I beg your pardon, madam, if you consider I have insulted your family. I do not think that the honest labour of a man's — or even a woman's — hand is to be despised. Where should we be if all children were permitted to play all day, and never learned the habits of thrift and industry?'

'Industry?' Her several chins wobbled as she spoke,

and Cecilia watched fascinated. 'I don't think anyone can teach me anything about industry, as was left a widow twenty years ago, and brought up six children alone, aye, and kept my poor husband's farm as it should be kept, until my son was old enough to do it! And my niece's children just the same! Don't the girls bake and sew near as well as a woman grown! And as for the boy, I never saw such a one!'

She was obviously quite prepared to enumerate all their virtues one by one, but her opponent pulled out his handkerchief and silenced her with a loud trumpet blast as he blew his nose.

'I am sure that the children are paragons of all that is good, my dear madam. In that case, might I suggest that it would be a great loss to the world should they, by some mischance, be dashed to pieces among the hoofs of our horses, or by the wheels of a passing carriage? For that, madam, is what they risk by playing on the road!' He gave one last blow to his now reddened nose, took a book from inside his coat, and buried his face in it. Cecilia suppressed a smile, and was somewhat relieved to find that they were pulling up at the Bear Inn in Devizes. Though the halt was but for a few minutes she was glad to climb down and walk up and down while those passengers joining the coach saw to the loading of their luggage, and fussed over whether it was properly roped on.

The young man who had been sitting beside her also alighted. He had been able to see little of her charms, since her bonnet had most effectively hidden her lowered face and her figure was bundled into an old-fashioned travelling cloak rather than a more modish pelisse. He had seen, however, a few wisps of her brown curls, gleaming with tawny lights where the sun caught them, that had escaped springing from within the brim, and he was young and brash enough to take an interest in any female over fifteen and under twenty-five. He made sure that he was in place to hand her back into the coach, and received for his pains a smile that made him blink and blush behind his pimples. Cecilia, whose experience of young men was nugatory, had no idea of the effect of that smile, with its irrepressible dimple in one delicately pink cheek.

The increase in their numbers meant that all the passengers were somewhat squashed, though the fine weather had tempted two of them to sit outside. Cecilia was glad to see another man now sitting between the stout lady and her former adversary, and if her young neighbour was sitting rather closer to her than necessity dictated she was not aware of it. As the coach swept out of the inn yard the stout woman's basket gave another dangerous wobble, and for a second time Cecilia put out her hands to save it.

'Thank you, my dear! And to think I never said anything when you was so good as to help me before! What you must think of me!'

Cecilia smiled and murmured a disclaimer, while her new friend beamed at her, liking the candour in the wide eyes that were the darkest grey she had ever seen, and thickly fringed with lashes that owed nothing of their sooty hue to art, and all to nature. A nice, unaffected young lady, she thought, noting with a quick glance that the gloves, though darned, were of the finest kid, and the half-boots that showed, primly side by side beneath the voluminous hem of the cloak, were of the best quality. Her own mother, who had risen to lady's maid in an earl's establishment before marrying a local farmer, had always told her that a true lady might be known by the quality of her shoes and gloves, however poorly she might be dressed.

'Are you going far, my dear?' She already felt a proprietorial interest in the girl who had smiled so nicely at her niece's children.

'Yes, to London,' Cecilia answered. 'And you? But no, I recall that you said you were going to Newbury, to visit your sister, was it not?' Her bearing was quiet, but lacking in the shyness of a very young girl, and the stout woman cast a quick glance at the left hand, which was ringless so far as she could tell through the well-fitting glove. She mentally revised her companion's age up from the seventeen at which she had originally set it.

'That's right, my older sister she is, a good ten years older, but just as spry as I am, I'm happy to say! She has a little milliner's, in Newbury. Perhaps you know it?'

'I am afraid not. I have never been so far out of Bath as this, at least not since I was very young.'

'You're not so very old as yet, miss,' broke in the youth beside her, with what he fondly imagined was a man-of-the-world air. The thin man ventured another disdainful sniff, and the stout woman sucked in her breath in affront, preparatory to delivering a blistering snub, but Cecilia turned on the young man a look of such candidly shocked surprise that he blushed again, for shame, and mumbled an apology which she accepted with a nicely graded inclination of her head.

'Well! I should think so too!' said the stout lady. 'You don't want to put up with *that* kind of thing, my dear.'

'Oh, I don't think he meant any harm,' said Cecilia with calm kindness, which somehow made the poor youth squirm still more. 'And it is true that I am not very old! But I was only five years old when I came to school in Bath, so you see I am a deal older than that now!'

'Sent to school at five years old! Fancy! Poor little mite, that's just the age of my niece's youngest, and I'd not like to hear her carry-on if someone suggested that she should be sent away to school!'

'Was that the little blonde one who waved to you? She had a sweet little face. But she is lucky to have a good and careful mother in your niece, who will keep her at home and teach her what she needs to know. There is no need to send her away to school at so young an age. But I was so unfortunate as to lose my mama, and that is why I went, for my papa, you see, had died when I was only a baby.'

The stout woman leaned forward, her chins wobbling in sympathetic emotion.

'An orphan, and only five years old! Well I never! What a sad beginning to your life, my dear!'

Cecilia smiled at her.

'Yes, it is, but you must not think that I have been unhappy since then! Miss Herring, who was the governess of my school, was so very kind to me — indeed, she was quite like a mother! I can assure you that I had as happy a childhood as many, and think myself most fortunate.'

The stout woman nodded, but her expression was still sceptical. She had heard of Miss Herring, and knew that her establishment was of the first respectability, but it was inconceivable to her that a spinster lady, however kind, could take the place of a parent, or that a school full of children could be a happy home. Feeling that solace of some kind was called for, she lifted the lid of her capacious basket and rummaged inside, emerging triumphantly with a package neatly done up in clean paper, which she undid to reveal a goodly supply of small cakes and biscuits.

'There! Now, you eat as many of those as you care to, my dear, and you may be sure they will do you no harm, for I made them myself, and there's nothing but the best butter, and fresh eggs from the farm, gone into them.'

Cecilia hesitated. One of Miss Herring's maxims, oft imparted to her charges, was that a lady was never seen eating in a public place. On the other hand, the emotions of the morning had made it impossible for her to swallow any breakfast at all, and she was now very hungry indeed.

'Don't be shy, my dear! I made them for my sister, but she'll not grudge them to you! Now, I shall feel quite hurt if you say no! I'll have one too, to keep you company, and I'm sure you'll not say no, will you, young man? I never knew a lad of your age yet who could say no to food!' In her eagerness to comfort Cecilia with food her new friend was even prepared to overlook the youth's previous behaviour, and it was true that his eyes were sparkling a little, and the shake of his head was lacking in conviction. Cecilia saw that to refuse would cause offence, and with a mental apology to the shadow of Miss Herring she took a cake and a biscuit, and made no bones about enjoying them.

'That's the way! I like to see young people enjoy their food. There's nothing worse, to my way of thinking, than a girl who picks at what's on her plate. No child of mine ever did it, and no more do my niece's. Eat, and be thankful, that's what I say.' She suited the action to the words, and Cecilia felt no qualms in accepting a second piece of cake.

Much refreshed, the stout lady brushed the crumbs

from the ample shelf of her bosom, and set herself to learn more.

'So now you have finished at school, my dear, and are off to London!'

Cecilia swallowed her last mouthful, and wished she might have something to drink. Even in her grief of the morning she had been careful not to drink too much, being uncertain how often the stage would stop, or whether it would be possible to heed the calls of nature when it did so. Such things were never discussed nor referred to at Miss Herring's, and she could not bring herself to ask anyone, so rather than risk embarrassment or discomfort she had scarcely wet her lips with her breakfast cup of tea. Now, after the cakes and biscuits, her mouth was dry, and when her neighbour produced a paper of strong peppermint drops which he offered with diffident humility she was happy to accept one with another of the smiles he had hoped to receive.

'Yes, in a way,' she replied to the stout woman's remark. 'I have not precisely finished at school — that is, I ceased to have lessons two or three years ago. But Miss Herring was kind enough to say that I might stay at the school and help with the little ones. I was very happy to do so.' And relieved, she remembered. It had been a worrying time for her, for she knew very well that the money provided for her education was to cease at her seventeenth birthday, while the small allowance which was to replace it, though it would keep her from absolute destitution, would have been impossible to live on. All of her friends and contemporaries were taken away, one by one, returning to their homes in the joyful knowledge that their lessons were ended, and that ahead of them lay the heady delights of balls, and visits, and coming out.

She parted from each with sadness and tried to be happy for them, and it was true that most kept their promises to write to her. But three of them were now married, and all of them seemed, after a year of absence, to be living in a world so far removed from her own that she could find little of interest to tell them when she wrote. Their letters she enjoyed, reading them as she might have done dispatches from another land, but among the loving words she discerned an embarrassment, an unease that she and her friends could no longer meet as equals. To make it easier for them, she delayed her answers longer and longer, and allowed the correspondences to drop to a twice-yearly epistle.

With no home to return to, she had accepted Miss Herring's offer with relief and happiness. Since it had never occurred to her that she might hope for the pleasures other young women of her class expected as a right, it was no hardship to stay in the safe, happy environment of school, where Miss Herring made a companion of her, and allowed her to sit in her own little parlour in the evenings, and join in the sedate tea parties on Sunday afternoons. The younger girls both loved and respected her, and without realising it she had gained a certain dignity, a self-composure that the stout lady had remarked and wondered at.

The stout lady, who had heard Miss Herring's school spoken of as a place of the utmost respectability, where girls from the best families might be sent to pass their awkward adolescent years, was impressed.

'Miss Herring's? She must have thought very highly of you, miss. I am sure the little girls were lucky to be taught by you.' The young man beside Cecilia opened his mouth to agree, hoping to venture on another attempt at flattery, caught the stout woman's eye, and thought better of it.

'It is kind of you to say so. They were all dear, good girls.' For a moment Cecilia's throat tightened, but she swallowed and blinked away the threatening tears. They did not, however, go unnoticed.

'And now the school is to close! That's a pity, for it's very well thought of, I know.'

'Yes. Miss Herring had a fall, last year, and broke her leg. It has healed now, but she no longer feels able to take on the responsibility of the school. All the girls went home at Christmas time, and I stayed on to help her. You may imagine how much there was to do! We have been so busy, these last months, but now Miss Herring is happily settled, and she has let part of the house to a very nice family, so she will not be lonely.'

'And you, miss! Where will you go now?' Without really being aware of it, the stout woman had ceased to call Cecilia 'my dear', though she felt no less sympathy for her.

'I have relatives in London, who have kindly agreed to receive me.' If the stout woman had a low opinion of relatives who would allow a gently brought-up young woman, coming from the sheltered cloisters of a girls' school, to travel alone on the common stage, she did not express it, but her lips creased a little as if she was tightening them to keep the words pent up. Cecilia was not aware of it. Her eyes had strayed to the window, where the brilliant sunshine — too brilliant, the ostler at Bath had been heard to say — was now dimmed. The white puffs of cloud that had earlier disported themselves in the clear sky were gone, and in their place a thick bank of grey, so dark as to be the colour of slate, was advancing towards them. The outside passengers, who had thought themselves safe, could be heard asking each other's opinion, and that of the driver, in anxious tones, and it seemed that the answer they had did little to reassure them.

Cecilia, however, was impervious to the change in the weather. As the cloud had darkened the beauty of the day, so her companion's questions had darkened her own optimism. The end of her journey, about which she had determined not to worry, loomed more and more threatening with every turn of the wheels, and she found herself wondering how it would be.

Her father, who, as she had told her companion, had died when she was scarcely a year old, had been the younger son of an earl. Reckless, extravagant and pleasure-seeking, he had been the despair of his parents and when, at the age of thirty, he had announced his intention to marry the governess of his cousin's children, they had washed their hands of him completely. The daughter of an impoverished parson, she was good, clever and pretty. Indeed, if she had been better born, they would have been overjoyed to have his fancy light on a girl so well calculated to reform his profligate ways. The Earl, and more importantly the Countess, were, however, unable to see anything but that their son had disgraced his family by allying himself with one who in their eyes was scarcely more than a servant, and they had declined to receive the bride, or to have any further dealings with their son.

In his rage and hurt Cecilia's father had vowed that he would neither ask for, nor accept, anything from the family that would not acknowledge his wife. Untrained as he was for any kind of gainful employment, he had lived on his wits and succeeded in providing a respectable home for her and for the child that was born to

them, until the unfortunate day when, recklessly riding
a half-broken colt for a wager that would, if he had won
it, have given them several months of comfortable living,
he had been thrown and died instantly from a broken
neck.

His widow, too proud to go for help to the family that
had spurned her, had survived on her savings and the
income from the one thousand pounds that had been
settled on her at her marriage, and made what money
she could from her water-colour paintings, until when
Cecilia was four she had met and married her second
husband, a well-to-do attorney. As Mrs Ruspidge she
had known a year of contentment, and Cecilia herself
was kindly, if distantly, treated. All too soon, however,
she had found herself with child, and expired giving
birth to a baby that never breathed. With her last words
she had begged her husband to care for her orphan
child, and he had kept his promise to the best of his
ability. Unable, or unwilling, to keep Cecilia in his own
home, he had sent her to a good school, and conscien-
tiously paid her fees there. When he had married again,
his second wife was known to query the expense, and
complain that so costly an education was unnecessary
and took the bread from the mouths of her own little
ones.

Mr Ruspidge had steadfastly ignored such remarks.
Though certainly not born to the higher ranks, he was
still a gentleman, though his grandfather had been an
ironmonger. He had inherited a very comfortable portion, and had assured the wife of his bosom that he was
well able to support his stepdaughter at her school. If,
however, his dear wife wished to have the child home,
and bring her up with her own family, she was quite at
liberty to do so. This, not unnaturally, had given the

second Mrs Ruspidge pause, and when she had found
that her husband was quite prepared to pay for an
equally expensive education for a second stepchild, her
own son by her first marriage, her scruples melted like
snow on a chimney stack.

If virtue be rewarded, then it was certain that Mr
Ruspidge had his reward, for he had several peaceful
and happy years with his second wife, and when death
had come it visited him so gently that he did not even
rouse from his sleep, but let his soul go between one
breath and the next. His will had provided for the
continuing education of both his stepchildren, and his
widow was by then so used to the situation that she
scarcely gave Cecilia another thought.

When her own son had finished at school, and came
home to lead the life of gentlemanly leisure for which
she felt his education had fitted him, a few uncomfortable recollections did cross her mind. On enquiry,
however, she had found that the money for the young
girl she had never seen was to cease on her seventeenth
birthday, after which time she was to have the income
from her mother's one thousand pounds, which Mr
Ruspidge had scrupulously set aside for her to inherit at
the age of twenty-one. Since this amounted only to fifty
pounds a year Mrs Ruspidge had vaguely supposed that
the girl would find herself employment as a governess.
When a dutiful letter had arrived from Cecilia informing
her that she was to continue at Miss Herring's she wrote
an enthusiastic answer, warmly promising what she felt
sure would never be required, a welcome and a home if
need should arise.

Now, however, the need had most definitely arisen,
and Cecilia wondered uneasily what kind of welcome
really awaited her. When Miss Herring had first told

her of the decision to finish the school, she had taken
out that pleasant epistle from Mrs Ruspidge, and read
it over again. Two years older, and a great deal wiser
than she had been then, it no longer seemed quite so
sincere, but since she had no choice she wrote to her
stepfather's wife — the relationship so distant that it
could hardly be acknowledged as existing — and asked
whether she might come to her, stating plainly that she
had no one else to ask, and no other place where she
might reasonably expect to find shelter. The answer was
long in arriving, and reluctant in tone. Mrs Ruspidge
could not refuse to receive her, but quite obviously
expected that this importunate poor relation would
waste no time in finding herself a position in some other
household.

That had been before Christmas, and since then
Cecilia had heard nothing. Busy as she had been with
the winding up of the school, she had managed to put
her fears for the future out of her mind, but now they
recurred with horrid frequency. Perhaps the stout
woman read some of this on her face, for she delved
once again in her basket, and Cecilia was obliged to
stand firm in refusing a piece of soggy gingerbread that
she knew would make her thirst well-nigh unbearable
as well as making her fingers disgustingly sticky.

By now the outside world was growing darker by the
minute, though it was still a little short of midday, and
nasty gusts of wind were buffeting the coach, sending
little whistles of cold damp air through the interstices of
windows and doors. The hilly nature of the country,
which made the road far from straight as well as sending
it up and down some unnervingly steep slopes, now
became actively unpleasant. What, in fine sunny
weather, had seemed no more than a swaying motion

now took on the horrid connotations of a ship on a
rough sea. One of the passengers was looking decidedly
green, and Cecilia wedged herself firmly in her corner,
and set herself to endure.

It was with the deepest relief, therefore, that she saw
that they were coming into a town, which she thought
must be Newbury. Anxiously reckoning up the money
in her purse, she wondered whether she could afford to
stay there until the following day, in the hope that the
bad weather would have abated by then. At least, she
thought, she could have a drink of something, and a
breath of air would be welcome too. As they passed into
the yard of the inn their eyes were momentarily dazzled
by an incandescent flash of lightning, followed almost
immediately by the cracking roar of thunder. The
outside passengers were down from the roof almost
before the coach had come to a standstill, but not before
the rain had begun to fall. A flurry of heavy drops,
blown by the wind so that they hit the window almost
like shot, was its harbinger, and two seconds later the
sheeting rain was drumming and hammering on the
roof, while outside it rebounded from the cobbles as if it
had a life of its own.

It might stop within minutes, or it could go on for
hours. The warm glow from the inn windows could not
be resisted, and Cecilia lifted the hood of her cloak over
what was, though decidedly unmodish, her best bonnet,
clutched the rest of the cloak around her, and jumped
nimbly down from the coach, followed by her youthful
neighbour, and ran for the shelter of the doorway.

Inside, all was confusion. Several passengers from the
stage were vying for attention with the owners of other
vehicles, who had outrun the weather to get themselves
and their horses into shelter before the storm should

strike. All were wet, and cold, and demanding hot drinks, hot fires, hot bricks, and hot meals, while the landlord endeavoured to satisfy everyone and keep the various orders clear in his mind. Cecilia could see that she was unlikely to receive much attention at present, and since she rated her own claims to importance fairly low she was not at all affronted, but called to the coachman to have her box brought indoors, and calmly moved away from the doorway, where more and more people were crowding in.

At the far side of the room a further door stood half open, with a gleam of firelight shining through it. Abandoning, for the moment, any hope of obtaining something to drink, she moved towards it, in the hope that it might be a little quieter. As she reached the doorway, however, a shrill scream rang out, piercing through the clamour of voices in the tap-room and momentarily stilling it. Without stopping to think, Cecilia pushed open the door, and stepped forward.

A young girl, not a child, but still in the simple round gown of the schoolroom, lay back in a wooden settle, her fists tightly clenched and her face red. She was already drawing breath to scream again, and behind her in the corner of the room two little girls, aged, Cecilia guessed, between ten and seven years, huddled together, the elder holding the younger, who was also crying, but more quietly. Standing over them was a man, the type of man that Cecilia had only ever glimpsed in the distance in Milsom Street, or making his way to the Assembly Rooms. From the top of his fashionably cut dark hair, almost brushing the black old beams of the ceiling, to his gleaming hessians he proclaimed the non-pareil. Inexperienced though she was in such matters, even Cecilia could see that his neckcloth was tied to perfection, and the dark blue coat that sat so snugly across the broad shoulders had been cut by the hand of a master.

His dark brows were drawn together in a frown, and if he was aware of his audience or of Cecilia standing in the doorway he ignored them superbly.

'For God's sake, girl, stop screaming and listen to me! I tell you, I can do nothing about it!' The girl wailed and he turned away, smiting one fist down into his other open hand. 'What have I done to be persecuted like this? Can no one do something to quiet this wretched creature?'

As he finished this presumably rhetorical question there was another flash of lightning, so that for a moment he stood blackly silhouetted against its blue-white shine. The girl screamed, and screamed again, but the sound of her heels drumming on the floor was quite drowned by the thunder from without.

CHAPTER TWO

WITH a little exclamation Cecilia stepped briskly into the room, closing the door firmly behind her in the face of the interested spectators. The two little girls watched her round-eyed, and the gentleman with supercilious surprise, while she crossed the room to the window, ignoring for the moment the oldest girl, who continued to scream, her eyes screwed shut and her hands now clasped over her ears. The window, since it looked directly out into the road, was supplied with stout shutters which Cecilia closed and barred before drawing the curtains, dusty but heavy and thickly lined, as well.

'If I had wished to have the curtains pulled, I should have rung,' said the gentleman curtly. 'I have engaged this as a private room.'

'I beg your pardon, sir, but I think that you will find that it helps,' she said, stepping round his tall form to stand by the hysterical girl. Cecilia glanced at him as she spoke, but her attention was clearly on the eldest girl. Since she was, by nature, of a practical rather than a melodramatic turn of mind, it had not occurred to her to think that she was assisting in any kind of kidnap, or that the man whose handsome, aquiline features stared haughtily down at her harboured any violent or immoral intentions towards any of them.

She stepped over the kicking feet and took the girl's hands in her own, pulling them gently but firmly away from her head and holding them in a comforting clasp.

'Come, now, my dear,' she said, not raising her voice

but speaking distinctly and with authority, 'you are making yourself very ridiculous, you know.'

The girl drew in a breath, but the scream she was preparing for died away into a whimper and she opened her eyes. Curiosity stilled her drumming feet, and she considered what Cecilia had said. No one knew better than Cecilia that while girls of her age frequently courted attention rather than shrinking from it, nothing could more easily deter them than the prospect of being laughed at. To be the object of interest as one who was in the throes of tragedy or romance was one thing: to be ridiculous, quite another.

The lightning was hidden from the room by the shutters and the curtains, but they could not muffle the thunder, which chose that moment to erupt once again. The girl shrank back, her face contorted and her hands clutching at Cecilia's, and she gave a little cry.

'Good girl,' said Cecilia approvingly. 'You see, already your self-control is returning to you. You would not want, after all, to frighten your sisters, would you?'

It was a guess, but not a difficult one since all three girls shared the same ash-blonde hair and blue eyes. The elder of the little ones wrinkled her nose.

'*I'm* not frightened,' she said scornfully. 'Minty is, because she's only seven.'

'Quite so, and I expect you are—what? Eleven, perhaps?'

'Ten,' she responded, gratified. 'Well, ten and a half, nearly.'

'And you have been looking after Minty? What a very curious name, to be sure. Are you called Parsley?'

The girls giggled, the little one abandoning herself to laughter and rolling on the cushions, displaying in the process an amount of chubby leg, encased in well-frilled

pantalettes that would have had Miss Herring clicking
her tongue in horror. The gentleman, however, seemed
not at all shocked, though he declined to smile. He
folded his arms in a forbidding fashion, and kept his
smouldering glare on Cecilia. It had to be admitted that
she had succeeded in quieting the girls, and he had no
wish to be thrown back into the kind of scene to which
he had been treated a few minutes since.

'Parsley! Parsley! Sage and Onion!' chanted the child,
while the ten-year-old, less uninhibited in her mirth,
giggled behind her hands.

'No,' she said at last. 'I'm Sophronia, and she——'
pointing to Minty '—is Araminta. And she's Cleone,'
she added, rather as an afterthought.

'Goodness, what very. . .very unusual names,' said
Cecilia in admiring tones. The girl beside her, though
she still quivered convulsively with every crack of thunder, was no longer making any noise, and mercifully the
storm seemed to be receding a little, and the interval
between each rumble was longer.

'Well, if you are all feeling better, I might be permitted to order a luncheon, and then perhaps we may
continue our journey?' The gentleman spoke with what
he hoped were cheerful and encouraging tones, but
while the two younger girls looked happy at the prospect
of a meal the older snatched her hands from Cecilia's
hold, and threw herself back into the corner from which
she had started to emerge.

'Continue our journey! Oh, no, I can't bear it! It is
too much, you are too cruel, you are horrid, and a
beast!'

'That will do.' Cecilia spoke a voice that brought the
girl up short, and had her staring up into the stern face
of the person she had thought would support her.

'But you don't understand. . .' It was a wail for sympathy, but Cecilia shook her head.

'I understand very well, but nothing can excuse your speaking in such a fashion. I think you should apologise to your father at once. Think what an example you set your sisters!'

To her dismay this stern remark made the two little girls dissolve yet again into giggles, while the afflicted Cleone sat up once more.

'Him! My father! My father would never treat me like this! My father is the kindest man on earth, and would never be so cruel to me! My father——'

'Your father has allowed you to grow into an over-indulged minx!' put in the gentleman roundly. Cecilia had some little sympathy with this opinion, but Cleone burst into tears, real ones this time, and flung herself against Cecilia, clasping her arms round her waist and burying her face against her. Cecilia looked up at him in some dismay, seeing for the first time that he was a great deal younger than she had realised.

'I beg your pardon, sir——' she began.

'I should think you might,' he interrupted rudely. 'Did you really think me old enough to have fathered Cleone? I must be looking worse than I had thought.'

A little smile hovered at the corners of his lips, and Cecilia thought for a moment that she had never seen so handsome a man. His skin was rather dark, with the tanned look of the inveterate sportsman, and against it his eyes were a piercing blue, rather cold and hard at this moment, and surmounted by heavy dark eyebrows that gave his face, even in repose, a stern expression.

'I had scarcely seen you,' she excused herself, 'and then there was the lightning. It lit you up. . .' She saw again the tall figure rimmed with that unearthly glow.

Her face was more expressive than she knew, and for the first time he smiled a genuine smile.

'Did it? How very Mephistopholean.'

'Yes, it was rather,' she agreed, smiling candidly back.

'I always said he was a devil,' mumbled Cleone between her sobs. For a moment their eyes met in an instant of shared amusement, then Cecilia put the girl firmly away from her embrace.

'Well,' she said briskly, 'though your *manners* might leave much to be desired, I am glad to see that your *education* at least has not been neglected. The fact that this gentleman is not your father makes no difference to the respect you owe him. I am still waiting for an apology.'

Cleone gave a forlorn sniff, and was promptly handed a large handkerchief by her adversary.

'Come, now, Cleone,' he said, not unkindly, 'let us have an end of this wrangling. Confess that I am not always a horrid beast, and that there have been times in the past when I have been your favourite uncle.'

'But you are my only uncle!' she said with a watery smile.

'Then I must be the best one, mustn't I? Only you have not seen me for a year or two, and I had not expected to find you grown into a young lady while I was away.'

'Oh, dear, and I was so naughty to you! I'm sorry, Uncle Marcus, truly I am. Please, please forgive me!'

Cleone's apology bid fair to be as histrionic as her other moods, but when she would have thrown herself into his arms he put his hands on her shoulders, and held her at arm's length.

'Let us speak of it no more. It is more than time that

we ordered something to eat, and then I suppose that I must see about taking rooms for the night, since you will not travel further today.'

'I cannot, Uncle Marcus, I assure you. Please do not make me!' It was a cry from the heart, but he frowned.

'My dear girl, I am not trying to torture you,' he said in some irritation. 'It is only that I promised your father to get you home today. Ordinarily, I suppose, one day would be neither here nor there, but in the circumstances. . .'

'I know, and I would not for the world have Papa think that I am reluctant to meet his. . .that is to say, to meet my new mama. But if you knew how I felt!'

'I do not, but I can see that you are in earnest. Very well, I shall go and send word to the stables. Now do wash your face, like a good girl, and tidy yourself up. Perhaps this lady. . .?' He looked an enquiry.

'I shall be speaking to the landlord about a room, and will take the young ladies upstairs with me.'

'You are very good. I will see if there is not a private room upstairs, where we may eat. Perhaps you would care to join us in a luncheon?'

Cecilia withdrew a little, looking about her for her reticule, which she had cast from her on first entering the room.

'No, no, I would not intrude!' she said, flustered. 'I must speak to the landlord——'

'It is no intrusion, but the greatest favour,' he assured her. Cleone added her own assent, and the little girls were quick to cluster round her, the youngest putting a sadly grubby hand confidingly into hers, and hanging on it. 'I think my nieces would be glad of your protection,' he said wryly. 'I am quite well known in Newbury, and I am sure the landlord will vouch for me. My name is Inglesham.'

It had to be admitted that the prospect of luncheon was very tempting, the more so as her slender means would be stretched to the utmost if she must stay the night here, which she was hoping to do. The thunder had now died away to an occasional mutter, but the rain fell as heavily as ever, and it was quite obvious that the rest of the journey to London would be damp, slow and uncomfortable.

'Thank you, sir. I am most happy to accept,' she said, with a small reverence. 'I am Cecilia Avening.'

'Avening, eh? Any relation of the Earl of Syreford?'

'He is my grandfather, sir. But I should tell you at once that he doesn't acknowledge the connection.'

'Does he not? Well, it makes no odds. Stiff-necked old fellow, and as for the Countess. . . If you think me harsh and strict, Cleone, then just thank your lucky stars you do not have her for an uncle! I never met such a Gorgon!' He accorded his niece a careless flick on the cheek, and left the room.

'Well, really,' said Cleone, torn between anger and admiration, 'if I was rude, what was that? Imagine calling your grandmother a Gorgon!'

'The gentlemen, my dear,' said Cecilia, quoting one of the other great maxims of Miss Herring, 'must be allowed a licence that would be entirely improper in a female.'

'Must they?' Araminta was interested by this idea. 'Always? It doesn't sound a very good idea to me. Does that mean all gentlemen, or only lords like Uncle Marcus?' Cecilia felt unequal to the task of explaining, and shepherded the three girls up the stairs. She was thankful to have learned of her prospective host's title, before she had committed the solecism of calling him Mr Inglesham.

The landlord's wife took them to a pleasant room where a fire was already lit, and a large ewer of hot water awaited them on the washstand. They took turns to make use of the close-stool, modestly hidden behind a screen, and then washed faces and hands. There was scented soap, and an abundance of hot water and towels, and Cecilia revelled in what was, to her, luxury. All three girls brushed their hair, and Cecilia envied them its smooth waviness, taking off her own bonnet and surveying the result with dismay.

Her hair had always been a trial to her. It was very thick, and curled with such abundant vitality that as a child she had shed many a tear as she tried with comb and brush to smooth its tangles and knots. When she was no longer a schoolgirl, and might with propriety put it up, things became a little easier, but still she had to struggle, for brush and pin as she might the curls still resisted being ordered. However neatly and carefully she might arrange them in the morning there would soon be a halo of ringletted curls round her face and on her neck, while any sudden movement would invariably loosen the heavy mass from its moorings, so that it tumbled in a waterfall of springing curls down her back to her waist. When other girls complained of the discomfort of sleeping in curl papers, she was inclined to look at them in envy.

The removal of her bonnet did exactly that, and with an exclamation of dismay she hunted in her reticule for the brush she always carried with her, and the hairpins.

'Oh, what lovely hair!' exclaimed Cleone. 'I wish mine would curl like that!' She reached out a finger and twined one of the ringlets round it, pulling it down for the pleasure of seeing it spring back into place.

'You would not say that if it did,' said Cecilia grimly, setting her teeth while she dragged the brush ruthlessly through her hair, blinking away the tears that sprang to her eyes at the sharp tugs on her scalp.

'Oh, don't! You'll put it out at the roots, like that. Let me brush the tangles for you.'

'It would take too long. You have no idea what it is like! If I stopped to untangle it now, we should get no luncheon for at least an hour!' Swiftly Cecilia coiled up the recalcitrant curls, pinning them as firmly and severely as she could, so tightly that she could feel the tension in the skin at the side of her eyes. 'There, now my eyes are nearly as red as yours,' she joked to Cleone.

'Are they very bad?' The girl leaned to the glass, peering anxiously at her reflection.

'No, not at all! Hot and cold water, that's all they needed.'

'I know it is very silly, to be so frightened of thunderstorms,' said the girl, shamefaced. 'I don't know why it is, but I just feel so terrified, and the thought of being out in one, in the carriage. . .' She shuddered at the idea.

'I was frightened too,' pointed out Araminta kindly, rather spoiling it by adding, 'but I didn't make so much fuss, of course.'

'No, because I looked after you,' pointed out Sophronia, who saw it as her duty to depress any pretensions in her younger sister. 'Cleone has always been like that, Miss Avening,' she said in motherly tones. 'Grandmama says she can't help it.'

'My mama died in a thunderstorm,' said Cleone in a low, sad voice. 'Oh, not in it, you understand! She was not struck by lightning, or anything like that! Only there was a storm the night she died. Sophie and Minty don't remember it, they were so little — Minty was just a new baby. But I don't believe I shall ever forget it.'

'But now you have a new mama? I could not help hearing you say that.'

'Yes, and we have not met her yet! We usually live with Grandmama, in the country, and Papa comes to visit us as often as he can. He is very busy, you know. He is something to do with the Government, only he has never quite made me understand what he does. And he has been staying in Scotland, the past few months, and imagine how surprised we all were to hear that he has decided to marry again! It is to be next month, in London, and we are to be there.'

Cecilia was touched by the tone of determined cheerfulness in the girl's voice. For Cleone, at least, the thought of replacing a well-loved and still remembered mother was not an easy one. She found herself hoping very fervently that their father had chosen wisely, and that the stepmother would be kindly disposed to her new family.

'That will be very exciting,' she said, rising and leading the way to the door. 'And you know nothing of her yet?'

'Only that she is younger than Papa, though twenty-five is not very young, is it?'

Reflecting that to fifteen anyone over twenty was regarded as being elderly, Cecilia said solemnly that she thought twenty-five an excellent age for a new mama.

'Yes, for it would have been embarrassing if she had been too young, yet one would not wish Papa to marry an elderly lady.'

'And she might have dear little babies!' announced Araminta in clear, forthright tones.

'Oh, hush, Minty,' begged Cleone. 'It is not proper to speak of such things yet!'

'Why not? Mary at the farm has two dear little babies, and she was married when she was twenty-five. Shouldn't you like a little sister or brother to play with, Cleone? I think it would be lovely.'

'Yes, it would be, but one does not talk of such things before the wedding.' Cleone looked embarrassed, but Minty was not to be stopped.

'Why not? Mary was already talking about her little baby, before she was married. Well, of course, she was bound to, because she was already born. Cleone, why —— ?'

'I think you would do better to follow your sister's example, rather than Mary's,' said Cecilia with the quelling look that all good teachers could summon at will. Slightly chastened, the little girls followed them in silence, and they found their way to the private parlour that had been prepared for them. Lord Inglesham looked approvingly at the three girls, privately amazed that the dishevelled, travel-stained creatures could so quickly have been transformed into these models of cleanliness and decorum.

The meal passed without incident, largely because all the young ladies were very hungry and did full justice to the capons, the veal and ham pie and the ragout that the waiter brought them, along with a dish of early asparagus and another of neats' tongues. Their mouths were too full for speech, and Marcus Inglesham watched in some amusement as they worked their way through the courses. So many young ladies of his acquaintance, he reflected, merely toyed with their food, and it was quite a pleasure to see his charges eat. By the time they had made healthy inroads into some pippin tarts, and a syllabub, he was leaning back in his chair with a glass of wine in his hand. Cecilia, offered a glass of wine, had refused it with some confusion, and drank lemonade with the children. He suspected that she had never drunk anything stronger than negus, and he was touched when she candidly avowed, having refused a second portion of tart with reluctance, that she had never eaten so delicious a meal.

'Miss Herring believed that good plain food was best for young people,' she said, rather wistfully.

'So does Grandmama,' said Araminta. 'But when Papa comes, we have all kinds of treats! Maybe we shall always eat like this, now that we are to live with him!'

'I sincerely hope not,' Marcus Inglesham said, rising to his feet. 'You would become disgustingly fat, and wheeze like Grandmama's pug.'

'Oh, I would not, would I, Miss Avening?' The round blue eyes were turned on her appealingly.

'Well, you might, you know. And I don't believe it would be a treat any more, if you had all these dishes every day.'

Lord Inglesham, with a word of apology, took himself off to the tap-room to smoke a cigarillo, leaving the girls in Cecilia's care as a matter of course. She was quite willing, though she was beginning to worry about ordering herself a room, and could only hope that the landlord would find a corner for her somewhere. Cleone, exhausted by emotion, was quite content to lie down on her bed for an hour or two, and Cecilia kept the young girls amused with paper games and, when they tired of those, with stories. Inglesham returned to find her sitting and staring into the fire, while the two girls slumbered on either side of her as they sat on a sofa, each with a head on her shoulder.

'How very uncomfortable you look,' he said.

'Oh, hush, do not waken them!' she begged. 'A sleep now will do them good, for I think they none of them slept last night, for excitement. If you would just hold Minty. . .' Carefully she rearranged the cushions so that the two girls might lie each in her corner of the sofa, then stood up and walked to the window. It was almost dark outside, and the rain continued to fall.

'If you will excuse me, my lord, I must speak to the landlord. I must have a room and book a seat on the stage for tomorrow.'

'I am afraid you might have some difficulty,' he said. 'Several people have decided to break their journey because of the weather, and I know for a fact there is not a room to be had, for I heard others asking. The stage, too, is likely to be full, and I do not suppose you would want to travel outside.'

'Well, if I must, I must. But for tonight, what is to be done? I must speak to him at once.'

She would have hurried to the door, but he put out a hand to prevent her.

'Just a moment, Miss Avening. I have a suggestion to put to you that I think might benefit both of us. You are aware, I think, of the reason why I am taking my nieces to London?'

'Yes. Cleone has spoken of it to me. They seem happy at the news, although she is, I think, a little fearful, which is only too natural.'

'Indeed. It was a sad loss to us all when my sister died. She was. . .but there, that is all long in the past now. And my brother-in-law is to marry a second time, and has chosen most unexceptionably. His wife will, I believe, be a kind and careful mother to his children. And, I hope, a moderately firm one. Cleone, in particularly, has been much indulged by her father, and by my mother also, who has had the care of them since my sister's death. Not that I blame her, you understand, but still I would not like to see my nieces display such behaviour as I have seen today in the public eye.'

'Of course you would not, though in Cleone's case I think it is simply her age, which is an awkward one for many girls, compounded by her extreme fear of thunderstorms. Forgive me, but are you aware that her mother died during just such a storm?'

He frowned.

'No. To my everlasting regret I was abroad, at the time. I am glad you have told me. Did you think me very unfeeling?'

'Not at all. Merely lacking, a little, in experience of young girls.'

He thought he could have told her otherwise, but recollected that he was thinking of a very different class of girl.

'You had something to say to me?' she reminded him.

'Yes, I had digressed. Merely, I wished to beg your company on our journey tomorrow.'

'My company? But I am to travel on the stage.'

'Then I beg that you will reconsider. You have seen, I think, how ill-fitted I am to look after these girls! Normally, of course, I should not have been asked to do so, or at least only with the help of their governess, but she, poor woman, has been taken very ill. She is not a young woman, and took a severe chill while out walking with my nieces, which I fear has gone to her chest. My mother begged me, since I was visiting her for a few days, to see the girls safely conveyed to London, and I admit that I did not understand what I was taking on when I agreed to do so!'

She was silent, thinking. It was true that Lord Inglesham was finding his charges troublesome, and also true that she would certainly be far more comfortable travelling in what she felt sure was his own carriage, rather than in the crowded and chilly stage-coach, or worse still outside it. But should she do such a thing? She had so little experience of the outside world, but she was well aware that to be travelling with a gentleman of his lordship's age and undoubted attractions might damage the reputation that was her only recommendation.

'It would be quite proper, you know,' he said, as if reading her mind. 'I should not have asked you, if it had not been. Alone with me, of course, would be quite another thing, but I do not believe anyone could think you in danger of seduction with three such chaperons to protect you!'

Cecilia blushed a little, but did not turn away her head, and he thought vaguely that it was refreshing not to encounter any assumed coyness.

'I suppose it would be all right,' she said slowly, 'if you are quite sure. Will it not make you very crowded? You are not asking just out of kindness, are you?'

'My dear girl, I am afraid that it would not have crossed my mind,' he avowed candidly. 'The truth is, you have the knack of managing young girls, and I can see very well that, without you, my journey tomorrow will be almost as hideous as was that of today! I should in fairness warn you that Sophie, though she was not actually ill, felt very sick for much of the time, and that Minty never stopped talking!'

'In that case, I do not see how I can possibly refuse,'

she laughed. 'But where am I to sleep? Will you speak to the landlord for me? I feel that a word from you would go rather further than mine.'

'No need, if you do not object to sharing a room with the girls. An extra bed has already been set up in there, and there is plenty of room for another.'

He was rather high-handed, but she had to admit that it was a relief to have all the arrangements taken out of her hands, and to know that for tonight, at least, she would not have to worry about expenses. Cleone, entering at that moment, heard the news with flattering pleasure, and her exclamations woke the younger girls, who were full of excitement.

'Now you will be able to tell us more stories!' pointed out Araminta.

'So I shall,' Cecilia replied with commendable enthusiasm. The rest of the day passed amicably enough, and Marcus Inglesham surprised himself by joining in a simple round game with as much enthusiasm as if he were playing whist at his club. So amiable was his mood that Cleone ventured to tease him a little.

'I know why you were so eager to reach London tonight!' she said in a stage whisper. 'What will you give me not to tell?'

'A silver new nothing,' he responded promptly, 'since I have nothing to hide.'

'Had you not hoped to meet a certain lady this evening? Is there not a Miss C. watching the door for you?'

'If there is a Miss C., you may be sure she is far too well-bred to watch the door for any man. And where, pray, did you have this information from? Your grandmama, I suppose?'

'Yes, and she is so pleased! She says it is more than

time for you to settle down, and she is in constant expectation of hearing your engagement announced!'

He frowned a little, but did not seem too displeased. Cecilia was far from surprised to hear that so eligible and personable a gentleman should be contemplating matrimony. She did not even envy Miss C., whoever she might be. To be courted by a lord was so far beyond her imaginings that she could only look on it from afar, and wonder at it.

As for Lord Inglesham, it was true that he had expected to spend the evening dancing with Miss Chadworth. In his mind's eye he pictured her elegant figure, dressed always in the height of fashion, pacing the floor of Almack's. That she would not watch the door for him was certain, for her manners were too exquisite to permit such behaviour, but would she miss him? He rather thought that she would. He had recently begun to see, in her fine hazel eyes, a certain complacency when she looked upon him that he did not find displeasing. Well-born, well-educated and well-dowered, she was precisely the kind of woman that a man in his position should marry, and he was already more than half inclined to ask her. With his father dead, and himself an only son, he was quite as alive to his duties to the family name as his mother was.

Such a wife would grace his house, his table and his bed, and he did not think that she would frown on his continuing to frequent such places of pleasure as he was accustomed, from time to time, to go to. As long as he was discreet, he felt sure that she would maintain her air of well-bred calm, and provide him with exactly the sort of peaceful, well-organised home that he had always known.

CHAPTER THREE

CECILIA thought that she was only able to appreciate how very uncomfortable the stage-coach had been after she had spent an hour travelling with Lord Inglesham. For one thing, her fears about cramping them by her presence proved completely groundless. Though the conveyance appeared smaller and neater, to the outward eye, than the public coach, inside it seemed almost spacious. Cleone sat beside her uncle, while Cecilia was opposite them and between the two younger girls, and it seemed to her that, should the necessity arise, there would be room for both the girls to curl up on the seat, and sleep with their heads against her. The seat itself was soft, upholstered in fine leather that felt as smooth as silk to the touch, and there were foot warmers as well as woollen lap rugs, so they need not fear any sudden April chill.

The storm had vanished overnight, leaving a muddy road well mirrored with puddles, but at least Cleone need not fear for a recurrence of the previous day, and a night's sleep had restored her to what Cecilia assumed to be her usual good-humour. Thatcham and Woolhampton were soon passed, and the flatter nature of the countryside meant that their ride was much steadier, and Sophronia's cheeks kept their pretty pink colouring. As Lord Inglesham had warned her, Araminta kept up a flood of conversation, most of it quite inconsequential, and straying between Mary at the farm's babies, Grandmama's bad chest and the sundry remedies recommended for it, the new clothes they would all have for Papa's wedding, whether they would be permitted to visit Astley's Amphitheatre as they had done when last they went to London, exactly how fat the Prince Regent was, and her conviction that Cleone's singing was prettier than any ever heard in Covent Garden.

'Oh, hush, Minty!' Cleone blushed. 'It is not so very good as all that!'

'Well, you told me yourself that Mrs Hartfield told Grandmama that you could rival anything she had heard in London! And Mr Minchin said that you were the most promising pupil he had ever taught! And. . .'

Cleone frowned, and shook her head, but did not attempt to deny her sister's claims, and Cecilia could see that she was in fact a little proud of her talent.

'How very fortunate you are, to possess a good singing voice. It is something that can always give pleasure, to you and to others. I should so much like to hear you sing, but perhaps now is not the moment! What about you, Sophie? Are you musical, too?'

Sophie shook her head.

'Not really. I learn the pianoforte, of course, and I like well enough to play tunes, but how I hate all those exercises! I do not see the point of them, they are so boring!'

'Not as boring as listening to you prosing on about Jack, and how he jumped the fence, or the stream, or some such thing,' said Minty with feeling. Sophie's face lit up.

'That reminds me, Uncle Marcus! You know, you promised to take me driving in your phaeton next time I came to London! You will not forget, will you?'

He groaned theatrically.

'And to think I hoped you might have forgotten all

about it! Very good, but you must not pester me night and day. And before you ask, you may not drive my new bays! So it is no good asking me.'

His niece accepted this excuse with a good grace.

'Uncle Marcus has a pair of match bays which are. . . oh, perfect!' she explained solemnly to Cecilia. 'So fast, they would win any race they went in for, I'm sure.' She eyed him speculatively. 'Will you let me drive them when I'm bigger? Do you let Miss Chadworth do so?'

He frowned a little, but answered her equably enough.

'She has never asked to do so, and I don't suppose she ever would. Young ladies do not commonly do such a thing, at least not in public, in London.' Sophie screwed up her nose in disgust that anyone should be so lacking in initiative. It looked as though she might say something blighting, and Cecilia was opening her mouth to change the subject, but she was forestalled.

'I'm hungry,' broke in Minty, earning, though she did not know it, her uncle's deep gratitude. 'Starving,' she amended. 'I shall die of inundation.' Lord Inglesham's lips twitched, and her sisters groaned.

'Another of your new words, Minty?'

'And very impressive it is,' said Cecilia diplomatically, 'but I fancy you meant to say inanition, did you not?'

'That's it. Whatever. Anyway, I'm hungry.'

Cecilia, well versed in the ways of the young, had provided for just such a contingency, and produced from her effects a little basket, packed by the landlord's wife, with bread and butter, and cakes, and a flask of lemonade. With this they made a little feast, and they were able to enjoy a few minutes' quiet while Araminta's mouth was too full for speech. Lord Inglesham drew their attention to the window.

'That is the turning to Ritchings, where Lord Bathurst lived,' he informed them. 'My grandfather was acquainted with him, and often stayed there. He met the poet Pope, on several occcasions, and also Addison and Steele.'

'Oh, dear, how dull!' Cleone sympathised.

'He did not find it so, I can assure you! He counted himself fortunate to have made the acquaintance of such men.'

'Then I dare say he was not required to learn their poems, as we are,' pointed out Sophie. 'Though at least Pope rhymes, and has a nice rumty-tumty rhythm to it,' she added, anxious to be fair. 'Not like Shakespeare,' she added in disgust.

'Perhaps you are a little young for Shakespeare,' suggested Cecilia, hiding her amusement. 'It is a pity to form too definite a dislike for any writer, at your age.'

'Well, I am older, and I think Pope and Addison and all those old-fashioned people are sad stuff indeed! But I like Scott, and Cowper, and I think I should enjoy Shakespeare if I were permitted to see it performed, instead of merely reading it!' Cleone cast a sidelong glance at her uncle, who declined to rise to this bait.

'I will allow you Cowper, but I can see little that is great in Scott, though it is easy enough to read, I suppose. What of you, Miss Avening? Are you an ardent lover of the poets?'

'Yes, indeed, though I can understand that schoolgirls do not always care for the passages they must learn by rote. It has always seemed a pity, to me, that so many people set such work as a punishment. How can that foster an appreciation of beauty, when it is associated in

a young mind with the consciousness of having misbe-
haved, and perhaps missing some other treat or
holiday?'

'You have strong feelings on the subject of education,
I see.'

'Well, it is the only thing I know about. I have seen it
from both sides, you see — the pupil, and the teacher. Of
late, while Miss Herring was feeling unwell, she allowed
me to try out some of my ideas for teaching the younger
girls, and, though some of them were failures, I think
that with others I was able to help some of the little
girls to master things that had puzzled them, and to
find their lessons more interesting, too.'

'Then I wish you might teach us, for our lessons are
never interesting, are they, Sophie?' Minty had found
her tongue again. 'Though I don't think anyone could
make those prosy old poets interesting. All they ever
talk about is love.'

Her tone was disgusted, and her hearers could not
refrain from laughter.

'That, too, you may find less boring when you are
older,' said Lord Inglesham.

'But they're never about anything that I find interesting,' she protested.

'Such as what? Food? There would be something, a
poetical cookery book. And what about Sophie — ponies
in verse? You would learn that easily enough!'

'Yes, indeed! I still remember the first poem I ever
learned, because it had my name in it,' said Cecilia.

'A poem about you? How exciting! Who is it by?'
Cleone was intrigued.

'No, no, not about me! Why should anyone bother?
But Addison wrote one entitled "A Song for St Cecilia's
Day". Only think, your great-grandfather actually met

Addison! What a pity he did not also write odes to Cleone, Sophronia and Araminta!'

'I don't suppose anyone ever would,' said Sophie sadly. 'They are such very odd names.'

'My sister's name was Jane,' explained Lord Inglesham, 'and she suffered from having so very dull a name, so she gave her daughters the most unusual ones she could think of.'

'Well, it could have been much worse. Euphrosyne, for instance. Or Sophonisba. I suppose few of us are satisfied with our names. As a child I was called "Cissy", which I abominated.'

'Well you might! I should say that Cecilia is a delightful name, particularly when it has a poem to go with it! And she is the patron saint of music, Cleone, so you should be pleased.

'"*Let all Cecilia's praise proclaim,*
Employ the Echo in her name".'

He quoted the words with a smile, and Cleone gazed at him with astonishment, while Cecilia blushed pink as a rose. 'Well you might look amazed! I should think you would like this poem, at least, since it is in praise of music! And, come to think of it, so very appropriate to yesterday! Let me see:

'"*Let no rough winds approach, nor dare*
Invade the hallowed bounds,
Nor rudely shake the tuneful air,
Nor spoil the fleeting sounds.
Nor mournful sigh nor groan be heard,
But gladness dwell on every tongue".

How does that sound to you? It is not apt? But I have to admit that I was myself made to learn it, while in the schoolroom! Nothing changes, as you see!'

'But at least you have not forgotten it,' pointed out

Cecilia, a little embarrassed but determined not to show it.

'Well, I can't see that it does you any good, unless you should want to flirt with Miss Avening,' said Cleone, thereby drawing down her uncle's wrath on her head by her unladylike talk. Fortunately, before she had a chance to cry, they pulled up at the White Hart at Cranford Bridge, where they alighted for a luncheon. Afterwards, full of good food, the girls were all inclined to be sleepy, and even Cleone nodded off with her head pillowed on her uncle's shoulder. Cecilia, however, was too anxious to sleep. The inn at Newbury, and the morning's luxurious journey, had seemed like an interval out of reality, set quite apart from her everyday world. Now, however, they were crossing Hounslow Heath, and her head was buzzing with worries. Not, of course, that she feared an attack by highwaymen—in broad daylight as they were, and well protected by the coachman and groom, both armed. It was her arrival that loomed nightmare-large in her imagination.

Lord Inglesham stared lazily out of the window. It did not occur to him that he had any duty to entertain Cecilia, and in fact he was glad that she was silent, remembering with horrid clarity that his nieces' governess was afflicted with a tongue that was never still, though rarely with anything of interest to say. It had been a relief, he reflected, to have the girls so suitably looked after on the journey, and he thought idly that she was a pretty little thing with her starting dimple, even if more opinionated and managing than women of her age should be.

His thoughts strayed once again to Miss Chadworth. This evening, at least, he would be sure to meet her, and he would see from her demeanour whether she had

missed him while he was away. Or would he? She was
not, after all, a demonstrative woman—it was one of
the things he particularly liked about her—and as he
had pointed out to Cleone she was far too well bred to
allow her feelings to appear. They had never, naturally,
been alone together, unless you could count sedate rides
in his phaeton, with his tiger perched behind them. If
he had occasionally found her conversation dull, it was
probably because he took more interest in political
affairs, and in his horses, than he did in the gossip of
the drawing-room, though such gossip was eminently
suitable for young ladies.

They were nearing London now, and, glancing up, he
saw that a little frown creased Cecilia's forehead.

'Tired, Miss Avening?' he enquired civilly.

She started, his words sounding loud after their
prolonged silence. She had almost forgotten that he was
there.

'No, my lord, not at all. I would never have believed
a journey could be so comfortable, and I am most
grateful.'

'For goodness' sake, stop calling me "my lord", like a
servant,' he said.

'But that is what I am, really,' she said patiently, as
one explaining matters to a child. 'A governess, you
know, is no more than a superior kind of servant. And
you are, after all, a lord.'

'And your grandfather is an earl! And a dashed top-
lofty one, at that! Your father was the younger son, I
suppose? And married to disoblige him?'

'He married a governess,' Cecilia said stiffly.

'So that's why you have such a bee in your bonnet
about being a servant! Seems to me, Miss Avening,
you're as stiff-necked as your grandfather, but in the

opposite direction. There's nothing disgraceful about being a governess.'

'Certainly there is not. It is what I mean to be, and I think I could be a good one.'

'I am sure you could. The way you quieted Cleone, when she was screaming. . . I'd rather face a cavalry charge, myself! It was very impressive.'

'Then I wonder. . .would you be so kind, Lord Inglesham, as to recommend me to some good post?'

'Me? Recommend a governess?' He threw back his head in laughter, and Cleone stirred. 'My dear girl, I hardly think that my recommendation would help you!'

'I suppose not.' She was crestfallen.

'But I will speak to my mother. She will be coming to London herself, in a few days. She may be able to help you.' He spoke with careless kindness, and she wondered whether he would remember.

'Thank you. I should be very grateful.'

'I should have thought you'd do better to apply to your grandfather, however. Nothing would horrify him more than to think of a grandchild of his earning her bread looking after someone else's children! I should think he'd make you an allowance on the spot.'

'Nothing,' she said firmly, 'would induce me to accept one penny from the Earl.'

'No, I suppose not. But you cannot mean to be a governess all your life?' He shuddered.

'Not all my life, no. What I should really like to do. . .' She paused, looking at him enquiringly. Miss Herring had been firm on the subject of The Gentlemen, and how easily they were to be bored by conversations that did not relate to themselves. She had been accustomed to speak of The Gentlemen as if they were of a rare and different breed, rather like the ancient

Pharaohs, to be feared and placated, but lacking in some of the veneer of civilisation that A Lady should possess. Cecilia herself had encountered so few men that she had no way of knowing whether her instructress was right or not. At the school there had been only the drawing master, who had been small, bald and elderly, and the music and dancing master, whose cheeks were always shaved to baby smoothness, whose person was always fragrant with scents and pomades, and who had so little of the masculine about him that the girls were apt to regard him more in the light of a visiting aunt than a Gentleman.

Other than that, only the vicar of their small church was admitted to the select tea parties that Miss Herring held on Sunday afternoons, and he carried about him the aura of ecclesiastical propriety like armour. Lord Inglesham was the first gentleman with whom she had exchanged more than two words, and it had to be said that so far he had conducted himself so much in the manner suggested by Miss Herring's maxims that Cecilia was inclined to be wary of annoying him.

'What you would really like to do. . .?' he prompted, his face expressing more than a polite interest. He had never before encountered a young lady who would admit to any aim in life other than marrying as well as possible, and even that aim was never openly referred to.

'I should like to have a school of my own,' she admitted.

'A school of your own?' It seemed an unlikely wish for a pretty young girl.

'Yes. Girls must be taught, as well as boys, you know. After all, who is responsible for the upbringing of little boys, and overseeing their early years? Their mothers, surely? And if those mothers have been well educated, both morally and intellectually, surely society must be the better for it, in the end?'

He was amused by her vehemence, and inclined to tease her.

'But many mothers of my acquaintance see little or nothing of their children when they are small, beyond a daily visit to the nursery to be sure that all is well. They leave all that to nurses, and to governesses.'

'And you think that that is right? Did your mother do so, or your sister?'

'No. No, they did not.' He was thoughtful for a moment. 'You think, then, that girls should be as well educated as their brothers?'

'I see no reason why they should not be. But you must not encourage me — I am afraid I am too inclined to run on, when once I am started on my hobby-horse. There is, after all, little hope that I could start my own school. I am far too young, and though I must undoubtedly get older there is little likelihood that I will ever get richer!'

She spoke with cheerful insouciance, and there was no question that she was in any way angling for financial assistance. He knew a fleeting desire to say that he would set her up with a school of her own, until his own good sense told him what the world would be likely to say of such an arrangement. Nevertheless, he determined that he would speak to his mother, and find this unusual and enterprising girl a good position, if he could.

Cleone stirred, and opened her eyes.

'Where are we? Are we nearly there?' She looked much younger than her fifteen years, her cheek flushed pink where it had rested on his coat, and her eyes still heavy.

'Not far now. To what address may we take you, Miss Avening?'

Cecilia, who had in fact been wondering how she was to find the house, demurred at once.

'You must not go out of your way for my sake, my lord! I may very well take a cab from your brother's house.'

He raised one of his heavy eyebrows.

'All by yourself? That is carrying humility too far, Miss Avening. You must have a very poor idea of my manners.'

'Oh, no! That is. . .the young ladies are tired, and. . .'

'A few extra minutes will do them no harm. What address may I give the coachman?'

Flustered, she named the house in Harley Street where Mrs Ruspidge lived. It was not a fashionable area, but he merely opened the sliding hatch and directed his coachman. Cecilia woke the little girls, and took out the damp cloth she had packed, and a small, dry towel, and proceeded to freshen their hands and faces, and brush their hair. It was done in so matter-of-fact a way that they made no objection, and by the time they reached Harley Street all three were neatly brushed and tidied, their stockings straight and their gloves buttoned, a sight to gladden the eye of any prospective stepmother.

The carriage drew up outside the house, and the groom came round to let down the steps and open the door. The three girls kissed Cecilia.

'We shall see you again, Miss Avening, shan't we?' Minty, newly awake, was inclined to be tearful.

'Maybe, one day. But you will be so busy, you know, you will have very little time! Think of the new clothes that must be bought, and the visits you mean to make! And, of course, you will want to get to know your new mama, and learn to please her.'

'I shall come and visit you, even if she will not bring me,' pronounced Cleone, at which the two smaller girls protested that she was not to come without them.

'I hope you will do no such thing,' said Cecilia firmly. 'If your mama permits you to come, then well and good. If not, you must be sure to do as she wishes.' They agreed, though reluctantly. Her box was now standing on the step, and the groom was waiting to hand her down. To her great surprise, Lord Inglesham himself descended first, and in spite of her protestations helped her out of the carriage, and accompanied her to the door.

'Oh, pray. . .there is no need. . .' Now that the moment had come, her heart was beating painfully hard, and she could feel the palms of her hands sticking clammily to the inside of her gloves. He paid no attention to her, but nodded to the groom to knock again, since no one had come to the door.

It was beginning to grow dark. Looking up anxiously, Cecilia could see no gleam of light from the gloomy windows, and her heart misgave her. Surely she had not journeyed to an empty house? Her letter must long since have been received, stating the day of her arrival, and, if she was a day later than she had hoped, surely they would have waited for her, or left at least one servant to greet her? At last a welcome shuffling noise and the dull glow of an approaching candle signified that their knocking would be answered. An undersized maid opened the door a tiny crack, peering suspiciously round

it until her eyes widened at the sight of the coach, with
its four gleaming horses and its crest picked out on the
panels of the door.

'Lor!' she exclaimed in nasal tones, allowing the door
to open further and releasing a waft of polish-laden air.
'I mean, good afternoon, miss and sir, and won't you
step in?'

The words came out in a breathless babble, her eyes
still fixed on the conveyance. Lord Inglesham, satisfied
that he had done his best to convey a good impression
for the girl beside him, smiled a little.

'I am Miss Avening,' said Cecilia with composure,
though she could feel her legs trembling. 'I believe Mrs
Ruspidge is expecting me.'

For the first time the slightly popping eyes turned to
her, taking in her appearance and the fact that she had
with her several band-boxes, and a well-corded box.

'Dunno, miss, I'm sure,' she said doubtfully.

'Well, if you are not, I am, ' said Cecilia firmly,
feeling that she could not bear to stand like a beggar on
the doorstep any longer. She held out her hand to Lord
Inglesham. 'Thank you, my lord, for being so kind as to
bring me. I hope that the young ladies will be none the
worse for their journey.'

'If they are not, it will be thanks to your care,' he
said, bowing gracefully over her hand under the fascinated eye of the little servant. 'I shall do myself the
honour of calling on you, to offer my thanks in form.'

'There is no need. . .' she tried to say, but he paid no
heed to her. He strode back to the carriage, pausing
before stepping inside to bow once again. He had seen,
if she had not, that a corner of the curtain was twitching
in one of the upstairs windows. The groom carried the
box inside, Cecilia gathered up her band-boxes, and

with one last glance behind her stepped through the door, which the girl hurriedly opened wider and as hurriedly closed again.

The hallway was bare and rather cold, though very clean. The only light came from the candle the servant had been carrying, which she had set on a small side-table next to a silver tray containing visiting cards, some of them rather creamy-coloured with age. Cecilia and the girl stared at one another, each uncertain what should be done next. In the end, Cecilia realised that it was up to her to make the first move.

'Will you tell Mrs Ruspidge that I have arrived?' she said with as much authority as she could muster.

'Fanny? Who is it, Fanny? Why have you let this person into the house?'

The voice came from above, where a flight of stairs rose into Stygian darkness. Cecilia peered upwards, unable to see the speaker, who ignored her presence completely and confined her remarks to the maid.

'I have particularly told you, Fanny, not to allow anyone into the house without consulting me first! What can you be thinking of, girl? Nothing at all, as usual, I suppose. I should never have taken you in. I should have known that it would not do, to take you from the parish.'

The hapless Fanny lowered her head, and shuffled her feet. Cecilia's heart sank still further. Was she about to be thrown out of the house?

'Good afternoon, ma'am,' she called up. 'I am Cecilia Avening.'

There was a pause.

'Who?'

'Cecilia Avening, ma'am. Your. . .that is to say, the

late Mr Ruspidge's stepdaughter. Have you not received my letters?'

'I have indeed. I expected you yesterday, and when you did not arrive I presumed you had made other arrangements.'

'I beg your pardon, ma'am. There was a dreadful storm, and I stayed overnight in Newbury. It was not possible to inform you.'

'Stayed in Newbury? At an inn, and on your own? I never heard of such a thing.'

'I own it is not something I would have wished to do, but as it fell out I was not alone. Lord Inglesham, who was kind enough to convey me here today, was staying there with——' She was interrupted by an outraged shriek.

'You do not mean to tell me that he took you under his protection? Wretched girl, I knew how it would be! With a father such as yours, it was bound to be so! Well, you shall not stop here! I have my own daughters to consider, you know!'

'Madam!' Cecilia's clear, shocked voice broke through her tirade. 'Madam, you wrong me! Lord Inglesham was travelling with his three nieces, and it was with them that I stayed the night. He asked me to travel with them today, in place of their governess, who is ill. I own I was very glad to do so, for the inn and the stage were very crowded and uncomfortable. His lordship behaved with the greatest consideration towards me, and not the least suspicion of impropriety.'

There was a thoughtful pause. It was true that she had seen, while reconnoitring through the upstairs window, the pale shadows of three faces at the windows of the carriage. Mrs Ruspidge was far from eager to have this, to her, indigent relative under her roof, but she could scarcely turn the girl out into the night. Particularly, she thought, if her story was true. Who knew but what some good might come of it? One night, at least, could do no harm, and she would soon learn whether the girl was telling the truth or not.

'My dear girl, you should have made yourself clearer! What, after all, was I to think? I know nothing of you, after all, and seeing you arrive, as I thought, alone in a carriage with a strange man. . .but you will explain it all to me presently. Bring Miss Avening upstairs, Fanny, and then send Arthur up to carry her box. She may sleep in the bedroom next to the young ladies.'

Fanny, who had stood by without apparently understanding the exchange between her mistress and the guest, obediently took up the candle and led Cecilia up the stairs. On the landing, Mrs Ruspidge awaited them. She was a tall, bony woman, dressed in the lavender tones of distant mourning but with a good deal of finery. She examined Cecilia from head to foot.

'Well, my dear, you may kiss me,' she said, inclining her face. Dutifully Cecilia pressed her lips to a smooth, chilly cheek. 'Now, you must come and meet my family.'

Cecilia stiffened her knees, straightened her spine, and followed her hostess.

CHAPTER FOUR

THAT night Cecilia laid an aching head on her pillow, and a few tears trickled down on to the linen that was so fiercely starched that any semblance of comfort was lost in its shiny stiffness. She had seldom passed a more uncomfortable evening, and would have been hard put to it to say whether Mrs Ruspidge had been more disagreeable when she was hostile or friendly.

On reaching the room that was rather grandly named as the upstairs drawing-room — she was soon to learn that there was no other — she had paused on the threshold of a small parlour that seemed, to eyes dazzled by the dark of stairs and hallway, to be thronged with people. A second look showed her that it was in fact very full of furniture, much of it in the fashionable Egyptian style that combined opulent elegance with an almost total disregard to comfort. Ranged round the room, in various attitudes denoting surprise and disdain, were a young man, and three girls.

She was puzzled for a moment by the young man, introduced as 'My son, Augustus Hatherley', as she had quite forgotten the existence of this child of Mrs Ruspidge's earlier marriage. Of medium height, he had a very smart appearance, his clothes cut to fit like a second skin, and he wore a quantity of fobs, chains and other adjuncts to gentlemanly elegance. His dark hair was as heavily pomaded as had been that of the music master in Bath, and was swept back from his forehead in ordered swaths. He lounged across the room and lifted his chin to look appraisingly down at Cecilia, his lip curling a little at the sight of her outmoded gown.

'So! The little sister I have never yet met! How d'ye do, my dear?'

His voice was a would-be aristocratic drawl, which somehow failed to convince. She gave him the tips of her fingers, and dropped a small curtsy. Mrs Ruspidge gave a titter of laughter.

'Hardly a sister, my dear Augustus! One would be at a loss to name the relationship, if indeed there is one at all!'

He gave her fingers a little pinch, and rolled up his eyes in an expression of conspiracy against his mother. Cecilia, however, lowered her eyes and did not respond, so he went back to the fireplace, where a pack of cards and a half-empty glass testified to his earlier occupation.

The three girls clustered round. They were dressed in silk, even the youngest, with a great many flounces and a deal of trimming, and the widest, longest sashes Cecilia had ever seen. At twelve, ten and nine they all bore a powerful resemblance to their mother, though the strong-boned features were still partly hidden beneath the childish chubby overlay. Cecilia searched their faces in vain for a resemblance to the kindly stepfather she still dimly remembered.

'Is that your best gown?' queried Charlotte, her position as the eldest giving her the right to speak first. 'It is very out of date.'

'No, it is not my best,' Cecilia answered equably. 'It would be foolish to wear a good gown to travel in, wouldn't it? My best gown is in my box, but I am afraid you would think that out of date, also.'

Charlotte smirked at that, indicating that the answer did not astonish her. Georgina, the middle girl, looked at the cloak that Cecilia now carried over her left arm, since no one had offered to relieve her of it.

'A cloak! Only look, Mama, Miss Avening has a cloak! I did not know anyone still wore them, but servants, and poor people!'

'Well, I am not very rich,' Cecilia admitted cheerfully, 'though I wouldn't call myself a poor person, precisely! But a cloak is very much warmer than a pelisse, Georgina, and in a stage-coach that is a great advantage, you know.'

Mrs Ruspidge drew in her breath with a little hiss at this candid admission of poverty, but Amelia was too quick for her. Alone of the three girls, she still retained some of the candour and straightforwardness of youth.

'But you did not come in a stage-coach, I saw you from the window! There was a grand carriage, with a crest on the door, and Mama said it must be a lord, at least!'

'Your mama is right, for it was Lord Inglesham's carriage, Amelia. His nieces were travelling up to London with him, and he was so kind as to ask me to journey with them, since their governess was ill.'

'His nieces, eh?' Augustus looked up lazily from his game of solitaire. 'That would be Maisemore's girls, I suppose?' Cecilia inclined her head in assent. 'Thought so. Seems he's to marry again. He's found himself some Scottish heiress, they say. Long on money, and short on sense, if you ask me. Who'd want to take on three stepdaughters, one of them all but grown-up? He's hoping for a son, of course, no question.'

He offered these opinions in a throw-away tone, very much the man of the world. Cecilia forbore to point out that Mr Ruspidge had taken on not only herself, but

Augustus as well, and tried not to allow herself to be irritated by his tone of spurious familiarity.

The formalities of introduction now being considered complete, the three girls went back to their former occupations by the fire, namely reading a Gothick romance—Charlotte—and bickering over the possession of a grubby but finely dressed doll—Georgina and Amelia. Their mother cast a fond glance at their well-upholstered forms, and offered to lead Cecilia up to her room. Cecilia was rather surprised by this courtesy, having expected to have such a duty delegated to a servant, but she soon learned that her hostess wished to have the opportunity to take her to task for addressing her daughters by their first names.

'As one who stands, however distantly, in relation of a mother to you, you will not mind if I venture to give you the hint,' she said calmly. 'I like to be so very particular, you see, that my girls' manners are those of the very highest ton. And nothing, to my way of thinking, is more vulgar than this modern habit of addressing new acquaintances by their given names!'

'I beg your pardon, ma'am. It is merely that they are still children, and I am so used——'

'That is just what I mean! You are used, after all, to a rather different class of girl! And you were their teacher, were you not? That, of course, is a very different matter. I think, Miss Avening, that you would do well to be guided by me. An older woman, you know, and one who is accustomed to mixing with the highest in the land...'

Cecilia reflected that Lord Inglesham's nieces had been happy to be addressed by her by their pet names, and that his lordship had appeared to see nothing wrong in this. She was not in a position, however, to argue, and meekly agreed to follow Mrs Ruspidge's request.

They dined at five, Mrs Ruspidge explaining the unfashionably early hour as a concession to her girls.

'I like them to dine with me, when we have not company,' she said. 'It is so much better for them to have the benefit of adult conversation, don't you agree, Miss Avening?' Cecilia dutifully did, but thought privately that the girls would have benefited from the plainer diet that had been usual at Miss Herring's. The twelve-year-old Charlotte had several spots, and all three of them were plump to the point of fatness. The food was smothered in rich sauces, though it seemed to Cecilia that the fish or meat thus concealed was not always of the first quality. Mrs Ruspidge had hinted that her unexpected presence at their table would upset Cook, and Cecilia was obliged to say that she was not very hungry, and required only a little food. She was taken very much at her word, though she could not see that there was any shortage of dishes, and it was fortunate that she had eaten a substantial luncheon, or she would have risen from the table almost hungry.

When they had finished eating, Mrs Ruspidge rose and withdrew, very stately, her daughters and Cecilia trailing behind her, leaving Augustus in solitary splendour to make inroads on the wine. Back in the drawing-room the three girls eyed Cecilia's evening gown, of plain white muslin with a simple embroidered edging, and looked scorn at the string of small pearls that were her only ornament. Cecilia offered to play a game with them, but after a short while they declared that it was too difficult, and therefore dull, and she was left to stare at the fire while Mrs Ruspidge made pointed remarks about idle hands, and she resolved to unpack her work-box as soon as possible.

Augustus reappeared, closely followed by the panting Fanny with a heavy tray of tea and coffee. He drank two cups, quite quickly, then stood up.

'Well, I'll be off now!'

His mother looked fondly at him.

'Where is tonight, Augustus? I declare I can scarcely keep pace with your social life these days!'

'Lord, Ma, a fellow doesn't have to account for his every moment to his mother, does he? As a matter of fact, I meant to go to the club, and see what's afoot. Does that suit you?'

She gave him a deprecating look.

'My dear boy, I do not mean to pry! Only, if you should see the Duke, pray give him my regards, the dear thing! Only last week he was quizzing me that I was never to be seen, and that I had not called on the Duchess for this age!'

'Well, if I should see him, I might remember.' With this uncertain promise he left the room, without according a farewell to his sisters or Cecilia. She could not help wondering what Miss Herring would have made of this behaviour, and whether she would have considered it allowable in A Gentleman. The conviction had already grown in her mind, however, that Mr Hatherley's claims to that title rested on very inadequate foundations.

Now that the lord of the household had departed, his three sisters set to work to interrogate Cecilia about her former life. Since they did not scruple to ask even the most vulgarly intrusive of questions, and since their mother made no attempt to control their inquisition, Cecilia found herself unable to escape. They showed an

unflattering surprise when they learned that several of
the young ladies at the school had been titled, and when
they found that one of Cecilia's former particular friends
had married the heir to an earldom they were almost
impressed, until Cecilia told them that the friendship
had dwindled to an annual exchange of letters.

'But you might write to her, and say that you are now
in London! Surely she would have to ask you to visit, if
you hinted that you would like to?'

Cecilia tried to explain that she could do no such
thing, but the girls only stared at her. Mrs Ruspidge
looked annoyed at losing the possibility of so valuable a
connection.

'Maybe I should write on your behalf. As your
mother, you know. . .'

'I beg, ma'am, that you will do no such thing,' said
Cecilia earnestly. When pressed, she stubbornly refused
to divulge her friend's name, or that of the illustrious
family to which she now belonged.

'Well, I must say I think you are most ungrateful,
Miss Avening. I would have thought that so small a
thing, in repayment for my taking you in. . .but it is
always the same. Beware, girls, of this kind of pride! For
that is what it is, after all, no more than a false pride,
which to my way of thinking is a most unpleasant trait.
But there, I shall say no more about it. Let no one ever
say that I am one to bear a grudge, however badly I am
used.'

Charlotte tossed her head, while the younger girls
looked round-eyed at the sinner. Cecilia, her cheeks
burning, bit her lip and raised her chin, determined to
keep back the tears that thickened her throat.

'I beg your pardon, ma'am, for vexing you. I am
afraid that even to please you I cannot do what seems

to me to be wrong. I hope, however, that I may be of use to you in some other way. Certainly nothing is further from my wish than to impose myself as a burden. I have hopes of finding myself a position as governess, but until that time may I be of service by teaching Miss Ruspidge, Miss Georgina and Miss Amelia?'

The formal reference to her daughters went a little way to soften Mrs Ruspidge's ire.

'By chance, it is the case that they have no governess at present. The last young lady proved to be most unsuitable, so much so that I had to ask her to leave at once. Can you believe that she had the impertinence to fancy herself in love with Augustus?'

'Oh, no, Mama,' put in Georgina pertly. 'It was quite the other way round! It was Gus who was in love with her! He was forever coming to the schoolroom, and trying to kiss her! It was so funny, we laughed ourselves into stitches! Once we held her still for him, so that she couldn't push him away, and she stamped on his foot! You wouldn't believe the things he said, he was so cross! It was as good as a play!'

Cecilia was stunned by this candid admission, and was not surprised to see her hostess flush with annoyance. It appeared, however, that her anger was directed only at encouragement of her son in an unsuitable affair, and not at the lack of delicacy shown by her little daughters.

'Really, girls, I had thought you would know better! A person of that class, and Augustus fancying himself in love with her! The next thing we will find is that he will be wanting to marry her, and then where should we be?'

'No danger of that, Mama,' said Charlotte coolly. 'Gus will never marry any female who has not a sizeable

fortune, and good connections. I have often heard him
say so.'

Mrs Ruspidge's flush subsided.

'Well, he is a good son and an excellent brother, my
dears. You are very lucky to have a brother who will be
in a position to do you so much good, when it is time
for you to come out.'

Cecilia rose to her feet.

'Will you forgive me, ma'am, if I go up to my room?
I must unpack the rest of my things, and I am very tired
from my journey.'

An indifferent permission was given. Cecilia was
thankful that none of the girls thought to offer to help
her unpack — the thought of them picking over her few
precious treasures, and perhaps laughing at them, was
more than she could have borne. She found herself
remembering the pleasant evening she had passed —
was it really only the day before? — with Lord Inglesham
and his nieces. The thought of them hearing such a
conversation as the one she had just heard made her
cheeks burn with shame, and she found herself hoping
passionately that they would not keep their promise of
visiting her.

She would have been surprised had she known how
much, and how warmly, she was spoken of in the course
of that same evening. Lord Inglesham had taken his
three charges to their father's London house, and stayed
to witness their rapturous reunion with the father they
had not seen for some months. Sir Edward Maisemore
was a kindly, pleasant, unassuming man, who had been
devoted to his first wife and heartbroken by her death.
His grief had been so violent, and so prolonged, that it
had been agreed by all that it was better for his three
children to be separated from his misery, and he had

listlessly allowed them to be removed to their maternal grandmother's care.

No one could be more pleased than Marcus and his mother that their brother- and son-in-law had at last surfaced from the profound melancholy that had gripped him for the past eight years. Neither of them had met his prospective bride, who had been brought up exclusively in Scotland and made her come-out in Edinburgh, but she was from an unexceptionable family and, as Augustus Hatherley had impertinently pointed out, would bring with her a large portion. Not that Sir Edward had any need to marry a fortune, but no one could deny that it was a pleasing addition to his own estate. There was also the unexpressed hope that his new marriage, as well as providing a mother for his daughters, might bring him an heir.

The three girls were rapturous in their pleasure at coming to live with their father. Probably because he felt guilty at not being able to keep them in his charge, he had always been the most indulgent of parents, and had it not been for the good sense of their grandmother he would have showered on them every gift, great or small, for which they ever expressed a passing fancy. It had been agreed that the rest of the day should be kept for the children alone, and that they should not meet their mama-to-be until the following day, by which time she would have been presented both to the Dowager, and to Lord Inglesham, a man of whom Sir Edward stood in some awe, though he was several years the younger.

'I shall leave you in peace—if that is the word for it,' said his lordship, when the first greetings had been spoken.

'Thank you for bringing them, Marcus! I only hope

they did not make the journey quite hideous for you,'
said the fond parent, secure in the knowledge that his
children were so perfect that it could not but be a
pleasure to be cooped up in a carriage with them for the
best part of two days. Lord Inglesham saw all of this,
and raised his fierce eyebrows at Cleone, who blushed
and laughed.

'I am afraid I was very naughty to Uncle Marcus,
Papa! But by the greatest good fortune we met Miss
Avening, and then everything was all right! We had
such a pleasant journey!'

Sir Edward looked worried, and his brother-in-law
hastened to comfort him.

'It was no more than a thunderstorm, which frightened poor Cleone so badly. You know how she has
always feared them, so she is not to blame. And it is
true that I managed to find a splendid companion for
the girls, a lady who has taught for some years at what
sounds like an excellent school in Bath. She was so good
as to stand in for poor Miss Dixon, and she soon had us
all organised!'

Without meaning to, he gave Sir Edward the
impression that this helpful Miss Avening was a woman
of mature years, and he promptly dismissed her from
his mind. There was, after all, so much to talk about.
He watched with approval while his daughters thanked
their uncle for his care.

'We are to meet at Almack's, I believe?' queried Lord
Inglesham as he turned to leave.

'Yes. I own I should have preferred a less public
place, but Lady Inglesham professes herself starved of
gossip, and my—that is to say, Miss Cameron—also
expressed a wish to visit the famous place! She has never

been to London, you know, and so everything is new to her.'

'Well, that suits me very well. I look forward to meeting Miss Cameron. She is a lucky young woman, Edward.'

His brother-in-law demurred, but Marcus felt that it was true. He knew how very happy his sister Jane had been with this gentle, generous man, and his only hope was that Miss Cameron would not take advantage of his good nature.

He need not have worried. Arriving at Almack's later that evening, correctly attired in the black silk knee breeches and black evening coat that, with the dazzling white of his linen, enhanced his rather saturnine good looks, his eyes fell instantly on Sir Edward, who was dancing with a woman of almost blinding beauty.

'Good God! Can that be she, Mama? If so, she is going to take the town by storm! How is it that such a piece of perfection has been allowed to remain, unappreciated and unwed, in Scotland?'

His mother gave his arm a small admonitory pinch. The Dowager Lady Inglesham was tall, like her son, and though her hair was now iron-grey the resemblance between them was still very strong. A woman of forceful personality, she had ruled her husband, her children and her household with a rod of iron that was wielded with such delicacy and tact that they were almost completely unaware of it.

'Hush, Marcus! You will be heard, and you must remember that dear Edward is in a peculiarly delicate position! It must always be awkward to present one's present love to the family of a former one. You are right, though. She is very lovely! I see an empty chair over there, next to dear Emily. I do believe she has kept it for me, and we shall be able to see everything from there! What fun!'

Though her movements were slowed by age, the Dowager had lost none of her youthful interest in the doings of Society. While living for the better part of the year in the country, she still kept well abreast of events through her numerous correspondents, and as she made her way across the room on her son's arm she had to pause at almost every step to acknowledge greetings. Once seated, she arranged the deep violet silk of her skirts, unfurled her fan, and inclined her head with its startlingly fashionable melon cap in quilted violet satin to exchange news with her friend. Lord Inglesham stayed at her side, idly watching the dancers. Miss Chadworth was present, he saw, moving with her usual grace through the dance with an elderly peer. Her attention was, very correctly, given to her partner, and he did not know whether or not she had marked his entrance.

The dance came to an end, and Sir Edward was seen to be approaching. As they drew nearer, the young woman's beauty became even more apparent. Her hair was of a shade so bright that it fully deserved that overworked adjective 'golden', and one might almost have suspected that it had been assisted to that glorious colour had not her eyebrows and eyelashes been identically coloured. Another woman might have chosen to darken, discreetly, those golden lashes, to display their thickness and length to better advantage, but, with innocence, or perhaps wisdom, Fiona Cameron had left them alone, and they shone like a precious setting for the sapphire-blue of her eyes. Her skin was the white of skimmed milk, flushed a delicate wild rose on cheeks that owed their glow to good health and exercise, rather than paint. Her beautifully shaped mouth smiled happily, displaying pearly teeth, and it was not to be wondered at that the crowd parted like the Red Sea to let her pass, while even other women stopped to admire what their menfolk could scarcely withdraw their eyes from.

Presented to Lady Inglesham, she dropped a pretty and respectful curtsy, and sat obediently in the chair indicated for her. Marcus listened with half an ear to their conversation while ostensibly chatting with Sir Edward. Miss Cameron responded with shy gratitude to her ladyship's congratulations, and owned that she thought herself the most fortunate girl in the world.

'We have so much in common, you see!' she said artlessly. 'Poor Edward lost your dear daughter, and I myself lost the man I had loved, and thought I should have married. I was so very unhappy; I thought I should never find another man I could care for in that way. Is it not wonderful that we should have found one another?'

'Very wonderful, my dear. I am so pleased for you both.'

'You are so kind, Lady Inglesham! I confess that I was very nervous of meeting you tonight! I know that Edward regards you almost as if you had been his own mother, since his parents died when he was so young. I hope he may continue to do so. I have no mama either, you see, so I shall be much in need of your advice, if you will be so good as to help me. Of course I know I can never replace your daughter! Edward has told me so much about her! But I mean to do my best to be a good mama to his girls, and I am sure I cannot do that without you!'

Lady Inglesham was touched by this moving speech.

Marcus, listening to the soft, pretty voice, wondered if she could really be as good as she seemed — it seemed almost excessive, coupled with such astonishing beauty. He could find no shadow of insincerity in her face or tone, however, and chided himself inwardly for being so cynical. His mother, after all, was far from gullible, and he need not fear that she would be taken in. It was hard to see, in any case, why Miss Cameron should go to the trouble to deceive a woman who was, after all, no true relative of Sir Edward. He came to the conclusion that she was, in fact, all that she seemed, and he congratulated his brother-in-law on his good fortune.

After a little while he asked Miss Cameron to dance, and she accepted with a pleasure that was completely lacking in flirtatiousness. During the dance they talked, and he soon discovered that any opinion she might express was bound to be prefixed by 'Edward says'. It was almost a relief to find that this paragon, though certainly good-natured and undoubtedly beautiful, was almost completely lacking in the kind of intelligence and wit that he was used to in the women of his family. He returned her to Edward with secret relief, thinking that, though she would ornament any room, he would die of boredom after two days in her company.

His duty done, he made his way towards Miss Chadworth. By contrast to the astonishing Fiona Cameron her light brown hair and brown eyes looked almost dowdy, but she welcomed him at her side with a decorous pleasure that made him think that she must have missed him. She was an excellent dancer, and conversed agreeably, though he found himself noticing that she was reluctant to put forward any firm opinion until he had given his own, and that then she was inclined to follow his lead. On the few occasions when she differed slightly, he had only to reason with her for a few moments for her to come round to his way of thinking. In the past, he had with masculine arrogance taken this as an index of her intelligence, but now he found himself wondering.

'You are so very agreeable, Miss Chadworth,' he complimented her. 'I am always able to persuade you that I am right.'

'I do believe that gentlemen know best in most matters,' she said with a graceful inclination of her head. 'And you, of course, explain things so clearly and well that I cannot help agreeing with you.' He could not but be a little flattered, and after their two dances he walked her back to her mother, and stayed chatting with them for nearly half an hour until he saw his mother signalling to him. He made his farewells, and went to her.

'Are you tired? Do you want to go home?'

'Yes, but that is no reason for you to leave! I hope I am not such a poor thing that I cannot spend a few minutes alone in a carriage!'

'Nonsense, Mama, you know I am longing to discuss the divine Miss Cameron with you! Besides, I am tired too. Travelling with your granddaughters is a wearing business, I find.'

She was amused, and thought privately that it was a pity he had not children of his own to pester him. There were times when she feared that her son was growing a little selfish—oh, never with her, but in his attitude to others. Now she asked about the journey, and listened with interest and pleasure as he described it in detail.

'I might have known that you would find someone to take on your responsibilities! You are incorrigible, Marcus!'

'Not at all. I did my best for my nieces, and, if that included finding them a companion who could amuse, instruct and control them, so much the better! You would have been pleased, I think, to have seen how easily she made them mind her, particularly when Cleone was being so very — that is to say, when she was so frightened of the thunderstorm.'

'Yes, poor child. It is a very real fear, Marcus, silly though it might seem to you, who fear nothing.'

'No one fears nothing who is not a fool, Mama. I admit that I was not very sympathetic, but I had never understood that there was a storm on the night that Jane died.'

'Yes, a very bad one.' The Dowager fell silent for a moment, remembering that past grief. 'So, your schoolmistress found that out, did she? I would not have expected Cleone to tell it to a stranger; it is something she does not speak of readily.'

'Well, I am glad she did, for it helped me to understand the poor child. But you must not be thinking of her as my schoolmistress, Mama. Though I rather hope you will be able to do something to help her. She is, I think, much in need of a position in some pleasant family. I did not gain a very happy impression of the place where she is — relatives of some kind, but I did not altogether understand the connection.' He had not thought to ask, he realised with a slight pang, and Cecilia had been singularly unforthcoming about her private circumstances, though perfectly happy to tell the girls about Miss Herring's school.

'Of course, I will do my best. My friends, though, Marcus, are rather beyond the days of needing a governess — they are all grandparents, rather than parents. She has obviously impressed you. Is she pretty?'

He laughed.

'You ask me that, when I have just met Miss Cameron! Really, Mama! I scarcely noticed her looks. She is well enough, I suppose. Rather dowdy, as one would expect, but neat and pleasing in her appearance. Really, I can scarcely recall her face.'

As he said the words his fickle memory gave him the lie, for suddenly Cecilia's face appeared before him. He was surprised to find that he could remember every detail—the dark grey eyes, so expressive of her moods and thoughts in spite of her self-control and privacy. The fine skin, not as white as Miss Cameron's, of course, but with a creamy glow that set off the glowing tawny brown of those wild tendrils of hair forever escaping from the demure hairstyle and clustering round the neat ears, the broad, thoughtful forehead, and the slender, childlike neck. The face he saw in his mind's eye was thoughtful, serious, and he knew a sudden longing to make it smile. It would not do so, however, and he was obscurely dissatisfied.

CHAPTER FIVE

THE week that followed was one of the unhappiest of Cecilia's existence. Without having any undue pride, she knew that she was a good teacher, and she had never found any difficulty in making her lessons interesting, or in controlling and even inspiring such girls as she had in her care. Naturally, at Miss Herring's, there had from time to time been difficult children, those who were hard to teach for one reason or another, or those who were inclined to naughtiness. There, however, the general tone of the establishment had been such that disobedience and unruly behaviour had been frowned on by the majority of the girls and that, together with the calm good humour and kindly understanding of Miss Herring, had often succeeded in performing what might have appeared to their families to be a miracle in transforming their problem daughters into happy, dutiful, well-educated young women.

Cecilia felt that she had never sufficiently appreciated Miss Herring until now. Even when the pain and worry of her broken leg had been at its worst, Cecilia and the two other resident teachers at the seminary had always known that they could rely on her support, encouragement and wisdom. The fact that she had run so successful a school for so many years, without any jokes of a piscatorial nature relating to her name, spoke volumes for the respect in which she was held. No child, after the first few weeks at the school, was ever known to make pointed remarks about kippers, or red herrings, or

Yarmouth bloaters. Such impertinent jokes, and many
others, Cecilia was now forced to endure, ever since on
her first morning in the Ruspidge schoolroom she had
made mention of her friend and preceptress.

Charlotte, Georgina and Amelia had laughed wildly
at the comical notion of Miss Herring's name.

'And to keep a school! A school of fish!' giggled
Charlotte. 'Even in such a dowdy place as Bath, you
must have been the laughing-stock of the place.'

'I do not think so,' said Cecilia mildly. 'Miss Herring
was much respected. Now, Miss Ruspidge, if you will
kindly open your grammar?'

'Oh, pooh to that,' Charlotte said rudely. 'I hate
grammar. It's boring, and there's no use to it that I can
see. Me and my sisters all hate it.'

'My sisters and I,' corrected Cecilia gently. 'You see,
my dear, that you must have a knowledge of grammar
if you are to speak correctly.'

'Why? You understood me, didn't you? So what does
it matter?'

'A young lady of birth is expected to know how to
speak correctly,' said Cecilia with cunning. This gave
Charlotte some pause for thought.

'Well, I'll do a bit. But only a bit, mind. Mama
always says we shouldn't strain ourselves, doing too
much at a time. You have to do what Mama says.'

It was all too true. Cecilia soon learned that there
was no point at all in appealing to the girls' mother for
support in anything. She would always, no matter what
the circumstances, take her daughters' side in any
dispute, and her own education was such that she could
see little point in many of the lessons that Cecilia
devised.

'Now, do not be overworking them with all that

history, and geography and such stuff,' she said firmly. 'I do not like them to study too much, it makes their eyes red. And plain sewing, too! That is for servants to do. A little pretty embroidery, or netting a purse, is all very well, and I do not like to see a young woman with idle hands. But as for making poor little Georgina mend that great rip in her pinafore — it is unnecessary, and quite out of the question.'

In the end, Cecilia was forced to confine her teaching to such subjects as Mrs Ruspidge thought necessary in a young lady, and these were for show, rather than for use. That they should be able to pen a pretty hand was naturally of the first importance, and speak enough words of French and Italian to enable them to sing in those languages, and smatter their conversation with a few fashionable phrases. A little ladylike drawing, a slight acquaintance with the fashionable poets and novelists of the day — no need to read them, just to have a few names and little quotations got up — these were the height of her aspirations.

In music, also, Cecilia failed to satisfy. Though she played prettily on the pianoforte, and possessed a singing voice that was slight but true, her insistence on scales and exercises, and on having all the notes correct instead of merely some of them, earned their scorn.

'Only think, Mama,' said Charlotte loudly, 'Miss Cecilia plays only the piano, and nothing else! She has never even tried the harp!'

'Well, my dear, you must remember that not all girls have your good fortune,' replied her mother complacently. 'She does her best, I suppose, and if she can teach a few pretty little pieces to Amelia it will be better than nothing. It is only for a little while, after all, and then I shall have a proper governess for you.'

'I don't want to have lessons with her,' pouted
Amelia, who was not slow to follow her elders' lead.
'Cecilia! Sealy! Silly Sealy! That's what I'll call her!'

'Hush, dear,' said Mrs Ruspidge without much conviction. 'She will hear you.' In fact the entire conversation had been clearly audible to Cecilia, as she was
sitting in the schoolroom, where there was at least a fire,
mending Georgina's torn hem, and Mrs Ruspidge was
on the landing just outside. Cecilia could scarcely be
hurt by such ill-informed and ill-natured words, but it
was uncomfortable none the less.

Mrs Ruspidge did, however, find it very convenient
to have someone to be with her daughters, after two
months of being without a governess. She herself was
very busy, every day, with shopping and calls. The
shopping was very time-consuming for, although the
late Mr Ruspidge had left her very well provided for,
she was greatly addicted to finery. Added to this, she
longed to break into that magic circle of 'Society', on
the fringes of which she was constantly hovering. By
dint of being assiduously helpful and friendly to a few
impoverished but well-connected acquaintances, she
had managed to worm her way into the lower echelons,
and now she was working hard at improving on this,
wasting no opportunity to make new acquaintances, and
sticking like a leech to anyone who might help her.

All of this was expensive. She was convinced that in
order to succeed she must be dressed in the height of
fashion, but at the same time she had no intention of
paying the kind of prices that were charged in the select
Bond Street shops where the leaders of fashion bought
their gowns, bonnets and other clothes. She had found
a dressmaker, one of the indigent French gentlewomen
who had escaped many years before from the Terror,

and employed her to make up gowns for herself and her daughters, relying not only on illustrated magazines but on the clothes that she observed when she walked in the park, in Bond Street itself, and in as many fashionable haunts as she could reach.

In spite of all these efforts, Mrs Ruspidge's expenses were considerable. The greatest of them was, of course, her son. Augustus Hatherley was no less determined to cut a dash than his mother. His presence at an expensive school had ensured that he had made the acquaintance of a number of well-born bloods, but he had never succeeded in forming a close friendship with any of them. He was accepted as an acquaintance by several, but only so long as he could copy their extravagances, their clothes, their gaming, and their horses. He had to compete as slightly more than an equal: to smile while he dropped a monkey or a pony on the turn of a card; to be prepared to lend a bit of the ready to a well-born, temporarily embarrassed young man, without being too quick to demand repayment; to pay for merry little supper parties after a visit to the theatre or the opera, without counting how many bottles were being ordered or drunk.

As a result his mother, who refused him nothing, tried to keep her own spending as low as possible. She was, after all, obliged to remember that in a few years Charlotte would be making her come-out, and that she must keep money available to set her afloat in the world, and endow her suitably for the kind of marriage that would enable her, perhaps, to help her sisters in their turn. She missed no opportunity, therefore, of a bargain. A new warehouse offering silk or muslin at competitive prices; a little back-street shop with laces, ribbons, feathers or beads; anywhere selling cut-price gloves, or bonnets, or slippers, all of these places were sure of her custom. And if, as often happened, it did not suit her to be seen in such a place, she was delighted to be able to send her daughters, duly chaperoned by their governess, in her stead. Charlotte had as sharp an eye for a bargain as her mother, and was quite happy to bicker over the price of a flawed length of muslin, or a packet of smuggled lace.

Tiring though these trips were, for many of them involved a lengthy walk as well as a great deal of standing around when they reached their objective, Cecilia still found them preferable to spending time in the schoolroom with her unrewarding pupils. She very soon gave up hope of being able to teach them much that was meaningful, and while they were out the girls were obliged to treat her with the appearance, at least, of civility, patronising though it might be. Then, too, she was having the opportunity of seeing London, and, although the districts that they visited were often not very salubrious, their journey thither could, if carefully planned, be made to take them past places of interest. Since the girls themselves were in no hurry to return to their studies, they could sometimes be persuaded into a church, or a gallery, particularly if the latter might be presented as fashionable and, therefore, of importance.

It had long been a theory of Cecilia's that the study of history could be made more vivid to the young by taking them, whenever opportunity presented itself, to places of interest. Accordingly she persuaded her reluctant pupils, on one of their shopping expeditions, to accompany her to Westminster Abbey, a place she had long wished to see. She had assured them that they would find the great building both beautiful and interesting, but while she had hoped that this would be the case she was not altogether surprised when, after only a few minutes, all three declared themselves bored to distraction.

'It's so dark, and cold, and it smells. I won't go any further, and you shan't make me,' declared Georgina.

'My neck aches,' whined Amelia. 'Why did they have to build it so tall? And all those horrid statues give me the shivers. I don't see what it matters who they are, if nobody's ever heard of them.'

'Well, I am sorry that you do not care for it. It is generally thought to be a very fine example of Gothic architecture, and I had hoped. . . Since we are here, however, I do not mean to waste my opportunity. If you do not care to walk round any more, you may sit quietly here, and wait for me to return.'

'Sit here alone? I am sure we should do no such thing, and Mama would say you should take us home.'

'I think there can be no impropriety in the three of you sitting here together, in such a place. It is, after all, one of the most important religious buildings in our country.'

'You are supposed to look after us, not please yourself. I think you should take us straight home.'

'Oh, no, Charlotte, let us sit for a while!' Amelia lent unexpected support. 'My feet are tired, and my legs ache so,' she explained in response to her sisters' surprised looks.

'That is not surprising, at any rate! I am sure we must have walked several miles out of our way, coming here.'

'Not above half a mile,' Cecilia corrected her, 'and you were happy enough to walk more than that out of your way yesterday, to purchase that trimming for your bonnet. But I will make a bargain with you,' she added hastily, seeing that the issue would otherwise be argued interminably. 'Only allow me time to look round for a while, and I will pay for us to go home in a cab. Out of my own money,' she elaborated, seeing suspicion in Charlotte's eyes. It was a sacrifice, for she had so little money of her own left, but she was determined to finish her circuit of the Abbey, and in particular to see the monuments to the poets and writers to be found there. Her offer was grudgingly accepted, and she made haste to avail herself of what time she had.

The great church lived up to all her expectations, and it was a relief to see it alone even if hurriedly. Absorbed in what she saw, Cecilia scarcely noticed the scattering of other visitors, whose murmuring voices made a wash of sound that echoed against pillar and vaulting, ebbing and flowing like waves on a beach. On reaching Poets' Corner, however, she was startled to perceive a tall figure standing pensively before a monument to Pope.

'Lord Inglesham!'

He turned.

'Miss Avening!' His voice was as suave as ever, and she was not to know that he was astonished, even put out, by the pleasure he felt in seeing her again. 'You are well, I hope, and recovered from the rigours of the journey?'

'Perfectly, thank you, my lord. Though thanks to you, my journey was not as uncomfortable as it would otherwise have been.' She scarcely knew what she was answering. As she looked at his tall, handsome figure, her eyes fixed on that politely attentive face bent down to hers, she felt suddenly that he was somehow more real than her surroundings. The memory of Mrs Ruspidge and her disagreeable family became as insubstantial as shadows in the blinding certainty of his presence.

'I could say the same to you. You are visiting some of the better known sights of the metropolis, I collect? But alone? Did none of your relatives see fit to accompany you?'

'Oh, I am not alone!' She was quick to take up his implied criticism. 'My — that is, Mrs Ruspidge's three daughters are with me.' He raised an eyebrow, looking pointedly at the empty spaces around them. 'They were tired,' she explained. 'It was a long walk, and they were not interested in the Abbey. Only I felt I could not leave without seeing this part, at least. So here I am,' she concluded inanely.

'Here you are,' he agreed, and she was not to know that the irony in his voice concealed a kind of surprised discomfort at his own behaviour. He was, in fact, very well aware that she was not alone, having seen her and her charges enter the Abbey as he was driving past in his phaeton. He had pulled up his horses almost before he was aware of his conscious decision, and, pausing only to tell his astonished tiger to wait for him, followed her into the building. Impulse had carried him there, but fortunately the few moments that had elapsed meant that Cecilia was not immediately visible, and he had had time to realise what a spectacle he would make of himself, running after a chance-met young woman in this way.

He would almost have turned and gone again, but the acoustics of the place were such that Cecilia's conversation with the girls had floated back quite clearly to him over the ecclesiastical hush. With some hope of managing an accidental meeting, and one moreover unencumbered by her young ladies, he had taken him-

self to Poets' Corner, correctly guessing that Cecilia
would not leave the Abbey without visiting it.

Now that she stood before him, he could almost have
laughed at himself. Behaving like some kind of lovesick
schoolboy, forsooth, to manipulate a chance of meeting
with a governess! If Miss Chadworth should hear of
this. . . He tried to picture himself behaving like this for
her, but his imagination was unequal to the struggle.
He frowned, and Cecilia saw it.

'I must not delay you with my chatter,' she said
coolly, wondering why they were standing there in
silence. 'I expect you are with your nieces, are you not?'

'No.' He spoke abruptly, still frowning. 'They are
with their father. Do not go,' he added brusquely as she
made a move to withdraw. 'Please,' he amended when
she raised her eyebrows at his tone. 'Do you not want to
hear news of them? And they would never forgive me if
I did not take back some message from you — they speak
of you constantly.'

Cecilia could not help being pleased.

'Do they? What delightful girls they are; please give
them my love. And have they met with their new mama?
Will they be happy with her, do you think?'

'I hope that they will. She seems to be a kind young
woman — and she is certainly very beautiful. Quite a
paragon, in fact!'

Cecilia thought privately that beauty of person might
be of secondary importance to the three girls, however
delightful it might appear to their uncle, but she murmured a platitude.

'Yes, they were stunned by her appearance, to the
extent that all three of them — yes, even Minty! —
became completely tongue-tied for as long as half an
hour. After that, of course there was no stopping them.

"Oh, Papa, our new mama is as beautiful as a princess in a story!" was what Sophie said, so of course Minty came in with, "As beautiful as an angel!" without even bothering to whisper.' He smiled at the memory, and Cecilia smiled also, thinking that it must be a hard woman indeed to resist such flattery.

'Miss Cameron blushed like a rose, and gathered the little girls into her arms to kiss and pet them, in the most natural way in the world. For the moment, at least, she can do no wrong in their eyes. Edward stood by, with the bemused expression of a man who has somehow stumbled into Paradise, and is not quite sure how he has managed it. Only Cleone, of them all, held back a little. At least she was neither rude nor unwelcoming. Someone who did not know her would probably have thought her merely shy, and I trust that Miss Cameron thought so. Certainly she took great pains to draw the girl out, asked her about her interests, and said she was eager to hear her sing.'

Cleone had smiled, and answered, and kissed the rose-petal cheek that was offered to her, but she had volunteered nothing. It was hard for her, of course, who of all of them remembered her own mother. And then, how unfortunate for a girl who in two years would be making her debut that she would be appearing in the care of one who would inevitably outshine her, as the moon did a star. Fiona Cameron's corn-gold hair paled her own ash-blonde into insignificance, so that it looked almost pale mouse, while the brilliant blue of her eyes made the younger girl's seem faded and lack-lustre.

'It is hard for Cleone,' said Cecilia softly, unconsciously echoing her thoughts. 'She will need very gentle handling.'

'I wish you might talk to her,' said Lord Inglesham impulsively.

'Me? But I am not acquainted with Sir Edward Maisemore. It would be intolerably intrusive.'

'But if I were to suggest it?'

'Then it would be you that were intruding. I could not agree to such a thing, my lord.'

He knew that she was right, and that made him all the more irritated by her firm refusal.

'There you go again, calling me "my lord"! I wish you would not do so!'

'I beg your pardon, Lord Inglesham. I really should go now. My young ladies will be becoming impatient.'

The meeting which he had wanted now seemed to him to have been a mistake. He found it hard to accept that she was not, had never been, involved in the life of his family. In the short time that they had spent together she had fitted in so naturally that it seemed quite normal to him that she should want to help and advise Cleone, and her refusal to do so annoyed him more than was reasonable.

'Very well. I bid you a good day, Miss Avening.' He strode off, and Cecilia watched him go. With all her heart she longed to go after him, to say that she would do anything that he wished, however ill-advised. Sternly she told herself that she was nothing to him, and that he could be nothing to her. In the circumstances, it would be better if she should forget him and his family completely, never see them again, and concentrate on building herself a new life with her new family, disagreeable though they might be. With a heavy heart she rejoined her complaining charges, and took them home.

Her resolve was sorely tried. Mrs Ruspidge treated her more as a servant than as a member of the family, and her daughters were not slow to take her example. More trying than this to bear, however, was the behaviour of Augustus. Having already heard the edifying story of his behaviour with the former governess, she was not altogether surprised when, coming downstairs from the schoolroom at the end of one afternoon, when that part of the house was in total darkness, he had stopped her on the stairs, and taken her hand.

'Well, if it ain't Miss Mouse!' he said, his hand gripping hers when she would have pulled it away, and his thumb caressing the inside of her wrist in a most disagreeable fashion.

'Mr Hatherley, how you made me jump! Leave go my hand, if you please. I am in a hurry, and I believe that your mother is waiting for me.'

'And I don't believe it! Haven't I just seen her this very moment going downstairs to speak to Cook? As a matter of fact, I made sure of it, for I told her I had a desire for a dish of sweetbreads tonight, and that nothing else would satisfy me. So, you see, she will be busy for quite a while, for where they'll find sweetbreads at this time of day there's no knowing!'

He seemed very pleased with his cleverness, and as he pulled her closer she could smell the wine on his breath, and turned away her face.

'What's the matter, then? Playing coy, are we?' He jerked on her hand, then, so that she almost lost her footing. She grabbed for the banister, and her sudden movement upset his own precarious balance. He went down a step, and swore, and for a moment his grip loosened and she was able to pull free. Surer-footed than he, she ran down the stairs and made her way to the safety of the kitchen. Mrs Ruspidge looked up in surprise as she came in.

'Whatever are you doing in here? Have you no work to do, Cecilia?'

'Yes. . .that is, not a great deal, ma'am. I came to enquire if I might be of help to you.'

'Well, that is something, I suppose! As a matter of fact, you may. I particularly want to have a dish of sweetbreads for dinner, and here is Cook saying she has no time to buy them, if she is to finish the other dishes. Just pop on your bonnet, and see if you cannot fetch some.'

Normally Cecilia would have been dismayed at being asked to go out, in the half-darkness, but anything was better than risking another encounter with Augustus.

'Very good, ma'am. To which shop should I go, Cook?'

'I'm sure I don't know,' said that much tried domestic. She was, she knew, very important to her mistress, and could certainly afford to be surly with this poor relation. 'You'd better just go from shop to shop, till you find some.'

Cecilia did just that. At shop after shop she was met with a shake of the head, a polite negative or, on one occasion, an impolite one. It was dark, and she found she had strayed much further than she had noticed, and was in a place she did not know. It seemed to be very busy, almost rowdy, and she shrank against the wall as a group of young men swaggered past, talking very loudly and shoving at one another as they went. One of them cannoned into her, and clasped her in his arms in a pretence of needing support. She struggled fiercely, which made him laugh, then, remembering her hapless predecessor, stamped heavily on his foot.

By good fortune she had had the forethought to wear stout country boots, knowing that the kind of streets she was likely to be in would be dirty. Now he swore and let go of her. His friends laughed and jeered, and in rage he raised his arm and gave her a blow on the side of her head that sent her reeling into a doorway. Her head buzzing, she was aware of the support of other arms, but when she would have struggled a female voice spoke quietly in her ear.

'Don't worry, I have you safe. Now, then, boys — ' she raised her voice to a commanding, authoritative tone ' — you don't want any trouble, do you?'

'Why not, eh? Thass wot I say, why not?' Her attacker still seemed belligerent, but his friends were pulling him away.

'Sorry, Mrs E! Taken too much daffy, ain't 'e! No offence, missis?'

'Very well. But he could find himself in serious trouble, attacking innocent women in this way. Be off with you, and keep clear of the Watch!'

'Thank you, ma'am,' said Cecilia shakily. Her head clearing, she was able to look properly at her helper. She was dressed with great propriety, almost severity, and her face was soft and wrinkled, so that her aquiline nose stood out proudly against the lined cushions of her cheeks. Her voice had been educated and ladylike, and she looked with concern at Cecilia.

'You are bleeding, my dear. Come inside for a moment, and I will wash away the blood.'

Cecilia put up a shaky hand, and felt the stinging dampness on the side of her face.

'It is nothing, ma'am, I assure you. I must have done it when I fell against the wall, and it is only a scratch.'

The other woman looked at her consideringly.

'It is quite safe to come in,' she said, a remark Cecilia considered odd since she had never considered that it

might not be. However, it seemed to her that to continue
to refuse might give offence, so she meekly followed her
saviour into a pleasant sitting-room. Its aquamarine
walls were simply decorated with a Greek key pattern,
and the furniture was chosen with care and taste. There
were several bowls of flowers around the room, scenting
the air, and there was an atmosphere of calm and repose
that was balm to Cecilia's spirit after the crowded,
vulgar drawing-room of Mrs Ruspidge.

Her injury was cleaned and salved, and Cecilia
answered such questions as were put to her, explaining
why she was out on her own.

'My dear girl, it is most inadvisable! And to have
come so far! You have been most unwise, and are lucky
to have escaped with so little hurt.'

'I know it,' said Cecilia ruefully. 'I am afraid I have
lost my way.'

'You are lucky that is all you have lost. I am afraid
that I thought you had come here on purpose, perhaps
even to see me.'

'To see you, ma'am? Why is that?'

The lady smiled, her cheeks creasing up in a network
of arbitrary wrinkles that seemed not to follow the usual
pattern of facial lines but had invented their own
pathways quite independently.

'My dear child, there are so many young girls who
have no way of keeping themselves — even, sometimes,
girls of your class! I do not wish to shock or frighten
you, but this house is a place that I should like to think
you have never heard of, let alone visited. I did very
wrong to ask you in.'

Cecilia looked at her in amazement.

'You mean that this is a. . .that you are a. . .? My

goodness, I should never have guessed! I mean. . .' She
floundered to a halt, and her hostess smiled.

'I do not work, any more, as you might guess from
my age and appearance. But I do have girls living here
who do, and I admit that I am always on the look-out
for nice, pleasant, well-spoken young women. Oh, do
not be afraid! I have no intention of keeping you here
against your will! But you may believe that many of the
girls who come to me are safer, and happier, than they
would have been elsewhere.'

'I do believe it, ma'am, for you are very kind.'

'Well, I made a mistake tonight, but perhaps it was
lucky for you that I did. Now, you must be off home,
and I will send one of my boys to see you safe back.
Don't be alarmed! When I say boys, I mean just that!
Johnny is no more than eleven, but he will keep you
from harm, I am sure.'

'It is very good of you, ma'am. I know I should not
rob you of the use of your servant, but I cannot refuse.
Only. . .'

'Only what? You may give him a shilling, if you like,
and he will be very content.'

'Oh, I will, I will! But it is not that. Do you suppose
he might know of a place where I might be able to buy
some sweetbreads? I have been gone so long, and if I
should return without any. . .'

This time the other laughed out loud.

'My dear child, whatever next? You shall have some
from my kitchen, and welcome. Only be sure you do not
tell where they came from!' She opened her door, and
called some instructions. 'Now, you must forget that
you ever met me.'

'How could I do so, when you have been so good to
me?' Cecilia held out her hand, and after a moment's

hesitation the older woman took it in her own. 'Please tell me your name, at least.'

'I am Mrs Elham.' The well-bred voice was a little husky, and she turned away for a moment, blinking rapidly.

'And I am Cecilia Avening. It is unlikely, I know, but if ever I can serve you. . .'

'You can best serve me by never returning to this street! However, if ever you find yourself in need of help, you will not call on me in vain. A message will always find me. And meanwhile, if you should have more trouble with the young gentleman where you are staying. . .' She beckoned Cecilia closer and whispered in her ear. Cecilia, after a first startled glance, listened intently, and looked a question. The older woman nodded reassurance, and Cecilia gave a half-embarrassed giggle. It was certainly not the kind of thing she would ever have learned at Miss Herring's, but there was no denying that, for a girl alone in the world, a few basic suggestions about self-defence did not come amiss.

With Johnny's guidance, Cecilia was soon back in Harley Street, where she found that nobody had so much as remarked her absence, let alone been worried about her. Cook sniffed at the sight of the sweetbreads, but they came to the dinner table none the less, and Cecilia for once made sure that she received her share. She ate them with a smile, and mentally toasted her unusual new friend as she did so.

CHAPTER SIX

A FEW days later, Cecilia arrived back from yet another visit to a little shop that Mrs Ruspidge had heard of. She was loaded with parcels, since the three girls had not scrupled to buy quantities of ribbons and trimming, as well as several pairs of silk stockings and a number of branches of artificial flowers. They had not, of course, wished to carry their purchases, and although none of them was heavy Cecilia's hand ached with the effort of holding the fragile flowers in such a way as to protect them from harm.

Tired and depressed, she was in no way cheered to find that Lord Inglesham had called during her absence and left his card. She did not know whether disappointment or relief was the stronger of her emotions. It was true that she would have welcomed the chance to talk to Lord Inglesham, who now represented to her a link with all that was happy and safe in her past, as well as a hope of a more pleasant future. At the same time, she was relieved that he had not met Mrs Ruspidge, who she knew would have latched on to him at once, and attempted to force herself into his family as a friend. Nor, she thought, did Charlotte, Georgina and Amelia present a good advertisement for her teaching skills. Their names might be royal, but their behaviour, even when it was at its best, was impertinent, vulgar and intrusive.

She looked at the little rectangle of pasteboard.

'He never come in that carriage this time, miss,'

volunteered Fanny, who as usual had been detailed to open the door since Mrs Ruspidge went nowhere unaccompanied by a liveried footman. 'Frightened me, 'e did, miss, with them eyebrows an' all.'

'Silly Sealy's lord, and to think that we missed him!' complained Georgina. Cecilia's name was now common usage in the schoolroom, and even in the drawing-room where Mrs Ruspidge only tutted slightly when she heard it. 'If only Mama hadn't sent us all that way we might have been back! Won't she be cross, too, that she was out! What'll you bet she'll make you return the call?'

'Nothing, for I shall not do so,' said Cecilia calmly, hiding her feelings.

'You must, if Ma tells you to! Mustn't she, Char?'

'She'll go herself, if you don't,' volunteered Charlotte, 'and if you do she'll go with you.' Cecilia knew with a sinking feeling that it was true.

She started to walk up the stairs, but was stopped by an outraged shriek from Charlotte.

'The card! His card! You mustn't take that away; Mama would be furious! I do believe you were trying to steal it, you wicked thing!'

It had not occurred to Cecilia that it had any value, and she could not admit that she wished to keep the thing as a memento of a happy evening. She realised, however, that Charlotte was right, and knew that the card would be kept, prominently displayed, for as long as possible, and Lord Inglesham's name brought casually into many a future conversation. She hoped very much that she would be able to prevent Mrs Ruspidge from making her return the call, and so she did, but not without saying quite bluntly that such a thing was out of the question, and that his lordship would only be disgusted by such behaviour. In this she was unexpectedly supported by Augustus Hatherley, who had once been roundly snubbed by his lordship and had never forgotten it.

'It won't do, you know, Ma,' he drawled. 'Makes a girl look fast, that kind of thing. Can't be done.' As his mother was rather in awe of his superior education, she accepted his words. Cecilia was so relieved that she could almost have been grateful to Augustus, if he had not been such a trial to her.

Lord Inglesham strode away from his visit to Harley Street in no very good mood. It had never occurred to him that Cecilia might not be at home when he called, and if Fanny had not been so patently lack-witted that she was incapable of telling a convincing lie he might have wondered whether Cecilia were not simply declining to receive him. As it was, he went away unsatisfied, declaring that he would certainly not put himself out to come to this out-of-the-way street again. It was not that he was disappointed—certainly not! Merely that he had hoped to make another attempt to persuade Cecilia to see whether she could not help Cleone come to terms with the idea of her new mama.

That his niece was unhappy he was sure, though he thought it unlikely that she would confide in him, the uncle she had not seen very often in the last few years. Pale and quiet, Cleone spent long hours at her piano, going softly over the songs she had been taught before. He thought that she was using her music as an excuse for not joining in the games and discussions that Edward and Miss Cameron set time aside for each day.

This, too, he would have liked to have told Cecilia. He had been very impressed by her handling of the three girls, and would have welcomed her advice, could she have been persuaded to offer any. Earlier that same day, he had taken Miss Chadworth for a ride in his phaeton, drawn by his famous bays, and had told her of his nieces, and his fears for Cleone. She had looked at him in amazement.

'Surely the girls are not your responsibility, Lord Inglesham? They have a papa of their own, and your mother, as I believe, has always been very close to them. I do not see that you need to concern yourself with them.'

He persisted, going so far as to ask her advice about Cleone.

'Edward — their father, you know — will do nothing, for he will be quite unaware that there is any difficulty until it is too late. My mother will not wish to stay too long in London, and I know she will be reluctant to interfere. As for Miss Cameron, I cannot speak too warmly of her goodness and kindness, but she is not, I am afraid, very clever.'

'What has cleverness to do with it? Your niece is what, fifteen?'

'Yes, fifteen.'

'A child, then. And as such she must be obedient, surely, to her father and to Miss Cameron, who will be her mother. I see no difficulty in that. She owes a duty to them, and if she fails in that duty she must be told. It is quite simple.'

'I do not see it as quite so simple. You have only met Cleone once, I think, but I know her well, as is only natural. She is a warm-hearted, emotional girl, devoted to the memory of her mother.'

'But her mother has been dead for years! And now she is lucky to have a new mother, who will be kind to her, surely? This is not the age of wicked stepmothers, Inglesham.'

'No, it is not.' It did not occur to him that she was doing as he had wished, and disagreeing with him. He might, then, have thought that he would like it, but he certainly did not care for it on this subject. 'But she is a sensitive girl. She suffers, for instance, from a great terror of thunder.'

'What has that to do with it? Pray, Lord Inglesham, do not take the corner so fast! I was quite frightened!'

'I beg your pardon. I assure you that I am considered to be a fairly safe driver.'

'I am well aware that you are considered to be one of the best exponents of the art — or is it perhaps a science?' she complimented him warmly. 'I am afraid, however, that I am not quite used to being so high up! It is quite an experience, however, and I shall strive to quell my fears. Which, by the way, is what your niece should be encouraged to do. A fear of thunder is quite irrational, since it can hurt nobody, and so she should be told. It is quite ridiculous to pander to such ideas, for in time they can easily turn into a fixed habit which started merely as an affectation.'

'I do not call it an affectation. She was in great fear. My sister, you know, died during a thunderstorm.'

'But not because of it, surely? I should have heard if it were the case. No, Lord Inglesham, she should be encouraged — made, if necessary — to behave in a seemly and ladylike fashion. That is what my mama would have done, and that is my only advice.'

Her calm complacency irritated him. There seemed no reason to prolong the conversation, and he drove her home as quickly as she would allow. They spoke of neutral subjects, and if she was disappointed that he did not take the opportunity of having her alone with him to propose to her she did not show it. Her mama, he thought, had taught her well. Too well, perhaps?

Marcus went home again in no very pleasant mood. He found his mother sitting alone in the small room she favoured when she was at the London house, since she had decorated it herself to suit her colouring, and it was, besides, small enough to keep at the constant warm temperature which best agreed with the tight discomfort she so often felt now in her chest. She was writing letters, and finished a sentence before she looked up with a smile.

'I believe you would finish your sentence even if the house were to be on fire,' he said, rather crossly.

'I expect I should. The habits of childhood, you know, are inclined to stay with one forever, and your grandmother was very insistent that one should finish a thing properly, before beginning another. I have never seen any reason to differ from this.'

'Come to think of it, I do exactly the same!' he realised, never having been aware of it before.

'And I have no doubt your children will do so, also,' she said peacefully, laying aside her letter. 'How was your drive?' she continued, with an unusually obvious connection of ideas.

'Very pleasant,' he answered shortly. The Dowager waited quietly, her hands folded in her lap, and watched him kick moodily at the logs in the fire. She did not care for the odour of burning sea-coal, and her fireplace was always supplied from the country estate with the sweet-smelling wood that she loved. Although he was thirty years old, she could still see within him the small, determined toddler he had been. When, as now, his formidable eyebrows were drawn together in that irritable way, she knew to expect, if not a tantrum, at least an outburst of some kind or other.

'Mama, what do you think about Cleone's fear of thunder?' he asked abruptly. She was surprised. It was the last thing she had expected him to want to talk to her about.

'That it is unfortunate, of course, for her more than anyone. She suffers from it: not only from the actual terror, and from the anxiety of waiting when a storm is on its way, but from the knowledge that she ought to be able to control herself better than she can.'

'You do not think she should be made to do so?'

'I cannot see how it is possible. How can one make someone cease to be frightened of something that they know is not inherently fearful? She can learn self-discipline, and indeed has made some improvement, though not always, as you have seen. Why do you ask? We spoke about this not very long since. Have you just seen Cleone?'

'No, but she has been on my mind. Before I went away she was only a child, and though I was fond of her it was only in the way of buying her little gifts, or taking her to the pantomime at Christmas. Now I come back from the West Indies to find her a young woman, and so very like Jane! In looks, that is. Jane never had her volatile nature, and really one wonders where it came from!' His mother looked at him, seeing in him the living reflection of her own highly emotional and volatile husband, and suppressed a smile. 'I cannot help but be anxious for her,' he continued. 'I am afraid that she is far from happy with her father's new marriage.'

'But in the long run, it will be better for her. As you say, she is becoming a young lady, and it is not good for her to be only with old women like myself and Miss Dixon.'

'Miss Dixon is a good governess, is she not? She taught Jane, after all, and I still remember learning my letters from her when I was a little boy.'

'That is just it! She is an excellent woman, and I would never consider her leaving me. But I have been wondering whether she would not be better suited for a companion for me, someone to help me with my letters, than to be in charge of three lively girls. I fear she does not control them as well as she should, and they do not respect her, though they are fond of her. So the influence of Miss Cameron will, I believe, be a very good thing.'

'So, she should be made to mind Miss Cameron? I suppose it is her duty to do so.'

If his mother found his choice of words unusual, she did not remark upon it.

'I hope that in this case her sense of duty will go hand in hand with her own wishes. Of course it will be difficult for her, just at first. That is to be expected. But though she may be self-willed, a little over-emotional, she is at heart a thoroughly good, loving girl. I think that if she is carefully treated she will come through this test with flying colours. And no one, you know, could be a more careful parent than Edward.'

He nodded his agreement to that, but he still had not sat down. The fire, which had been burning perfectly brightly, had not responded well to his attack, and was glowing sullenly. She did not think it would survive another assault.

'My dear, will you not take a chair, if you intend to stay here? The room is too small for you to take your exercise in it, and my neck is getting tired with having to look up at you all the time.'

'I beg your pardon, Mama.' He dropped into a chair, crossing his legs and swinging the uppermost foot backwards and forward, just out of time with the tick of the clock. Her husband had had just the same trick, when he was worried or ill at ease, and the familiarity made it dear to her, though she still found its arhythmic quality unsettling. Quietly she moved the small round table near him so that he would not kick it if the movement became any stronger.

'Do you not think the girls should have a new governess?' he burst out at last.

'Perhaps, but I would not be inclined to hurry things too much. For one thing, it would never do to hurt poor Miss Dixon's feelings, and, for another, they are surely enjoying a little holiday, until after the wedding. There is no need for them to be doing lessons just now, and getting used to a new governess, when they are already having to adjust to living once more with their father, and to their new mother — do you not think it might create more problems?'

'Not if they knew her already.'

'Ah, you are thinking of the young lady you met on the journey? But my dear Marcus, the acquaintance of a few hours! They cannot be said to know one another.'

'They liked her.' He was, she could see, almost pleading with her. She filed the knowledge away, to be pondered upon later, in privacy.

'I dare say they did. But they must learn to like, and to love, Miss Cameron herself. Besides, the question does not arise.'

'You would not recommend Miss Avening to Edward, then?'

'My love, I should not dare to. Oh, not that Edward would be cross — when is he ever? But it would be impossibly interfering of me. I am, after all, only his mother-in-law, not his own mother! It was one thing to have the girls, when he felt himself unable to do so, but quite another to be pushing myself into his new marriage! Miss Cameron might never forgive me, and I should not blame her. She does not deserve to start her marriage under the shadow not only of the memory of Edward's adored first wife but of that wife's family also.'

He knew that she was right, but his foot was still swinging.

'I have not forgotten the young lady, Marcus. I promise you that I have asked among all my friends, and you know they are numerous! I am sure that something can be done for her. Have you been to call on her?'

'Yes. She was out.' His tone expressed all the irrational anger he felt at her absence, but he was unaware of it. He stood up. 'It is not a fit place for her, Mama. I do not think it is good for her to be there.'

If she wondered at his vehemence, she hid her feelings successfully.

'From what you have told me, she is a young woman of character and good sense. I do not think she will come to too much harm, for a while, at least. Call again, and bring her to see me. Or ask her to come and call on me — you may explain that my state of health makes it difficult to do a great deal of visiting. I shall be much better able to place her, if we have met.'

His look expressed gratitude, but she could see he was not satisfied. With a word of farewell he left her room, but she did not at once resume her abandoned letter. Instead she sat, staring at the log fire, a little frown between her eyes.

She had known Miss Chadworth since her come-out

three years earlier, for her grandmother had been one of her own friends. There was no doubt that the girl would make a most suitable wife for Marcus, and she had been pleased when she had heard, from her friend, that he had been paying his attentions to her. At twenty-one she was everything that a mother might require in a daughter-in-law: cheerful, calm, good, and from a similar background to his own. She would bring ten thousand pounds with her—respectable, though not a fortune, but Marcus did not need to marry a fortune. She would be a good mother to his children, a good mistress to his house, a good hostess at his table. But would she be a good wife for Marcus?

That he himself had some doubts was obvious, since he had still made no formal proposal. He danced with her, took her walking and driving, visited with flowers and small gifts, all the actions of an accepted lover. But his face did not change when he saw her, and he seemed unworried if she did not appear at an evening function. The Dowager Lady Inglesham remembered her own youth, and a little reminiscent smile trembled on her lips. She had been so fortunate as to fall in love with a man who was welcomed by her parents as a son-in-law, and her marriage had been, if tempestuous at times, supremely happy. She did not want some kind of cold-blooded, respectable match for her only son, however suitable.

Yet did she really want him to marry a governess? She hoped that she was not the kind of person to mind about such things, but there had been some nasty rumours flying about, she remembered, at the time of young Avening's marriage. That most of the rumours had emanated from his own mother had made them more unpleasant but also more credible. And here was

Marcus, thoroughly out of temper because he had been
to call on the girl and she had been out! She thought it
likely that he was not, as yet, aware of the trend of his
own feelings. Certainly she had better do some investi-
gating of her own, before he became so. Meanwhile, the
fire was definitely in need of mending. She rang her bell.

Cecilia did her best, from that unfortunate evening
on, to keep as far away from Augustus Hatherley as
possible. Fortunately he did not spend a great deal of
time at home, which he regarded merely as a place to
sleep, eat, and have his laundry done. During the
hunting season he had not infrequently managed to get
himself invited down to the country estates of his
wealthier friends. He earned his keep by riding their
more difficult horses, for it had to be admitted that,
objectionable though he might be in many respects, he
was an excellent rider. Any man who had a horse with
bad habits, or one which he was wishing to sell, was
glad to have Augustus ride it out twice or thrice. If the
bad habits could be cured, he would exhaust the horse
into submission, and overcome it by the force of his will.
If the horse was to be sold, he would be sure that it was
seen to its best advantage, sailing over fences, always up
with the leaders.

Now, however, such sports were at an end for a while,
and the season was beginning in all its glory. With the
abdication of Napoleon the French King Louis, grown
old and fat in his exile, unexpectedly found himself
Louis XVIII, and was received in London where flags
of the Bourbons flew everywhere, and everyone wore
white cockades in his honour. Paris, of which the
English had been starved for so long, was now once
more available, and English visitors were flocking there
by their thousands. Augustus toyed with the idea of

going himself, but not very seriously. For one thing, his knowledge of the French tongue was minimal, and, though everyone knew that one had only to shout more loudly in English to make foreigners understand, still there was the inconvenience of travel, lodging and servants. Nor, of course, was he a connoisseur of the arts, so the Corsican Monster's looted treasures held no allure for him.

All in all, it seemed good to him to stay in London. A personable young man did not find it too difficult to make himself welcome to the many anxious mamas who were about the difficult and expensive business of launching their daughters into society and, if possible, matrimony. Augustus had no interest at all in settling down in marriage, but if some wealthy heiress — preferably already in control of her fortune — should cross his path he would not be averse to making his way in the world that way.

London, after all, was to be the social capital of the world that year, if the Prince Regent knew anything about it. Though the Emperor of Austria had refused an invitation, still King Frederick of Prussia and Czar Alexander would be coming, along with many more minor members of royalty. It was true that these could be an embarrassment — so many of them were related to the Regent's impossible and inconvenient wife, after all! — but they still promised a glittering array of celebrations, and the Russian advance guard, in the shape of the Czar's sister Grand Duchess Catherine of Oldenburg, was already in residence in Pulteney's Hotel. All in all, it was very promising, and Augustus was looking forward to a great deal of enjoyment and, he hoped, profit.

To be part of all this would, however, be expensive.

It was true that a gentlemen had not the problems of the opposite sex: nobody, for instance, would be likely to remark on the fact that he was wearing the same evening coat that he had worn the previous week. But still one must have everything new, from top-boots to hats and gloves, and one must have at least access to a good horse to ride in the park, and the possibility of hiring a respectable carriage. With the cream of the foreign visitors expected in June, it seemed to Augustus to be a good idea to live rather more quietly in May, saving one's money and one's energy, while indulging in a little lucrative gaming of an evening. And, if he should lack for amusement, he might renew his pursuit of the elusive Cecilia. While he scarcely expected to be able to 'know' her, in the biblical sense, some kisses and perhaps a little exploratory caressing were always pleasant.

As May progressed, therefore, Cecilia found that it was more and more difficult to avoid Augustus. He waylaid her on the stairs and in passages, until she found herself leaving a room only with the protection of the girls, or Mrs Ruspidge, whenever possible. For the first few hours of the day she was safe, since he rarely woke before twelve, and she tried as far as she could to do such schoolroom studying as she could induce her charges to perform during those hours. She knew only too well that he was not averse to coming into the schoolroom, and that the presence of his young sisters would inhibit him not at all.

She could not prevent a few encounters with him. Once he had found her alone in the schoolroom, and she had been obliged to dodge round the chairs until she could run from the room. A second time he had cornered her in the hall, and succeeded in landing a kiss, not on her lips, but on her averted cheek. That time the sound of Mrs Ruspidge coming down the stairs had saved her from his continuing embraces. A third time he had lain in wait for her when she went up to her bedroom at night. This room was not one of the guest rooms, but a small chamber on the third floor, near to the schoolroom. Cecilia had not minded being put in what was to all intents and purposes a servant's room, for she was only too glad to be away from the family. With the onset of warmer weather, it was no hardship to read or sew in her little haven, when she had the freedom to do so.

It gave Cecilia a severe shock to find her tormentor hiding round the corner from this little room. She had thought that Augustus was still down in the dining-room with his wine, or had gone to his club. Instead here he was, his breath heavy with port, reaching out for her as she was already beginning to relax in the expectation of peace and privacy. He held her firmly, one hand pinning her arms to her sides while the other gripped her chin so that she could not turn away her face.

She gripped her lips tightly together, so that when his hot, wet mouth came down on hers it found them hard and unresponsive. He let them wander over her neck, and she had time to be thankful that her evening dress was cut so unfashionably high. He pulled her hard against him, pressing her body against his own, while his free hand left her chin and wandered down, feeling her breast through the layers of clothing, weighing and pinching it.

'It's all real, then,' he congratulated her thickly. 'Wasn't sure. Could have been padding.'

If she had not been so upset and angry, Cecilia could almost have laughed. That she should attempt to emphasise her feminine attraction at all was unlikely; that she should do so while living in this house was unthinkable. She did not speak, but held herself rigid and away from him. It seemed likely that she would have to put into practice some of the instructions that Mrs Elham had given her, but she wished to hold them in reserve for as long as possible. For one thing, they were the kind of actions that no young lady ought to be capable of, and, for another, she was afraid of what might be the consequences.

Mrs Ruspidge, of course, was devoted to her son and he could do no wrong in her eyes. There was no doubt that were he to complain of Cecilia's behaviour he would be believed whatever Cecilia might have to say in her own defence. It was true that Cecilia's presence made it unnecessary for Mrs Ruspidge to look for another governess for her girls, but Cecilia did not think that such a consideration would sway her for long, if she thought that her son was in danger of being seduced by a penniless interloper. With no other prospect in view, Cecilia could not face the thought of being put out into the street. While she did not fear that she would be driven to the lengths of applying to Mrs Elham for help, still she would have to ask for what was scarcely more than charity, either from one of her old school-friends, or from Lord Inglesham. Either would be intolerable.

'Let go of me, Mr Hatherley,' she said between clenched teeth, 'or I shall be forced to call for assistance.'

'Call away,' he grunted. 'They'll not hear you, two floors down, and Charlotte screeching that infernal song.' He gave her breast a final pinch, then his hand roved round to her back and down, cupping her buttock and pulling her hips against him. They were too tightly pressed together to allow her to move her legs other than to kick him, and she was wearing only soft kid evening slippers that would hardly be likely to do much damage. Instead she did the next best thing, hoping that he might take it as an accident.

'Oh, I feel so faint!' she said in failing tones, and allowed her weight to sag against the arm that was still around her. His other hand ceased his exploration for the moment, as he needed both arms to support her weight. His head, which had been nuzzling at her neck, lifted so that he could look at her face. There was an expression of avid excitement in his eyes that made her words almost come true. Rolling up her eyes, she let her head loll sideways and then brought it heavily forward, so that the full weight of her skull fell against his nose.

With a yell he released her, both hands coming up to clutch at the nose that was already spurting blood. Cecilia, mindful of her gown, stepped neatly backwards.

'Dear me,' she said calmly. 'You had better go and put a key down your back, Mr Hatherley.'

'You little bitch!' he said indistinctly. 'You did that on purpose.'

'Sir, I was fainting! And I still feel a little unwell, so you will excuse me if I do not help you.' She whisked herself into her room and locked the door, thankful that it had a key and that the door itself was stoutly made. Leaning with her back against it, she listened to his feet stumbling down the stairs, and hoped that he retained enough sense to say that he had bumped into something, or fallen downstairs. His male pride, she thought, would scarcely allow him to admit that he had been beaten by a woman, and it would be difficult for him to claim that Cecilia had thrown herself at him, when she had so obviously managed to protect herself.

He kept to his room for the whole of the following day, and when he came down to dinner there were still traces of blood round his nostrils, and bruising round both his eyes. The nose, rather to Cecilia's relief, did not appear to be broken, and though Mrs Ruspidge was loud in her lamentations he dismissed her sympathy curtly. His sisters, less sympathetic, thought it a great joke, and were inclined to tease him, but Cecilia said nothing, and kept her eyes on her plate.

CHAPTER SEVEN

CECILIA was even more careful after that. Fearing that the key might one day disappear from her door, she bought a stout bolt, and had it fitted by the boot boy one afternoon when everyone was out. After that she felt a little safer, and, whether because of her vigilance or because he had lost interest in her, Augustus seemed to be less of a problem. She dismissed him from her mind, and concentrated on looking for another post, searching the newspapers for advertisements, and going so far as to visit an agency that specialised in such things.

The result was not encouraging. Her age, for one thing, was against her. Wise mamas were far from willing to take attractive young women into their homes, to the detriment of their own peace of mind and to the temptation of husbands, or older sons. Then, although she had a glowing testimonial from Miss Herring, she had never actually worked as a governess.

'But how am I to get experience, if no one will employ me?' she asked helplessly. The manageress of the agency looked at her with little sympathy.

'The kind of position that you are seeking is rarely the subject of an advertisement,' she pointed out. 'Nor do such ladies come to us, except as a last resort. They ask among their family and friends, and invariably get someone recommended in that way. If you have no one to speak for you. . .' She let her voice tail off, and closed her ledger with a dismissive snap. Much discouraged, Cecilia returned to Harley Street. It was now almost two weeks since Lord Inglesham's call, and he had not tried to see her again. It had, of course, been no more than a courtesy, and naturally he must have felt that he had fulfilled his obligations. That his mother had been asking among her friends she was, of course, unaware of, and she felt sure that he had quite forgotten his promise of asking her to help.

Marcus had, in fact, called a second time. On that occasion he had been taken up to the drawing-room by the uniformed manservant, whose eyes had opened wide at the name and style of the visitor. Mrs Ruspidge, highly elated, had greeted him effusively.

'Lord Inglesham! I had so much been wishful of thanking you for your kindness to my girl! So very much obliged to you for bringing her to London in your carriage! Young girls today, alas, are sadly heedless, and to be travelling alone, as she was. . . I could not consider it wise! But there, you cannot expect old heads on young shoulders, can you, Inglesham?'

'I was not aware, madam, that she had any other choice in the matter. Were any other arrangements made for her?'

'The foolish girl quite forgot to inform me of her plans, you know, Inglesham. If she had, I should of course have told her. . .but she did not. Brought up as she was, one cannot expect her to have quite all of those ladylike little ways that you and me, Inglesham, are accustomed to! *Rather* too independent, to my way of thinking. She simply arrived! Without so much as a by-your-leave!'

'She is your stepdaughter, I believe, madam?'

'No, no, not at all! She was my husband's step-daughter — no relation at all, really! He was very good to her, but then he always was too good, too generous

to everyone.' She paused to raise a highly scented
handkerchief to her eyes, regarding him above it. He
had sat down, at her invitation, but refused to give up
his hat and gloves, since he had no intention of staying
if Cecilia was out. 'I hope I know my duty well enough,
Inglesham, to take her in out of Christian charity. Not
that she was any concern of mine, really, but I would
not have it said that I had refused her shelter. Of course,
it will not be for long. I know she means to look for a
position. It is not what I would want for *my* girls, of
course, but there, beggars can't be choosers, can they,
Inglesham?'

'So they say.' He was disgusted by her vulgarity, and
had enough experience of her kind of toadying familiarity to know that if he were not careful she would be
inviting herself to call on his mother. As it was, he
supposed she would hereafter claim him as a close
friend, and make much of his visit. He had, after all,
called twice at the house, and he had not missed seeing
his own card, displayed with careless artistry, on the
silver tray in the hall. He felt more than ever that this
was a wholly inappropriate place for Cecilia to live, but
it was hard to know what he could do. To pass on his
mother's invitation would be tantamount to inviting the
whole family; even to call for a third time would create
a presumption of friendship. He rose to his feet.

'Your dear mother is with you in London?' she
enquired hastily. 'I hear so much about her from the
dear Duchess—she quite raves about her, you know!
Only the other day, she said to me——'

'My mother has a great many friends, and numbers
among them several duchesses. I am afraid that I have
not the time to remain any longer, madam. Pray express
my apologies to Miss Avening.'

'But surely you will wait? She has but just now stepped out, with my little girls, for a walk. Such pleasant weather, is it not? And I know that she will be sadly disappointed to have missed you. Let me send for some wine, and cake. . .it is no trouble, no trouble at all.'

'You are too kind, madam. Unfortunately I am unable to accept your invitation.'

'Ah, you gentlemen — always on the go, as my son says. So naughty of him! But another time, perhaps?'

He bowed, but did not answer.

'You have a message for Cecilia?' She was not one to give up too easily, he saw.

'No message, except that I called.' He left the room, and she could almost have stamped her foot with vexation. She could be in no doubt that he wished to have nothing to do with her, or her family. Even her best card, the Duchess, had been played without effect. It was true that the Duchess had been no more than an opera girl who had trapped a drunken duke into matrimony and was now running him into his grave. Still, half pickled in gin though she was much of the time, she was a duchess, and Mrs Ruspidge prided herself on the connection, though she could see that it was unlikely to bring her further inside the fringes of society that she presently inhabited. Cecilia, had she played her cards aright, might have been very useful indeed, but Lord Inglesham had made it very plain indeed that he did not intend to pursue the acquaintance. Well, the girl should be punished by not hearing of his lordship's visit — not that she would even care, the stuck-up ninny. Mrs Ruspidge gave an exclamation of profound irritation, and rang the bell. She must make sure, before the girls returned, that the manservant did not let the cat out of the bag.

June was approaching, and the London Season was in full swing. Society, with its generous sprinkling of foreign royalty, and the promise of more and greater to come, threw its collective self into gaiety. Balls, soirées, picnics, breakfasts, masquerades — the list of private and public entertainments was endless. Romance, too, was in the air, for was not the young Princess Charlotte, only heir to the corpulent Regent her father, about to become engaged to the Prince of Orange? Of course, the Russians were hardly likely to be pleased with such an alliance, but Holland was a useful enough place, after all, perhaps more useful than the huge, but still largely uncivilised, Russia.

On the third day of June guns in Hyde Park fired salvoes to mark the signing of the definitive Treaty. The Napoleonic wars were officially over, and London prepared to receive the Allied Sovereigns. Landing at Dover three days later, the Czar was reported to have said, 'God be praised! I have set foot upon the land that has saved us all!' His arrival in London was less diplomatic, however. Refusing to stay at St James's Palace, he insisted on putting up at the Pulteney Hotel with the Grand Duchess, and then to crown the insult declined attending the magnificent banquet that the Regent had arranged at Carlton House, and dined with his sister at the hotel.

The Prince, however, was not to be deterred, and continued with his programme of sumptuous entertainments. London was in turmoil. There was almost no milk to be had because, said the milkmaids, the cows in Green Park had been frightened by the guns, the bands, and the parades. The very washerwomen were growing above themselves, and refusing to work for anyone less than a prince, or perhaps a general. At Almack's, Czar Alexander set the seal of approval to the fashionable dance of the day by performing the waltz, and Princess Charlotte was rumoured, now, to have lost interest in the Prince of Orange, to whom she was supposed to be bethrothed, and was making sheep's eyes at Prince Augustus of Russia, who had come in the suite of King Frederick.

Even in Harley Street, the waves of excitement generated by the events of the time were stirring up the stagnant backwaters, and bringing with them the heady ozone of worldly glory. Nothing would satisfy the girls, day after day, but to go to Hyde Park, where they were willing to loiter for hours in the hope of seeing a prince, a king, or even General Blücher. He, in the absence of Wellington, who was rumoured still to be enjoying himself in Paris, was much admired as a war hero, his propensity for over-indulging in strong beer and cognac seeming no more than the kind of bluff martial behaviour to be expected from such a man.

Cecilia was only too happy to be thus employed, and derived as much pleasure as they did from observing the fashions, and trying to recognise the faces of the great from the portraits printed in the public Press — no easy task. Her only concern was in managing to control the girls, and keep them from going beyond the line of what was pleasing. They had no notion of shyness, and did not scruple to comment on the appearance of passers-by in tones that could scarcely be called private. Cecilia had several times to blush for them, and once or twice actually to apologise, but by threatening to bring them no more she succeeded in taming them to a certain extent. No advice that she could give as to the advisability of refraining from personal remarks, or at least uttering them in quiet whispers, had any effect at all, for they had grown accustomed to treating her with all the disregard that their mother showed her.

It was with pleasure, therefore, that she learned that her three charges had been invited to go with their mother for a whole day's visit to a friend.

'Lady Aurelia — quite the most delightful creature, and a good friend of the dear Duchess — has invited us all. There is no need for you to come, Miss Avening. Lady Aurelia's children have their own governess, and I am sure that she will be more than equal to looking to my little angels!' Cecilia doubted it, but she wished them much pleasure of their visit, and welcomed the prospect of an entire day to herself. It was true that Mrs Ruspidge, with her habitual hatred of idle hands, had left a large number of the girls' clothes to be mended, and even stockings to be darned, but Cecilia was a quick and careful needlewoman. By dint of rising as soon as it was light, and working hard for the first few hours of the morning, she was able to leave the house as early as half-past ten, having made satisfactory inroads on the work.

The prospect of a holiday raised her spirits to a level they had never before reached since she had arrived in London. The weather was fine and warm, allowing her to wear her best pelisse over the simple sprig muslin gown that she had not been too proud to iron up herself. The pelisse was of deep rose-pink, very simply cut but fitting to admiration, and had been given to her two years earlier by one of her departing school-friends, who had admitted candidly that she had grown too stout to wear it any more. It was of excellent material, and Cecilia had taken good care of it, so that with her simple summer straw bonnet freshly trimmed with matching pink ribbon, she felt, if not fashionable, at least as smart as she was ever likely to be.

The brilliant sunshine had brought out crowds of people, both walking and riding. Cecilia was fortunate to see the Princess Charlotte herself, driven by at a spanking pace. So absorbed was she in watching the royal passer-by, and wondering what her life must really be like, that she all but bumped into another figure that was also absorbed in the spectacle.

'Oh, I beg your pardon! Why, it is Cleone! Miss Maisemore, I should say, of course.'

'Miss Avening! How wonderful this is! I had been so sorry that we have not seen you since our journey. Why did you not come and visit us? Papa has been so much with us, and Miss Cameron, that it has scarcely been possible for us to come and find you, but I did hope you would call.'

'You are very kind, Miss Maisemore, but I did not wish to intrude on your reunion. And I, too, have been very busy.'

'I wish you would call me Cleone, as you did before. Miss Maisemore sounds so very unfriendly. What have you been busy with? Have you found a new post? They are lucky girls, if that is so.'

'Not exactly a new post, but I have been acting as governess for the daughters of my stepfather's second wife. Dear me, what a mouthful! I do not think she would wish me to call her my stepmother, and of course she is quite right, for she is no such thing. I am very grateful to her for taking me in.'

Cleone seemed content to take these words at their face value, and certainly Cecilia was in good looks, and seemed cheerful enough. She tucked her arm confidingly through Cecilia's.

'Now I have found you again, I shall not easily let you escape! You are not in a hurry, are you? Please, please say you are not, and that you will come back to the house with me! Sophie and Minty will be wild to see you again!'

So warm and loving an invitation was balm to Cecilia's spirit, bruised as it was by the hard looks and harder words that were her continual lot in Harley Street. While she had been reluctant to interfere with Cleone's new life at Lord Inglesham's instigation, she still felt affectionately disposed towards the girl, and would not refuse her advice if it should be asked for. The sunshine, the festive air of the park, and the pleasure of being wanted all combined to make her throw caution to the winds.

'If you ask me like that, how can I refuse? But Cleone, how does it come that you are here like this? Surely you are not all alone, are you?'

'Of course not! I am here with my maid.' For a moment she tried to look like a young woman of the world, but then her sense of humour got the better of her and she giggled. 'That sounds very grand, doesn't it? She's not really my maid, of course. At least, she's all of our maid, me and my sisters. Oh, very well, Miss Avening, *mine* and my sisters'! She was one of the nursery maids, when we were small, and now she helps look after our clothes, and helps us with our hair, curl papers and that kind of thing. You know what I mean. She is a dear! She would have travelled with us on the journey, only she came on ahead with Grandmama.'

'And does she, in addition to her other perfections,

enjoy the unusual felicity of being able to make herself invisible?'

Cleone giggled again.

'You are so funny, Miss Avening — not like a governess, at all! No, she is here, but the truth is we became separated in the crowd. I am afraid I was too busy watching the Princess — did you see her go by? I ran ahead, to get a better view, and when I turned round Abby was gone!'

'Will she not be very much frightened? Should we not be looking for her?'

'No, for she is very sensible. It happened once before, when we were much younger, and she told us then that we should always stay quite still, and that she would come and find us. Otherwise, you know, we might each end up going round in circles, missing one another at every turn! There, now, what did I tell you? Here she is!'

The former nursemaid came trotting up, panting, and pink of face. She was very plump, almost fat, but her soft roundness had a most appealing quality to it. Cecilia could imagine what a haven her wide lap and generous soft bosom would be to an unhappy child, and how warm and comforting those chubby arms, which would certainly be as smooth and dimpled as a baby's. She fixed her eyes on Cecilia's face in a long, searching look, but seemed not to be alarmed by whatever she saw there.

'Now, Miss Cleone! Running away as if you had no more sense than little Miss Minty! And me, that can no more run than that bench there!'

'I'm sorry, Abby, truly I am! You should not have run after me; you will make yourself ill on this warm day! Come and sit on the bench a moment, since it is so

near, and rest yourself.' Cleone kept one hand on
Cecilia, and with the other took her maid's hand. 'Oh,
Abby, I am so glad I did run, though! For I have found
Miss Avening, who was so good to us when we came up
to London with Uncle Marcus! Is it not the most
fortunate thing in the world?'

'Very pleased, I am sure, miss,' said Abby, bobbing
a neat curtsy. Like many fat people she moved with
surprising grace and lightness. 'I heard all about you
from my young misses, and very grateful I am, too.
They've talked of you a lot.'

'That is more than I deserve, I am sure. But let us
follow Cleone's advice, and sit on this bench for a few
minutes. It is in the shade, too, which is quite welcome
on such a day.'

'Thank you, miss. I don't mind if I do. I'm not built
for running, and that's a fact.'

Cleone sat down, with her two companions on either
side of her, and sighed happily. 'What a morning I have
had! Seeing the Princess, and now finding you, Miss
Avening. The others will be quite jealous, only of course
they are so happy to have gone with Papa to visit Miss
Cameron that they will not mind it.'

Her voice, from being uncomplicatedly happy,
dropped to a carefully neutral tone.

'You did not wish to go with them?' Cecilia asked
casually.

'No, for I shall see her later today in any case. And
sometimes, you know, I like to do things without them,
though I am fond of them. Is that wrong of me?'

'Of course it is not,' reassured Cecilia. 'It is only too
natural. You, after all, are almost a young lady now,
and your feelings and interests are necessarily different
from theirs, when they are still children.'

On Cleone's far side Abby nodded, casting an approving glance at the stranger.

'They are quite. . .one could almost say, quite in love with Miss Cameron,' said Cleone quietly, her eyes fixed on her hands, which were now folded rather tightly in her lap.

'Are they? That is very good to hear. You must be very happy for them. Of course, it is not to be expected that you should feel quite as strongly as they do. I do not suppose even Sophie really has any recollection of her mother.'

The kid gloves were stretched tightly over her knuckles. Cleone carefully unclenched her fingers, and began absently to smooth the stretched leather.

'She is very kind, and good, and very, very beautiful,' she said with careful fairness. 'But. . .'

'But you cannot put her in your mother's place?'

Cleone shook her head.

'No. And I cannot — I *cannot* — call her Mama!' Her voice wavered childishly upwards, and her lower lip wobbled and turned down at the edges.

'There is no need for you to do so yet, since they are not married,' pointed out Cecilia with calm good sense. 'Even if Sophie and Minty do——' she paused while Cleone nodded miserably '—I think, from what I have heard of him, that your papa would not expect it of you, just yet.'

'I have seen him glance at me, looking — oh, I don't know — hurt, when I have called her Miss Cameron,' said Cleone in despairing tones. 'And then the others remark on it, and ask why I do so, and I don't know what to do!'

Two fat tears ran down her cheeks, and she wiped at them childishly with the back of her hand. Automatically, both Abby and Cecilia reached for a handkerchief, and she found herself with one for each hand, and laughed shakily.

'It is not really for me to advise you, but in your place I should go to your papa, Cleone, and tell him what you have told me. It is true that "Miss Cameron" sounds rather cold and distant, and I am sure you do not wish to hurt her feelings, do you? After all, only just now you begged me not to call you "Miss Maisemore". Supposing you were to try to call her "Mother", instead of "Mama". Could you do that, do you think?'

Cleone's hands fell still, as she considered this idea.

'Yes, I could. I really think I could! Oh, Miss Avening, thank you!' For a moment it looked as though she would cast herself intemperately into Cecilia's arms, quite forgetting where she was, but as once before Cecilia caught her hands in her own, and held them firmly.

'There, now! I am sure you would have thought of it for yourself, sooner or later. Or your grandmama would have done, if you had asked her. Did you speak to her about it?'

'No.' Cleone hung her head. 'It is so awkward, you see. If only she were Papa's mother, instead of Mama's, things would be so much simpler! I have scarcely seen her since we came to London; it is almost as if she was avoiding us!'

Cecilia mentally awarded the absent Dowager Lady Inglesham full marks for tact, even if she had perhaps taken her care too far.

'I feel so much better now! Do let us go back to the house and see if Papa and the girls are returned. Oh, I cannot wait to see their faces, when they see you!'

Sir Edward's house, near to Grosvenor Square, was a

haven of well-bred tranquillity after Harley Street. Cecilia's arrival, with Cleone and Abby, coincided with the return of her sisters and father. His face, even now, had the worn look that long physical or emotional suffering left behind it, but his eyes were kind and his smile welcoming as he held out his hand to Cecilia.

'Miss Avening! You cannot believe how pleased I am, and how very guilty I feel that I did not come in person to thank you for your well-timed services. My daughters have sung your praises, and even my brother-in-law seems deeply impressed by your abilities. He had no idea, it seems, of the discomforts and dangers of travelling with three young ladies! Yours was a rescue indeed!'

Cecilia laughed, and disclaimed, while the younger girls clung round her, asking for kisses. After so short an acquaintance as theirs had been, she was surprised to find herself feeling so at home with them, and when Sir Edward pressed her to stay for luncheon and spend the afternoon with them she made little demur.

'You find us very much *en famille*,' he said, laughing. 'Now that I have my girls with me, I grudge almost every moment that is not spent with them. Even to the extent of taking meals with them!'

'Not every moment, surely, Papa? I know you want to be with. . .with Mother, also!' Cleone's voice wobbled a little, but the unfamiliar word came out firm and clear. He cast a startled glance at her blushing face, and was wise enough to make no remark. The little girls, fortunately, were too busy trying to tell Cecilia, in minute detail, everything that they had done since their arrival in London. They began to drag Cecilia up the stairs, and, glancing back, she saw him put his arm round his eldest daughter and kiss her with great affection, an embrace that was warmly returned.

Cecilia shared their simple luncheon of cold meats, bread and fruit.

'If I had known you were to be here, Miss Avening, I should have had a better meal for you than this,' said Cleone with housewifely concern. Cecilia reassured her, and indeed she had not expected to eat at all until the evening, since she had intended to stay out all day, and she scarcely liked to go alone into a pie shop, or a chop house.

After they had finished, Sir Edward announced that he had papers to go through, and went off to his library, while the three little girls carried Cecilia up to their schoolroom, a comfortable if shabby apartment that was still furnished and decorated as it had been for Sir Edward in his own childhood. Cecilia admired their drawings and their needlework, tactfully suggested some books which she thought they might enjoy, and begged to hear Cleone sing. Nothing loth, Cleone took up her place by the elderly pianoforte that had been brought upstairs so that the girls might practise. Cecilia sat down to play her accompaniments, and for half an hour the two younger girls were content to sit quiet and listen.

Cecilia's playing was careful, and she excelled in the difficult art of accompanying, so that her music followed and complemented the singer rather than competing with her. She was amazed by what she heard, for, though she knew that Cleone must be good, she had not expected anything quite so lovely. It was a clear soprano voice, very true, with a richness and roundness of tone that was extraordinary in one so young. Cecilia had been accustomed for many years to attend the excellent concerts that were frequently given in the Assembly Rooms in Bath — Miss Herring regarding such outings as being an important part of her girls' training—but she thought she had rarely been so moved and uplifted.

As the last notes died away, Cecilia lifted her hands from the keys and let them fall into her lap. Even Minty, who must have heard her sister sing many times, was silent, and, looking at Cleone, Cecilia thought she was in another world. Then she gave a little sigh, and came back to earth.

'Well, that is enough now,' she said. 'I am afraid that I forget the passing of time when I sing, but I do not want to waste our day with you!'

'My dear, your singing can never be a waste of time! I have never heard anything so beautiful,' said Cecilia sincerely. Miss Herring had not, as a rule, been one to accord a great deal of praise for abilities that were, as she put it, gifts of the Creator rather than the fruits of endeavour. Nevertheless, even she would have been impressed, and Cecilia was pleased to see that Cleone blushed and thanked her quite inarticulately, rather than taking the praise as no more than her due.

'Papa has said that I shall have a proper singing master, now we are in London,' she told Cecilia, in awed tones.

'That is very good. Such a voice should be properly trained. Of course, a young lady in your position would not be needing to sing professonally, but for select concerts, and charity performances, I imagine you will be much in demand when you are older!'

'What a pity you may not sing in the opera!' said Sophie innocently. 'You might wear a lovely spangled dress, and have flowers thrown at you every night!'

Cecilia and Cleone exchanged a smile.

'Yes, or rotten oranges!' said Cleone. 'No, thank you very much!'

The minutes slipped imperceptibly into hours, and when a message was sent asking the girls to come downstairs she was amazed to find how late it was.

'Oh, dear, I must go! It would not do for me to be late back.'

'You must not leave just yet, Miss Avening. Here are Miss Cameron, and Grandmama, both come to visit. You must come and meet them!'

Cecilia could not deny that she was very interested to meet both.

'This is the first time Grandmama has come to visit us here since we arrived — though we have seen her several times, of course!' confided Minty, as Cecilia helped to brush her hair. Abby tweaked the girls' sashes into tidy bows — Cecilia could not help noticing how very much simpler they were than her present three charges' — and Cecilia tried in vain to order her own unruly curls. As usual she had a halo of springing tendrils round her face, and when she tried to tuck them back Cleone stopped her.

'Oh, do not pull your hair back so severely; it is so soft and pretty like that!'

'But so untidy, Cleone! I cannot appear before your grandmama, and Miss Cameron, looking like a hoyden.'

'Hardly that, Miss Avening! Besides, you know they will never stay!'

There was much truth in that, and reluctantly Cecilia abandoned her efforts and followed the three girls downstairs.

When they reached the drawing-room, the first person Cecilia set eyes on was Lord Inglesham. Since he had not been mentioned it had never occurred to her that he might have accompanied his mother. She would not have admitted, even to herself, how much he had been

in her thoughts, and now the sight of his tall figure
outlined against the sunshine from the window seemed
like the embodiment of a dream. For a moment she was
unaware of the other occupants of the room as she stood
stock-still, her eyes fixed on his face. His expression was
unreadable, and he accorded her no more than a small,
unsmiling bow. She thought that he must still be
annoyed with her for her refusal to help Cleone, and
found herself hoping that he would be pleased by the
small suggestion she had made.

Cecilia returned his greeting with a little curtsy,
which she hoped would convey some kind of dignified
humility. In her fresh muslin dress, with her curls
clustering round her face and neck, she looked absurdly
young and, he thought, remarkably pretty. She had
looked carefully away from him, and did not see how
warmly his eyes lit up with a little smile as they rested
on her. Lady Inglesham, quiet in her chair, saw an
expression on her son's face that reminded her irresis-
tibly of her late husband, and she gave an imperceptible
little nod to herself.

The two little girls ran to greet their new mama, and
Cecilia felt a pang of sympathy for the Dowager, who
had cared for them for so many years. However, she
could read nothing but dignified pleasure on the face
that was, she realised, so like that of her son that it gave
her quite a start. Miss Cameron bent to kiss the girls,
then sent them at once to greet their grandmama, which
pleased Cecilia. As the bride-to-be straightened up
Cecilia looked at her properly for the first time, and was
stunned by her appearance. Cleone had said that she
was beautiful, but Cecilia had not expected anything
quite as lovely as this. It was not surprising that Sir

Edward should be standing as he did, his eyes fixed
rapturously on that beautiful face.

Since the Dowager was still speaking to Sophie and
Minty, Cleone led Cecilia forward to meet her stepmother. She pressed a dutiful kiss to the delicate cheek
that was offered to her.

'This is Miss Avening, M-Mother, who was so kind
to us on our journey to London. Miss Avening, Miss
Fiona Cameron.'

Cecilia was relieved that Miss Cameron did not
remark on the new style Cleone had of addressing her,
and guessed that Sir Edward had already mentioned it
to his betrothed. She was glad to see that there was real
pleasure and fondness in the look that the young woman
gave to her new daughter before she turned to the guest.

'Miss Avening, the girls have spoken of you very
often.' Cecilia took the offered hand, and returned the
smile that dazzled from that lovely face. 'You are very
clever, are you not?' She spoke with simple admiration,
as if Cecilia had claimed to be able to fly.

'Not *very* clever,' Cecilia assured her. 'I am afraid the
girls have exaggerated.'

'Oh, no! They merely told me that you know a great
deal about poetry, and told them so many stories,
besides. I am afraid I am not clever at all,' admitted
Miss Cameron with disarming candour. 'Quite a dunce,
you would say.'

'I am sure Sir Edward would not agree,' said Cecilia,
thinking that, though it might be true, it could scarcely
matter with such an appearance. As if to bear out what
she had said, Sir Edward bent and murmured something in his betrothed's ear, which made her smile and
blush.

'It is no use expecting to hold any kind of sensible conversation with them, Miss Avening.' Lord Inglesham's deep voice spoke in her ear, and Cecilia turned to find him beside her.

CHAPTER EIGHT

CECILIA, who had had no idea he had moved and was standing so close to her, started. She made a quick recovery, however, and was determined to speak to him quite normally, ignoring the way his physical presence made her feel. 'How pleased you must be to see them so happy together,' she said politely.

'Yes, but there is something else that pleases me yet more. Do not think that I have not noticed how Cleone greeted Miss Cameron. Do I surmise that you have had something to do with that, in spite of what you said before?'

Cecilia could not help being pleased, but she would not show it, and gave him a very direct look.

'Cleone asked my advice, and I was happy to be able to give some,' she said. 'It was only a small thing, after all.'

'Yes, of course it was,' he agreed maddeningly. 'Yet you would not do that small thing for me, when I asked it.'

He sounded for all the world as though he was jealous of Cleone. Cecilia stared at him.

'But that is quite different! You must see that!'

'Of course it is. Quite different.' He sounded angry, and Cecilia was not to know that his anger was directed against himself, and not her. He was horrified to find himself behaving almost like a sulky schoolboy, instead of the assured man of the world he knew himself to be. 'I am glad that you have this opportunity to meet my

131

mother,' he continued, striving to behave normally. 'I had hoped to convey her good wishes to you when I called, but of course you were not at home.'

He made it sound as though Cecilia had been hiding from him, as if she should have known that he intended to call, she thought crossly.

'No, I made sure that I would be out, since of course I realised you would be sure to visit that day,' she said seriously.

His lips twitched into a rueful smile. 'I beg your pardon! Of course you had every right to be out. I was merely disappointed. On my mother's behalf,' he added.

'So was I,' she answered shyly. 'I saw your card. . .'

Their eyes met for a moment, and something flashed between them that was like a question, and an answer. Cecilia could feel her heart thudding beneath her ribs, and the breath caught in her throat. Then she remembered the gulf that lay between them, and thought with shame that she was making herself ridiculous. That she, who could not even find herself a respectable position as a governess, should imagine for one moment that the warm look in his eyes meant anything at all. . .why, he was probably engaged to Miss C., whoever she was, by now. She closed her eyes for a second, to hide her feelings, and when she looked back at him her face was blank.

'I am glad to have this opportunity of bidding you farewell,' she said rather coldly.

'Farewell? I am not going anywhere. Are you?'

'Oh, yes,' she said with cheerful mendacity. 'I expect to be taking up a new position very shortly.'

He frowned.

'A new position? Whatever are you talking about?'

'Why, a post as a governess, of course! That was what

I wanted to do, more than anything. Apart from setting up my school, naturally.'

'Naturally. But you are not seriously considering a place as a governess, are you? I thought you were settled with your stepmother for the time being.'

'You disapprove? That is doubtless why you have not asked Lady Inglesham to help me to a place. And yet you wanted me to advise Cleone, and were pleased to ask for my help with the journey.'

'So I was. But I do not wish for you to be a governess. It is most unsuitable.'

He spoke without thinking, aware only that he did not wish to think of her shut away in some household where she would be out of his reach. Cecilia saw only that he thought her unfitted for the work.

'Unsuitable! Lord Inglesham, I told you before that you had no right to interfere in your niece's life. You have still less right to interfere in mine! I am happy to tell you that I shall be a governess, and I expect to be a very good one. And I shall go where I wish. To Scotland,' she added wildly, as the most distant place she could think of. 'Yes, to Scotland, where I have been offered an excellent post!'

'In Scotland? You will be able to visit Cleone and the other girls, then. I believe Edward intends to buy a house there, so that they may spend part of the year near Miss Cameron's home.'

'Oh, no. This is in quite another part of Scotland,' she said firmly. His lips twitched. His original impulse to anger had died away. Her cheeks were pink, her eyes sparkling with annoyance, and he found it refreshing to be scolded by a young woman, instead of agreed with. He was fairly sure that she had been offered no such place, but he could not resist leading her on.

'Indeed? In which part of Scotland do the family reside?'

Since Cecilia had not the remotest idea where in Scotland Miss Cameron's family lived, she found herself unable to answer. Refusing to be daunted by this, she glared at him.

'I cannot see that it is any of your business, my lord,' she said stiffly.

'No, it isn't, is it?' he agreed blandly. 'But you have already told me that I am interfering, so I am doing my best to live up to your expectations.'

Cecilia bit her lip.

'I beg your pardon. I am afraid I expressed myself with. . .with an unbecoming warmth. I apologise, my lord.'

'Not at all. Your "warmth", as you put it, was very becoming indeed, Cecilia. But if you call me "my lord" again, as if I were a bishop, I shall be tempted to put you over my knee and smack you.'

He took her hand and raised it, unresisting, to his lips. The colour flooded her face and she looked at him, speechlessly. He felt a sudden urge to take her into his arms, so powerful that only the combined presence of most of his relatives prevented him. Startled by the intensity of the feeling, and unable to extricate himself gracefully, he walked back to his place by the window, where he was soon joined by the little girls, who clamoured for his attention. A few moments later he made his farewells and left the room. Cecilia did not know whether to be relieved or sorry at his departure.

'You must meet Grandmama, Miss Avening.' Cleone drew her away, and Cecilia made her curtsy to the Dowager. She felt flustered, and hoped that his mother had not seen Lord Inglesham's extraordinary behaviour. The Dowager greeted her with kindly imperturbability, and made her sit beside her. Cecilia was surprised by the number of questions she was asked, but they all related to her experiences at Miss Herring's, and Cecilia thought only that her ladyship might be able to help her to a post, and was happy to answer fully and freely.

The chiming of a clock in the corner of the room made her start, and look about her in horror.

'Good heavens! Was that five o'clock? I must be going!'

'Shall you soon turn into a pumpkin, Miss Avening?' asked Minty cheekily.

'No—a white mouse,' responded Cecilia instantly. 'And I deserve to be treated as one if I should be so rude as to be late for dinner!'

'Well, I should be very kind to a white mouse, if I had one! I should keep it in a dear little cage, and give it all the cheese it would like, and let it run up my arm!'

The Dowager suppressed a shudder.

'Heaven forfend! But if you have to leave, Miss Avening, would you give me the pleasure of your company? I am on my way to visit a friend, and only called in for a short time, to see the children. I should be happy to convey you home, and then perhaps the cat would not get you after all?'

Cecilia smiled, and shook her head.

'I hope you did not think I was implying that my hostess is a cat, your ladyship? It is most kind of you, but I am living in Harley Street, and I am well aware that, wherever you are going, it must be completely out of your way.'

'Well, I am in no hurry, and I expect the horses can manage a few extra paces. Come, Miss Avening, to please a lonely old woman?' The rest of the family cried out at this, and indeed, looking at the Dowager's bright eyes and sprightly mien, Cecilia could only laugh.

'I am afraid that this is blackmail, your ladyship! But I cannot resist it, as you must know! I accept with pleasure, and will keep you no more than a few minutes while I fetch my bonnet and pelisse.'

The three girls went with her. Sir Edward turned to his mother-in-law.

'That was kindly done, ma'am. I had meant to send her home myself, but if it is not inconvenient to you?'

'By no means. I welcome the opportunity. A pleasant, sensible young woman, is she not?'

'Delightful.' He looked a little puzzled at her interest. 'The girls seem very fond of her, don't they? Do you think we should ask her to come and be their governess, while Miss Dixon is ill?'

The Dowager smiled a little smile.

'Oh, no. No, I do not think that would be suitable at all.'

He would have questioned her further, but Cecilia returned, and in the bustle of farewell he forgot his suprise. There were often times, he found, when he did not understand his mother-in-law. She was just like Marcus, in that respect.

Lady Inglesham was kindness itself on the journey, asking many questions about Cecilia's former life, and insisting on conveying her right to the door. Cecilia was dubious, fearing Mrs Ruspidge's encroaching ways, but in the end she need not have worried. She bade a swift farewell to the Dowager and climbed out of the bar-ouche, to find that the door was opened to her by the adenoidal Fanny.

'Is your mistress not yet returned, Fanny?' She could not keep the relief out of her voice.

'No, miss. They sent to say they bin invited to stop to dinner. Master's invited, too. Cook says as you'll have to make do with a negg, she don't want to be bothered with kickshaws. What's kickshaws, miss?'

'Elegant trifles, Fanny. You may tell Cook that I shall be very happy with an egg, and some bread and butter. "Better is a dinner of herbs", you know.'

''Erbs, miss? Wiv your eggs? I dunno if Cook's got any.'

Cecilia sighed.

'Never mind, Fanny,' she said gently. 'Pray tell Cook that an egg will do very well.' One of the minor but more painful deprivations of her present home was, she thought, that there was no one who understood her little jokes.

The Dowager Lady Inglesham watched thoughtfully as Cecilia was admitted to the house in Harley Street, then signalled to her coachman to drive on, her mind turning over what she had learned. She was, she admitted to herself, impressed with the girl. Undoubtedly a gentlewoman, she had a strength of character and purpose that was akin to her own. Not, of course, a beauty, although there was something very taking about those dark grey eyes, so direct and guileless, and that untameable hair. Even making allowance for her natural pride in her son, Lady Inglesham could not believe that Cecilia could be quite indifferent to him as a man. That she was without any idea that she herself might be an object of interest to his lordship was one of her chief charms.

A day of freedom, and the pleasure of being with people to whom she was neither an encroaching poor relation, nor a menial, kept Cecilia's spirits high for the next few days. Lord Inglesham's odd behaviour she put resolutely from her mind, and, if on occasions she found herself shivering at the memory of his kiss on her hand, she told herself sternly that it was no more than a meaningless flirtation. The important thing was that Lady Inglesham seemed pleased with her, and there might be a chance of finding employment through her. Mrs Ruspidge and her daughters were also, if not pleasant, at least less inclined to find fault with her than usual. They had been made much of by Lady Aurelia, and were to visit again so that they and her daughters might spend some time together. As well as this promised treat, there was a delicious scandal to brood over and discuss.

The Princess Charlotte, deciding that she could not bring herself to marry the Prince of Orange, had summoned him to Warwick House to refuse him, giving as her excuse that there was no provision made for her to live in England, and that she did not want to leave her mother. Since all the world knew that the Princess Caroline had, among her other scandalous private and social failings, an almost total want of maternal feeling, this was regarded with derision by everyone, and as a severe rebuff by the unfortunate Prince.

The Regent, predictably, was furious, dismissed all his daughter's ladies-in-waiting, and doubtless berated her handsomely into the bargain. Charlotte, in a passion as great as his own, had rushed out of Carlton House, hailed the first free cab, and gave the driver a guinea to take her to her mother in Connaught Place. Princess Caroline, delighted by this opportunity to meddle, summoned the royal uncles, the Dukes of York and Sussex, and the Archbishop of Canterbury, to consult with her what was to be done. Charlotte was eventually persuaded to go home to Warwick House, but it was generally felt that she was the heroine of a very pretty little drama, in which the Regent was consigned to the part of villain. Even Caroline won some sympathy from the fickle public, who saw her — temporarily — as a wronged wife and mother, and cheered her when she arrived at a gala night at the Opera. A startling vision in a black wig, both it and her person liberally studded with diamonds, she sailed in after the close of the National Anthem, and graciously accepted both the plaudits of the audience and the bows of the Emperor and King Frederick.

All of this was common knowledge, but Lady Aurelia was acquainted with one of Caroline's ladies-in-waiting. She was, therefore, in a position to regale them with several choice titbits of gossip, and her ability to repeat these, under the promise of secrecy, to everyone they knew, made life very enjoyable indeed to Mrs Ruspidge and her daughters, who were quite as *au fait* with the scandal as anyone. With such delicious news as a pass, they were certain of a welcome even in houses where they had hitherto been denied admittance, and were in high fettle. Cecilia found her duties shrinking to mending and furbishing her charges' clothes, curling their hair, and writing an occasional letter for Mrs Ruspidge, who was aware that her handwriting was as poor as her spelling was uncertain.

If it had not been for Augustus Hatherley, her burdens would have been few. He, too, joined in the round of socialising, glad for once to hang on his mother's coat tails. It was useful, but it was also boring, for among the young women he met there were few who were rich or aristocratic enough to tempt him to a flirtation. He was too careful to respond to such lures as were cast by certain married ladies of his mother's acquaintance —

which could only lead to trouble in the long run, with
the possibility of a suit against him by some wronged
husband for 'criminal conversation'—and he found
himself starved of feminine company. Even the complai-
sant little whore he had been accustomed to visit, when
necessary, had found herself a titled protector and would
have nothing to do with him.

So it was that Cecilia, going around the house in a
glow of happiness at the prospect of Lady Inglesham
finding her a suitable position or even, perhaps, helping
her to start her own small school, appeared in his eyes
to be a more desirable conquest than ever. The fact that
she obviously found him unattractive was a challenge,
as was the baiting of his friends, who found it incompre-
hensible that he should have a halfway pretty girl living
in his house and not have managed even to get his hand
up her skirt, let alone anything else.

After an evening at his club, where it seemed to him
that the sole topic of conversation was ribald speculation
as to the incapable, or otherwise, condition of that
which was to be found within his breeches, he determined that he would achieve satisfaction with her, at
last. Though inclined to think highly of his own
charms—and certainly the little whore had seemed
happy enough, and had often praised his abilities—he
had no illusion that he would gain his object other than
by force. The idea of a rape excited him. And what,
after all, could she do? She might complain to his
mother, but Mrs Ruspidge would do nothing against
her precious son, and besides, would do anything to
hush up any hint of scandal. It would be his word
against hers, and, provided he could have the house
empty, there should be no difficulty. His years of riding
difficult horses had made him very strong, and he knew

that she would be no match for him in that direction. If he had to knock her out, he would do so, but it would be better, much better, if she were to be conscious and he could terrify her into obeying him.

It was not difficult to plan, and he set about it with care. His mother and the girls, he knew, were expected at Lady Aurelia's, and it would have needed for one of them to be at death's door to prevent them from going. Aware that, if she thought there was any danger of his being there, Cecilia would be sure to leave the house, he made it clear that he intended to accompany them. The footman would, of course, go with them, and it was easy enough to send Fanny and the boot boy out on long, impossible errands, while he suggested to Cook, with a wink and a half-sovereign, that she might like to have a day off.

As usual, Cecilia was given a pile of mending, as well as a bonnet of Mrs Ruspidge's to steam into shape and trim afresh. She had discovered that her charity guest had neat fingers and a natural taste that enabled her to revive an elderly bonnet and make it look like new. Cecilia did not mind: it was much less boring than mending rents in Georgina's petticoats. She had, indeed, half wondered whether she might take herself to visit the Maisemores, but she thought it was too soon since her first visit, and the last thing in the world she wanted was to appear encroaching. It was, besides, raining heavily and steadily, so that the roads would be wet and dirty, and she would inevitably arrive in a bedraggled state, with muddy hems and a wilting bonnet

It was quite cheerfully, therefore, that she settled herself in the drawing-room with the pile of sewing, and the bonnet which she intended to save for a *bonne bouche*. The light in this front-facing room was better for fine work, and the chairs more comfortable than in the schoolroom or her own bedroom. She hummed a little tune as she sewed, head bent over the neat line of stitches that was marching, in satisfying uniformity, along the hem of Amelia's frock. Unaware that Fanny had been sent out, she did not even look up when the door opened quietly, and Augustus slipped into the room.

Mrs Ruspidge, who, had the weather been fine, would certainly have saved herself a few shillings and walked, had been forced by the weather to hire a carriage to take her family to Lady Aurelia's. She did not grudge the expense, however, in such a cause, and was loud in her exhortations as they climbed down, obsequiously assisted by her footman, outside the door of Lady Aurelia's fashionably situated house.

'Take care, Charlotte! Do not, I beg you, let your petticoats drabble in the wet! And Amelia, if I see you set one foot in the mud, or splash your sisters by stamping in the puddle, as you did the other day, you will know all about it, I promise you! You cannot sit all day at dear Lady Aurelia's in dirty things! Hurry, girls. And Augustus, do help me, dear. Will you not give me your arm. . .? Oh, you are knocking at the door. Well, that is a good idea. Come, now, girls, be ready to hurry in out of the rain.'

So absorbed was she that she did not notice the tall gentleman riding by on the other side of the street, who checked his horse at the sound of her voice. It was strident enough for him to hear every word, and when he heard her say that their visit was to be for the day he hurried on. Only that morning the Dowager Lady Inglesham had asked her son whether he did not intend to call on Miss Avening again, and ask her to come and

spend the day with her. Now, it seemed, his way was
clear. Should he go now, straight away? But no, he was
wet, and dirty after his ride.

He thought he would prefer to change, and perhaps
it would be sensible to take the phaeton, so that he
might convey her back? The thought of Cecilia riding
beside him in his favourite vehicle engendered a surpris-
ingly warm feeling of anticipatory pleasure, so that he
squeezed the horse into a brisk trot, to the peril of
passers-by trying to keep their clothes clean. He did not,
therefore, see Augustus Hatherley leave Lady Aurelia's
house a few moments later, having made the excuse of
the onset of a sudden sick headache. Certainly his face
was flushed, his forehead lightly dewed with sweat and
his eyes over-bright, so his mother made no bones about
sending him straight home.

The first thing Cecilia noticed was a pair of highly
polished boots, topped by the skin-tight trousers that
Brummell had made fashionable. The second was a
strong smell of brandy. Mr Hatherley, letting himself
quietly into the house and elbowing the door to behind
him, had paused on his way up the stairs, and gone
back to the dining-room to fortify himself for the agreeable fray. With what he considered to be sensible
forethought, he had brought the bottle and two glasses
with him, and set them quietly down on a table near the
door. The warm glow of a large glass of brandy now
spread itself pleasantly from his stomach, wreathing
aromatically through his brain and engendering a
delightful heat in his loins. As he stood before her, in
the moment when she realised that he was there, that—
to him—important and interesting portion of his anat-
omy was just in front of her face, and he knew a
moment's temptation to unbutton, and display himelf

in all his magnificent tumescence before her astonished and, perhaps, admiring eyes.

While the little whore would, he knew, have reacted in the most gratifying manner to such an act, even under the influence of the brandy he was aware that Cecilia was unlikely to do the same. Since he still hoped, however faintly, for her co-operation, it was important that he should not startle her, just at first. He therefore beamed down at her, in what he hoped was a warm, charming way, and whisked the needlework from her hands, being dimly aware that even a needle might make an unpleasant weapon, if correctly applied.

'Miss Avening! Cecilia! Working so hard, and spoiling those pretty eyes! It shall not, it must not be!'

Cecilia was nervous, but not yet frightened. It was, after all, broad day, and she was a guest in his mother's house.

'Not at all, Mr Hatherley. The light is particularly good in here. I had thought you had gone to Lady Aurelia's?'

'So I did, but then I thought, there's poor little Cecilia, all alone, no one to speak to all day! Such a pity! So I came back, to keep you company.'

'You are kind, but I beg you will not deprive yourself of this outing on my account. I have, as you see, plenty to occupy myself, and I am by no means averse to my own company.'

She kept her voice calm and low, aware that he had been drinking, and unwilling to antagonise him.

'Deprive myself? My dear Cecilia, it is no such thing! How you can say such a thing, when you have a mirror to look in every morning. . .?' His hands came out, and plucked several hairpins out of her already loosely fastened hair. He giggled, and held them up out of her reach with one hand, while stealing two more with the other. She felt the heavy mass of curls began to slip, and put up her hands to hold it from falling down her back. 'No, no, dear Cecilia, let it fall!' he said in a caressing voice that sent a prickle of cold down her back. He was standing so close that if she should try to stand up she would be forced to press against him, so she held herself rigidly in place, looking at him disdainfully.

'Sir, you are drunk, and I find your conversation unpleasant. Kindly leave, or let me pass. I will not stay in the same room with you.'

'Come now, that's no way to speak to one who wishes to befriend you! I could be very good to you, Cecilia, if you were to be good to me. . .' Without warning his hands came out and seized her wrists, pulling her to her feet and against him. She struggled, but his grip was like iron bands, and he forced her arms down and behind her back until he was able to hold both her slender wrists in one strong fist. His other hand buried itself in the mass of hair that, when her hands were taken away, had tumbled down her back. Twisting his fingers in the curls, he pulled her head back and fastened his greedy mouth on her lips, sucking and biting at them so that she could scarcely breathe.

She was numb with terror, but still did not apprehend the danger she was in. He jerked her wrists upwards, so that her arms were bent out sideways, and wound the fall of hair that was now completely loose, twisting the fingers of the hand that held her wrists into its tresses. He had learned, at least, to be cautious of her head as a weapon. Once she was secured, his free hand moved to her neck. He pulled away the muslin fichu that filled in the neckline of her gown, casting it on the floor before attempting to slip his hand down inside her bodice. His hips moved, rubbing and pushing the hard lump of his member against her belly and thighs; his face was suffused, his eyes blind and fixed.

Her tight-fitting gown resisted his efforts to fondle her breasts, and with a hoarse, panting exclamation he grasped it at the shoulder, pulling and tearing until the muslin, worn with washing, ripped away. As he did so she found enough breath to utter one piercing scream, so that he jerked viciously at her hair until she thought he would pull it out by the roots.

The sound she made scarcely gave him pause, so sure was he that there was no one to hear it. That the windows were open at the top he either had not noticed or did not care, assuming that no one from the street would bother to interfere. He did not hear the answering shout, nor the sound of the front door crashing open. Nor did Cecilia, but her own scream had somehow woken her from her trance of fear. As his fingers bit into her exposed breast, she braced herself, then brought one leg up with all her strength, driving her knee into his groin.

At once her hands and hair were free. He reeled back, his face green-white, clutching himself with hands that could scarcely bring themselves to touch the agonised, white-hot pain at the centre of his being. Doubled over, he retched, bringing up strings of burning bile that seared his mouth. Suffocating, he whined as he dragged the painful breath in and out. Stunned, even horrified, Cecilia watched him, not knowing whether she hoped or feared that she had given him a death blow. She was still standing, wide-eyed, her hair in wild disarray down her back and her breast bared above the ruins of her gown, when Marcus Inglesham burst into the room.

CHAPTER NINE

LORD INGLESHAM closed the door behind him, as gently and softly as if he feared to disturb a sleeping baby. His eyes passed over the wretched Hatherley, who more by luck than judgement had fallen into a chair and was curled in it like a snail in its shell, groaning and wheezing. He looked at Cecilia, whose wide eyes were fixed on him and who made no move to cover herself. It was he who came forward, picked up the fichu where it lay abandoned in the middle of the floor, and held it out to her. She took it like an automaton, then stood looking at it as though she had never seen its like before.

Gently he took it from her hands and laid it over her shoulder so that it fell in folds on her front, keeping himself as far from her as he could and touching even the fine muslin only with the tips of his fingers, as if to disassociate himself, physically, from her body. When she felt its feathery touch she looked down to where her breast, round and white as a pearl, gleamed through the soft fabric, the nipple rosily pink like a rising sun through layers of cloud. Then her hands came up to clutch the fichu to her as if it had been armour, her hands shielding that private part of her that no man had ever, till now, seen.

He stepped back again, moving slowly like a man wading through deep water. She was, he saw, in a state of shock so profound that she might as well have been a sleep-walker, and he feared to startle her awake. The

approach of a man — any man — to one who had been so
brutally handled might drive her into an extreme of
terror. It was, of course, only too obvious what had
happened. He had been on the doorstep, waiting for his
knock to be answered, when her scream had come, clear
and high and full of fear, issuing from the windows
above. The street was all but empty; no one heard it but
he. Certain, without knowing why, that it was she, he
set his shoulder to the door, and, even as he told himself
that the stout wood could never be broken by such
means, the whole door gave to his pressure and he
stumbled, half falling, into the hall. Augustus, in his
excitement, had not checked it, and the lock had failed
to catch. Kicking the door closed behind him, Marcus
had raced up the stairs, and flung open the door on the
tableau within.

Inexplicably, his first emotion was guilt. He should
have been quicker — though his rational mind told him
that by the time she had screamed some harm had
already been done, and that until that sound warned
him he could not have known that he was needed.
Nevertheless, if only he had not gone home, like a
popinjay, to change his clothes and fetch his phaeton!
He would have been here — they might even have left
the house altogether — before the man's return. Again,
reason told him that what he might have prevented
today could have happened tomorrow or the next day,
and with worse consequences.

Beneath all these rational and irrational arguments
was the deeper guilt: that he was a man, a man like the
one who had done this. Useless to tell himself that he
had never forced his attentions upon an unwilling
woman in his life, that he would never consider laying
even the finger of one hand on a female without her

consent. Deep down he had felt, in that moment of first seeing her, how the blood had surged in his veins. Anger, furious anger; resentment that any man should dare to set hands and lips to this girl, to see and touch what should be seen and touched only by. . .yes, by himself! There it was, pure and uncomplicated, the blackest jealousy. And she, he thought, had seen and known it, so that now she shrank from him in fear.

He continued to retreat, trying to indicate that she need not be frightened of him, that he was no possible threat to her, until he reached the doorway. Her face, now, was as pink as it had before been white, but she did not drop her head and hide behind the wild curls that clustered on neck and shoulders. Head up, poised almost proudly, she continued to face him. He thought that she was so afraid of him that she dared not take her eyes from his every movement, and even as he moved away from her he admired the courage that kept her eyes steady and her face still.

Cecilia, in fact, was so lost in shame that she could not move. He was, of course, disgusted by her, that much was plain. No young woman should have been able to defend herself as she had just done. It was a whore's trick — literally; the trick of a woman of the streets. He could not bear to look at her; the sight of her naked flesh repelled him so that even her fichu, innocent and modest garment though one might have thought it, he could scarcely bring himself to touch. And when he had covered her — why, oh, why had she not been more modest, why had instinct not led her to pull up her gown, to hide that which should not be revealed with her hands or her hair? — he had snatched his hands back as if she were a red-hot coal that would burn his fingers.

Perhaps she was, deep down, the shameless harlot that he obviously thought her.

Now he had removed himself from her as far as he could go. He was not, of course, to know that, in spite of all that had happened, she wanted perversely to feel his arms round her, to be held and rocked against his breast and comforted like a child, to be kissed and told that it was all right, that everything was all right, that he would not let anything hurt her now, that he was here. And her shame was intensified that so soon after escaping from the clutching hands of one man she should wish herself to be touched, caressed, even kissed by another.

She saw the shame in his face, and read in it dismay at his presence, at his inability to comfort her, at his longing to be elsewhere.

'I'm sorry,' she said, since the silence between them was stretched so thin that it must soon tear and break of its own accord. He looked at her as if she had spoken in some hitherto undiscovered language.

'Are you. . .all right?' He hardly knew what he was asking her.

'Yes. Thank you. He did not. . .there was nothing. . . just my gown. . .' She gestured with the hand that was not clutching the fichu to her, then blushed yet more deeply that she had reminded him. 'I'm sorry,' she said again.

A groan from the man in the chair interrupted them, attracting their attention. She no longer feared that he would die, but her shame would scarcely permit her to look at him. Marcus's only feeling was disappointment that the wretch's state made it impossible for him to vent some of his rage upon him.

'Will he get better?' she whispered anxiously, embarrassed to ask, but needing to know.

'Yes — unfortunately,' he answered grimly. As if in response, Augustus Hatherley managed to uncurl himself a little. His face, still the colour of lard, had lost the bluish tinge round his mouth, and his breathing was easier, though still laboured.

'Brandy!' he implored in a hoarse whisper. 'Please! Brandy!'

With an exclamation of disgust Marcus picked up the bottle from the table where it had been left, and splashed a generous measure into the glass. Augustus put out a hand for it, and drank greedily, choking a little, then held it out wordlessly. Shrugging, Marcus filled the glass again, and watched while that, too, was drunk. By the end of the second glass, Augustus was well on the way to recovery. Angry, and frightened, his worst fear was the ridicule of his fellows, that he had so easily and successfully been floored by a young woman. If the story should ever get out. . . He shuddered.

'I say, old fellow,' he said confidentially, 'no need to talk about this, eh?' He stood up, rather shakily and not very straight, and tried to lay hold of his lordship's arm. Marcus shrugged him off.

'Talk about it?' Inglesham was incredulous. 'Talk about this? For God's sake, man, would I do such a thing? Allow this lady's name to be bandied about. . .!' Words failed him.

'No, but, what I mean is. . .man to man, y'know, no need to say what she did, eh? I mean, she'd never have managed it if I'd not thought her a lady, the little vixen! To think of her knowing a whorehouse trick like that! She's not new to that game, you may bet your life on it, innocent though she looks! I should think half of Bath

has been up that alleyway, at one time or another——
Ugh.'

His final and involuntary exclamation was caused by
a strong blow to his jaw from his lordship's fist. There
was a crunch as the knuckles knocked out several of his
teeth, and his head went back with so fierce a snap that
in the last, interminable moment of consciousness he
felt sure that his neck must be broken. He crumpled like
a rag doll, and his lordship looked down at him with
considerable satisfaction, meditatively rubbing at his
grazed fist.

Cecilia had not moved. She had listened without
surprise or even dismay to Augustus's stream of slander.
His lordship would, she thought, be almost certain to
believe it, so there was little point in denying the claims.
What did it matter, anyway? Nothing really mattered,
any more. She wished he would go away, that they
would both go away, so that she could be alone. That
was the only reasonable, the only safe thing. And now
Augustus was lying on the floor, and she could not even
hear him breathing. She caught her breath on a sob.

'It's all right. He'll not speak like that again, don't
you worry. I'll make sure of it.'

She thought he had already done so.

'Is he dead?' Through her fevered imagination ran
pictures: she and Inglesham, at dead of night, creeping
down to the river and tipping the cold and stiffening
body into its concealing depths. Weighted with stones?
Perhaps that would be better. Then Inglesham, in
danger of the hangman's noose, fleeing to France or—
no—had he not just recently returned from the West
Indies? Perhaps he could go back there. In any event,
he would have to go, and the Dowager's heart would
break. And the scandal, should it come, would end any

possibility of Sir Edward marrying Miss Cameron, so the girls would be disconsolate too. And she, as guilty as he, could not even go to comfort them! She stared at Inglesham with nightmares in her eyes.

'Dead? Of course not!' He bent to set his fingers under the angle of the jaw, where the heartbeat throbbed strongly and steadily. 'He's just unconscious. I'll take him away, and get rid of him, before he comes round.'

'Get rid of him?' The nightmare, which had been receding, came back with embellishments.

'Well, you don't think I'd leave him here with you, do you? He shall come to my house — well, the stables, anyway. Good enough for him. When he comes round I'll give him the choice: leave the country for good, with some money in his pocket, or be taken down to Portsmouth and be pressed for a seamen. Not that they're so much in demand, since the war is ended, but no doubt some captain would see his way clear, for a guinea or two, to take him on as crew. I think that's a fair enough offer, don't you?'

Relief made her giddy.

'Oh. . .yes. But what of his mother? She will wonder what has become of him. Suppose she sets the Runners after him?'

'I doubt if they'd ever track him back to me. I mean, why should they? In any case, I'll have him write a letter to her. A very careful letter, of which I shall check every word. She'll be surprised and upset, of course, but she'll get over it. The country will be a better place without him, that's certain.'

'Yes. Yes, it will.'

Her voice was faint, and he looked at her with concern. The satisfaction of exacting some vengeance, however short in its duration, had distracted him from his worries for her, but now he saw that she was almost as pale as that damned fichu.

'You are faint! Sit down; I will give you some brandy.'

Hastily he found a clean glass, and poured some for her, but when he would have taken it to her she shrank from it as if it had been poison. Nor, he saw, had she sat down, though her free hand gripped the back of the chair next to her.

'No, please, no! Not brandy, not anything!' Her pleading voice was pitiful, and he saw that she could not bear him to come near her. At once he lowered his hand, ashamed at his lack of sensitivity.

'Of course, I'm sorry. Some water, then? I will fetch it, and set it on that table for you. Oh, I beg that you will sit down! You are ill, I am sure that you are ill.'

'No!' In her despair she almost shouted at him. 'I do not want any water, and I will not sit down. Please go away, and leave me alone!'

'Go away?' He stared at her as if he could not believe his ears. 'I cannot go, and leave you like this! In this house, and alone, with no one but that woman—who is not even here—to care for you?'

'I do not need anyone to care for me.' In that moment, she believed it herself. 'I can care for myself. Take Augustus, if you want to, and go. Just go.'

'By God, I shall not! You shall come with me, back to my house, and my mother shall nurse you. I promise I will not come near you, once you are there, but you must come!'

'And you will make me, my lord? You will make me humble myself before your mother, who will despise me? You will drag me from the house—for I will not leave it willingly—and force me to go with you? Now I see that all men are truly alike. Their will must be paramount; they must have what they want. Just like him, down there.' She nodded at the inert body at their feet.

It was as if she had stabbed him in the heart. He felt the blood leave his face, physically felt it as if his head were a jug and someone were pouring the liquid out of it. Her reference to humbling herself to his mother, and to her despising Cecilia, meant nothing to him, except insofar as he vaguely thought she was referring to her position as a governess. But that she should think of him as kin to that — that thing! He thought he could have thrown back his head and howled like a dog at the pain of it.

In his pride, however, he said nothing. His lips tightened and his eyebrows drew together until they were one solid line of black above the eyes that were as blue, though he did not know it, as the lovely Miss Cameron's. Bending, he took Hatherley's wrists and pulled him up, so that he flopped at last over his shoulder, which was bent to receive him. Lifting the weight as if it were no more than a sack of cushions, he turned to Cecilia.

'Since it is what you wish, I bid you a good day, madam,' he said bitterly. She took his icy calm for relief at escaping from her.

'Oh, go away!' she said, her voice breaking on a sob that he could hardly bear to hear. 'Go away! You will never have to see me again!'

'If that is what you want.' He executed a clumsy bow, hampered by the weight on his shoulder, and, turning, walked from the room, shutting the door behind him as gently as he had done when, a lifetime before, he had first come in.

Cecilia stood without moving, listening to his steps

on the stair. Each sound was so infinitely precious that
she thought she could store it up in her heart — the last
thing she would ever hear of him. Dully she counted.
Ten, eleven, twelve. She could have kissed the treads
that his feet stepped on, that knew his touch. Thirteen,
fourteen. He was in the hall, his footsteps dulled by the
strip of carpet that led to the door. The wait was agony,
but soon — so soon! — she heard the door open, and close
again. Her eyes closed with it. Like the sleep-walker he
had compared her to, she drifted to the window.
Through the muslin of the curtain she could see him,
issuing an order to his tiger, lifting the inert body into
the carriage. And those were the bays — had Sophie ever
driven them? She would never know, now. The reins
were in his hands, the tiger climbing on to the back of
the phaeton. The crisp sound of hoofs splashing over
the wet road, the hissing rumble of turning wheels. He
was gone.

She watched until the puddles lost the last ripples of
his passing and reflected once more the dull grey of the
sky that still held more rain, though none fell at the
moment. Then, at last, she took herself up to her room,
locked the door, and emptied the ewer of water — cold,
of course, but at least plentiful — into the bowl on the
washstand. Slowly, as if she were undressing a child,
not herself, she took off her clothes, garment by garment,
until she stood naked and shivering on the bare wood of
the floor. All the time she did so, the tears were running
down her face, burning her cheeks where they tracked
down. Her breath came in little panting sobs, but her
mouth was still and straight. She folded everything
neatly — all but the gown, which she dropped in the
corner of the room.

She set the mat on the floor in front of the washstand,

precisely aligned as if it were some kind of test, then soaped and scrubbed and rinsed every inch of her body until the white skin glowed red and angry. Then, though the water was grey and scummy with soap, she bundled up her hair and dipped in her whole head, scarcely wincing as the icy chill met the warmth of her scalp. She rubbed fiercely, heedless of the knots and tangles that formed so easily in the wet curls, then squeezed out as much of the water as she could, and wrapped her head in the damp towel that had already dried her shivering body. Still naked, she went to the corner where she had left her gown.

She bundled it tightly, her hands as reluctant to touch it as if it had been a slug, or a snake. She pushed the mass into the empty grate of the small, never used fireplace, and, with the tinder-box set next to the candle beside her bed, set fire to it. Her fingers were steady and careful; she shielded the glowing tinder with her hands, blew on it gently, transferred the flame that was tender as the first flower of spring to a corner of the muslin, and crouched before it, watching as the fabric shrivelled and blackened, poking at it once or twice when it looked as though the thicker pieces would do no more than smoulder.

The flames flared up, primrose-yellow, their warmth unfelt by her skin, which seemed, to her, to have turned into a thin carapace of ice. When there was nothing more than a heap of black ashes, edged here and there with a glowing lace of sparks, she stood up and returned to the washstand. For one last time she washed her hands, turning the soap over and over in her hands, then rinsed and rinsed. Then, at last, she slipped her nightgown over her head, tying it firmly closed, and, conscious at last of the chill she felt, took out a warm shawl and wrapped it around her.

The tears, which had never ceased to fall, though they had at times been lost in the water of her washing, now dripped from her jawbone, making little damp patches on the linen of her nightgown. She brushed at them absently. She hardly knew what to do with herself. She longed for the oblivion of sleep, but now she was shivering with cold, and the effort to move was more than she could bear. So she sat on her bed, her legs hanging and her cold feet set neatly side by side on the minuscule mat that was the room's only pretension to comfort. After a time she heard steps on the stairs, and stiffened.

'Miss? Miss? Are you there, miss?' It was Fanny's voice, and she drew in a breath of relief, though it did not occur to her to answer. Fanny tried the door, found it locked, and called all the louder.

'Miss? *Miss*!' She rattled at the door. 'Open up, miss! Oh, please, miss, do open the door!' Slowly and with reluctance Cecilia did as she was bid, and the astonished little maid peered up at her.

'Whatever is it, miss? There's something dreadful bin and happened! There's two chairs turned over in the droring-room, and someone's bin at master's brandy, wot was locked away, as well I knows, in the dining-room.' She looked suspiciously at Cecilia, her pink, rather rodent-like nose wrinkling as she sniffed. 'Well, it ain't you, anyways, and ain't that a blessing! 'Ere, what you doing in your nightgown, miss? You ill?'

It seemed as good a reason as any.

'Yes, Fanny, I am a little ill. I shall go to bed.'

'But your 'air, miss, what you done to it?' Cecilia only looked at her in a dazed way, and Fanny stretched up a hand and tweaked at the insecurely twisted towel, which fell down at once. 'Lor! It's all wet, miss! You can't go to bed like that, catch your death, you would! You better come down to the kitching with me, and have yourself a sit by the range.'

Cecilia shook her head wordlessly, clutching the shawl round her.

'Come on, miss, *please!*' Fanny had always felt some fellow-feeling for the other girl, who, though inhabiting a world far removed from her own, still seemed subject to many of the petty tyrannies and miseries that she daily endured. 'Ain't nobody in, miss, nor there won't be, not for hours. Cook's gorn to visit her sister in Stepney, and that's a fair step.' She chuckled at her own little joke, and Cecilia smiled a tentative smile. 'That's right, miss. Bring your brush, and I'll 'ave a go at your 'air. Always fancied meself as a lady's maid, didn't I?' Chattering encouragement, she led Cecilia down to the dingy basement kitchen, ill lit and redolent of many meals cooked and washed up, but warmed by the dim glow of the range.

With unusual initiative, she opened the draught and added extra coal, hoping that Cook would not notice when she returned, and put the kettle to boil. Cecilia sat obediently on the chair set near the heat. She sipped obediently at the tea that was put in her hand, and with a feeling of comradely daring Fanny sat on a stool next to her, her hands wrapped round her own chipped cup, savouring the luxury of warmth, comfort and the two spoons of sugar she had stirred into her tea. Then she took up the brush, and gently teased out the drying hair, strand by strand. It was sticky with the soapy water, but in the end she had it so that she could run the brush from roots to tips without obstruction.

'There, now! Ain't that just luverly? Shall I plait it
for you, miss, if you're going to bed?'

'Going to bed? Am I?'

Fanny looked down at her. Cecilia's eyes were heavy,
now that the warmth, the drink and the soothing,
rhythmic hair-brushing had done their work. As docile
as a child, she allowed her hair to be plaited, and herself
to be led upstairs and tucked into bed with a hot brick,
wrapped in flannel, at her feet. She was asleep before
Fanny had left the room, and she did not stir when Mrs
Ruspidge and her daughters returned. Even the uproar,
when a letter from Augustus was delivered to the house
saying that urgent business had called him abroad, and
that he could not really say when he would be coming
back, did not ruffle the surface of the dreamless sleep in
which she lay drowned.

Mrs Ruspidge fell into hysterics, and her daughters
promptly copied her, so that it was as much as Cook
and the footman between them could do to keep the
neighbours from summoning the Watch. Fanny was
considered too lowly a being to have a part in these
important matters, but she watched and listened wide-
eyed. When, at last, Mrs Ruspidge was able to speak
coherently, she questioned her household. Cook said
that Master had given her the day off, which made her
mistress frown, and Fanny, summoned to the Presence,
said that Master had sent her on an errand, which had
taken her all morning. Mrs Ruspidge frowned again.
For the first time she remembered the other member of
her household, conspicuous by her absence. A horrid
suspicion crossed her mind, and she started to her feet.

'That girl! That Avening girl! Where is she?' She
would have stormed upstairs, but Fanny spoke up
quickly.

'She's asleep in her bed, mam. Went out in the rain, she did, and got soaked to the skin. Taken a nasty chill, I shouldn't wonder. She came in just after me, mam.' The easy lie slipped glibly from her tongue — Fanny was adept at telling the story that would be most acceptable.

'And the master? Was he here?'

'Oh, no, mam. I never saw him since you left this morning, mam.' Her eyes shone with veracity. Mrs Ruspidge sat down again.

'He did not come home, then. And yet he complained of a headache! Was that no more than an excuse, and he intending to meet someone?'

'He'll be off making his fortune, madam, a fine young man like him,' said Cook soothingly.

'Oh, Ma, will he come back with gold and pearls and diamonds? That would be lovely!' Amelia was still just young enough to believe, a little, in fairy-tales.

'We'd not see any of them, if he did, you may be sure,' muttered Charlotte. Her mother, for once, boxed her ears.

Marcus Inglesham passed the next two hours in a state of icy fury. His first care was for Augustus, who must at all costs be removed from Cecilia's orbit. He was beginning to come back to his senses by the time he was lifted from the phaeton by his lordship's carefully incurious grooms and carried into the stables. There he was put, none too gently, on to a bed of musty hay that had not been considered good enough for the horses. Lord Inglesham himself sat by him, sending them all out but one elderly groom who had worked for him, and for his father, all his life.

It was not very difficult to persuade Augustus. When he opened his eyes to the murderous glare that was Inglesham's face, and the solid, aggressive stance of the groom, he thought for a moment that his last moment had come. He had the sense to keep quiet, and indeed, if he had tried to protest, as he considered for a moment, that Cecilia had thrown herself at him in a frenzy of madness, and then attacked him, his fears might well have come true. Instead, he found himself being offered a considerable sum of money to do something which he had, in any case, been moderately tempted to do.

As a matter of form he blustered, and bargained, but when he found that his lordship was not to be moved he settled for five hundred pounds, and his fare. He reflected that once he was out of the country his debts, which were numerous and far larger than his mother had suspected, or that he could pay, would no longer be his responsibility. All in all, he was not dissatisfied, and agreed to write the letter to his mother, which Marcus dictated to him, with alacrity.

The groom took him in his charge, with instructions to travel with him to France, and not to give him a penny piece before they had disembarked from the boat.

'And if you ever dare to return to this country,' said Inglesham with a look that made him quake, 'you may be sure that I shall know of it. And you will not enjoy the consequences.'

'Come back here? And have my mother crying all over me, and the bailiffs dunning me? What do you take me for?'

'What do I take you for?' Lord Inglesham struggled for words, then turned away. Augustus walked shakily out of the stables, and out of his life.

When the sound of the receding curricle had died away, Marcus Inglesham went slowly into his house. He shook his head to all offers of food or drink, and, although he was told that her ladyship was in her sitting-room, he made no attempt to visit her. He went instead to his own bedroom, a large and austerely furnished apartment, where he sat for a long time staring into the empty fireplace.

He was in doubt of his feelings. The wonder of it was that he had been so unaware of them until today. He had never, of course, believed in love at first sight, and perhaps he still did not, but somehow or other he had managed to fall in love with this stubborn, self-opinionated, proud and altogether delightful girl after only a few hours in her company. It was true, he supposed, that the idea of marrying had of late been firmly settled in his mind, but he had gone about it, as he thought, in the correct way for a man in his position. He had picked for himself Miss Chadworth, who was in every respect suitable for the position. If he had never met Cecilia, he might have married her and been tolerably content, never knowing what he had missed. Now he shuddered at the thought.

The powerful surge of emotion that had swept through him at the sight of Cecilia and Hatherley had illuminated, like a lightning flash, his innermost desires. At that moment, he could have swept her up and carried her off himself, with as little regard for the niceties of social convention as the worm Augustus had shown. Maybe he should have done, he thought wryly; he could be in no worse position than he was now. She did not care for him, as she had shown only too clearly. And after all, why should she? What had he ever done, what was he, that she should love him? Other girls might hanker after a title, but all she wanted was a school, God damn it!

She was disgusted by what she had read in his expression, frightened of him as a man, unable even to bear his presence in the same room. Well, she should have her wish. He would not try to see her — for his own peace of mind, he could not afford to. He would see that she had what she wanted — her own school. His mother could easily enough arrange for a suitable house to be bought, perhaps in Bath itself once more, where she was known. An older woman as a companion, word spread about of the desirability of the place — it could all be done. And she would end her days, in all probability, a spinster, happy to care for the children of others, and knowing none of her own. Then, when all was settled, he would go abroad also. Back to the West Indies, perhaps, where the hot sun and the easy life might drive from his mind the memory of cold, damp Bath.

CHAPTER TEN

CECILIA slept until late the following morning. She awoke heavy-eyed, but clear-headed. There was no lapse of memory, no few peaceful moments before the events of the previous day rose up before her eyes. It was all there, ranged neatly before her. She could bear it. She must bear it. She arose from her bed with the devotion to doing right of an early martyr readying herself for the stake. Someone—doubtless Fanny—had emptied and cleaned the grate; it shone with blacklead, and the sour, sooty smell was quite gone from the room. Outside the rain had cleared, and the sun shone with painful cheerfulness. With the fresh water in her ewer Cecilia performed her morning ablutions, dressed, subdued her hair with ferocious severity, and went downstairs.

Mrs Ruspidge, she learned, was keeping to her bed. Her three daughters, not to be outdone, had also refused to rise, but had eaten healthy breakfasts carried upstairs by the luckless Fanny, and were now showing signs of boredom. The stern call of duty led Cecilia up to the young ladies' room, as the chamber they shared was known. She found them almost boisterous, and more than ready to get up and dress.

'Our brother is gone away,' Charlotte informed her with great self-importance. 'Poor Mama is quite broken up.' Her tone of voice indicated that she felt no such emotion, and Georgina echoed it.

'I don't care. He was horrid to me, the other day. He pulled my hair, and said I was getting freckles.'

'So you are,' Amelia pointed out with childish candour, pink-faced from the exertion of inserting her stout form into the froth of pin-tucked and lace-decked undergarments. Her sister made a move to slap her, and she whisked round to Cecilia's other side and stood to have her buttons done up, since none of them saw any reason why they should do such things for themselves if their governess was there to do them.

'I have not! And anyway, that's better than spots, so there.'

'I haven't got spots,' pointed out Amelia.

'But Charlie has, and so will you. I don't mean to have them ever.'

'Yes, you will. You'll have them worse than me. Mama has given me some Denmark Lotion to put on them, but I shan't let you have any,' said Charlotte spitefully.

'That is quite enough,' said Cecilia firmly. 'If you are worried about freckles, Georgina, you have only to keep your face out of the sun, as I always tell you to do when we go to the park. And you should ask Cook for some lemon juice, and put it on night and morning.'

'Will that help?' asked Georgina, easily distracted.

'Yes, it will, if you are conscientious. But not if you do not use your parasol and keep your bonnet on.'

She settled them in the schoolroom, with little hope that they would attend to the lessons that she had set them, but tolerably certain that they would be quiet, at least for a while. With a devious cunning that she had not known she possessed, she pointed out to them that while their mama was prostrate in her room there was no chance at all of their visiting Lady Aurelia, or anyone else. It was, therefore, in their interest to let Mama rest and recover as quickly as possible. Then, with a sinking heart, she went to visit Mrs Ruspidge.

The room was dark, and the thick velvet curtains were still tightly closed, keeping out both sunlight and air. There was a musty, closed-up smell overlaid with the scent of face powder and old perfume. Mrs Ruspidge lay curled up, the covers pulled up to her neck as though it were the middle of winter, her eyes determinedly closed. Cecilia tiptoed to the bedside.

'Go away,' muttered Mr Ruspidge without opening her eyes.

'I am sorry to see you thus, madam,' said Cecilia truthfully. 'May I get you anything? A cup of tea, perhaps? You must keep up your strength.'

At the sound of her sympathetic voice, Mrs Ruspidge's chin wobbled, her eyes screwed up, and her mouth turned down in a grimace of grief. Two oily tears welled from beneath the wrinkled-up eyelids, and rolled down sideways into the well-goffered frill of her night-cap. She gave a moan.

'Where has he gone? He said so little in his letter!' she whimpered. 'When will he come back?'

'I am sure he will return one day soon,' Cecilia said with false assurance. He would not, of course, but what could she say to this unhappy woman? 'After all, he will want to see you, will he not? And he will need. . . I mean, he has no fortune of his own, has he?'

There was a thoughtful pause. This aspect of the matter had not so far occurred to the grieving mother, and it was true that, while he had rarely shown affection for her, her son had had a sincere love of her fortune. She had never denied him his share of the money left to her by the late Mr Ruspidge, but she had been aware

that of late he had been having difficulty managing on
the generous allowance she made him. Twice, in the
last year, she had paid off the most pressing of his
gambling debts. She opened her eyes, and pulled herself
up on her pillows.

'That is very true. He never could manage without
his mother,' she said, with some satisfaction.

'So, you see, you are bound at least to hear from him
soon. And if he does not wish to return to England at
the present, might you not go to see him? Foreign travel
is a very fashionable thing, just now. He was talking of
going to Paris, was he not? Think of the clothes and
bonnets you might buy there! And they say that Lady
Oxford's soirées are delightful. You would enjoy that,
would you not?'

Years of dealing with the sometimes spoiled children
of the privileged classes had made Cecilia an expert at
this kind of subtle flattery. Mrs Ruspidge sat up.

'Yes. Yes, you are right, my dear. If you will ring the
bell, I think perhaps I will take a cup of tea, and some
bread and butter. Where are the girls?'

'In the schoolroom, ma'am, and studying. They are
naturally anxious for you, and are being especially quiet
so as not to disturb you.'

A few more tears ran down cheeks that were regaining
their colour.

'Dear, good little things. I am fortunate in my girls.
They are the image of what I was, at their age!'

Cecilia could well believe it.

'May I open the curtains a little, ma'am?' she asked
when she had ordered the tea. 'It is a lovely morning.'
Permission was granted, and Cecilia waited quietly
while the tea was brought and drunk, and a surprising

amount of bread and butter consumed. Mrs Ruspidge was lost in thought.

'Paris,' she murmured. 'Yes, it would not be impossible. But——' her eyes widened again '—I still do not understand why he went, and so suddenly. You do not think. . .it cannot be that there was any scandal, was there?'

'I am sure there was not.' Cecilia spoke the lie firmly, feeling that the guilt of it was balanced out by the guilt she felt at having been, however innocently, the cause of Augustus's departure.

'It would be. . .oh, dear, it would be ruinous to my hopes for the girls!' Mrs Ruspidge, secure in the knowledge that Cecilia knew no one in her circle to tattle to, said what she could not have said to her closest friends. 'If he should be in any kind of trouble. . . He is, just sometimes, a little wild, you know! Just high spirits, of course, but still. . .' She looked this terrifying possibility in the face, and blenched afresh.

'I cannot believe that there will be any scandal,' said Cecilia as convincingly as she could. 'And if there should be any little rumour, it is up to you—to all of us—to scotch it. If you can only find the strength, ma'am, to get up, and to carry on as if nothing had happened only think how much that would reassure everyone! You might say, with truth, that Mr Hatherley had for some time been thinking of going abroad, and that there was a sudden possibility of going with a friend which was too good to miss. . .everyone knows how impulsive young men are! No one will think anything of it.'

Mrs Ruspidge could see the sense of this, and for the first time she looked almost with approval at her tiresome relative.

'Above all, it is important that the young ladies

should not suspect that there is anything amiss,' continued Cecilia. 'They are so. . .so innocent in their ways that they might let something slip—quite by accident, you know.' And may I be forgiven for that, she said to herself, knowing that her charges would not hesitate to vilify their brother in public, unless it could be shown to them that they would do themselves no good thereby.

Mrs Ruspidge flung back the bedclothes.

'Ring the bell for Fanny,' she said. 'I shall get up immediately. And be sure that the young ladies are dressed for visiting—I shall go out, and make some calls. My friends will be interested to hear of Augustus's journey, and they will be wild with envy when they hear I mean to go to Paris!'

Cecilia, seeing that her task was done, did as she was bid, and returned to the schoolroom.

The next two or three days were busy ones, for Mrs Ruspidge missed no opportunity to inform all her acquaintance of her son's invitation—by *such* a delightful friend, really one could name no names, but the son of a most distinguished house—to visit the Continent! Yes, indeed, an impulsive young man, but at that age, you know. . .and an opportunity not to be missed! Cecilia was kept busy teaching the girls what they must say, and keeping them turned out in the finery that their mother thought indispensable for London visiting. She had no time to think, and was glad of it. Later, when she could bring herself to do it, she would write to her old school-friend, and humbly beg her to assist her to a position in some household as far distant from London as could be found. Ireland, perhaps? Or Yorkshire, at the very least. But not, she thought with a shudder, Scotland. The name of Inglesham should never cross her lips or her mind, and in time she would cease to see his face in her dreams, and hear his voice and his step in every passer-by in the street.

Mrs Ruspidge, though it could not be said that she was precisely friendly towards Cecilia, was nevertheless far less inclined to find fault with her, and snub her, than in the past. When the girls had done the one or two hours of study that she tried to keep them to in the morning, she was allowed to come with them down to the drawing-room, if they were not going out, and employ herself with some needlework or letter writing while they practised the pianoforte, squabbled among themselves, or recited little poems for the edification of such visitors as might arrive.

Cecilia was thus employed, about a week later, when a knock at the front door, rather louder than general, indicated the arrival of a visitor.

'Who can it be, Mama? Do you expect anyone today?' Charlotte ran to peer out of the window. 'I can't see who it is, but there's a cab out there.'

'Now, come and sit down with me, Charlotte,' begged her mother. 'It don't do to be looking out like that.'

'But you do it, Ma,' said Charlotte crossly, doing as she was bid.

'Not when I might be seen,' hissed her mother, pulling her daughter down beside her and arranging herself in an attitude of gracious relaxation. The unmistakable sound of masculine feet running up the stairs brought her, however, to her feet.

'Augustus! It must be Augustus!' she cried. Cecilia shrank back into her chair. The door was flung open and Mrs Ruspidge started forward, her arms outstretched to receive her son, only to come to a sudden halt as she saw the man framed in the doorway.

'Lord Inglesham!' she said in astonishment. Her

recovery was quick, and in any other circumstances Cecilia would have admired the way she changed her embracing attitude to an outstretched hand of dignified welcome. 'Lord Inglesham, this is a delightful surprise! Girls! Make your curtsy to his lordship! Inglesham, my daughters Charlotte, Georgina, and Amelia. They have heard so much about you!'

He ignored her completely, brushing past her as if she were invisible and inaudible. His eyes darted round the room until he found Cecilia, frozen in her chair with her needle still raised from pulling the thread through her sewing. He strode forward, narrowly missing knocking Amelia flying, until he stood in front of her.

'Forgive me! Nothing but the direst necessity could have brought me to see you!' His voice was low and urgent. She could not speak, could scarcely bow her head in a gesture of acceptance. It looked, though she did not know it, like the haughtiest disdain. His frown deepened. 'Miss Avening, have you seen Cleone?' The abrupt words were so far removed from anything she had expected to hear that she did not at once answer. 'Cleone, Miss Avening; do you know where she is?' he repeated.

'Cleone? No. No, I have not seen her since — oh, since the day nearly three weeks ago, when I met her in the park.'

He gave a groan.

'I was so sure, so sure that she would come to you!'

She was shaken out of her shocked trance.

'What has happened, Lord Inglesham? Cleone is lost? How can this be?'

'She has. . .I very much fear that she has run away. She has not been seen since early this morning.'

'This morning. . .several hours, then. But not yet all night, thank God.'

'Not that, no. But if we do not soon find her. . .' He became aware, quite suddenly, of the presence of Mrs Ruspidge and her daughters, listening open-mouthed to this conversation. He stepped back to Mrs Ruspidge, taking her hand in his own and looking earnestly down at her. 'Madam, I beg your pardon. I have been inexcusably rude, invading your privacy in this way. I can only apologise, and beg that you will not speak of this unfortunate occurrence. As the mother of — three — young daughters, you will know how much damage, how truly ruinous to my niece's reputation and hopes of future happiness such a story could be. We must all do our best to shield her from the consequences of her folly.'

Mrs Ruspidge, a little awed by his solemnity and pleased at that inclusive 'we', dared to pat his hand in a motherly fashion.

'You need have no fear of that, Inglesham! I should not dream of mentioning such a thing, and nor, of course, would my girls! Poor young lady, it is a sad misfortune! I speak as a mother, Inglesham, who has recently known the departure of an only son for distant lands!'

Cecilia could have sunk with embarrassment at the reminder, but he seemed scarcely conscious of it.

'You are very kind. I must not, however, stand here talking. However hopeless the task, I must go and search for my niece. Edward — my brother-in-law, Sir Edward Maisemore, ma'am — sent for me only an hour ago, and this was the first place I could think of to come. Whatever her reason for going off as she did, I hoped and believed that she would have sought refuge with Miss Avening. Now I must look for her in earnest.'

'Of course, of course, Inglesham. If there is anything that we can do, any assistance that we may offer. . .?'

'There is one thing. May I beg Miss Avening's company for my other nieces? They are, as you may imagine, in a terrible state of anxiety, for naturally it was impossible to hide from them that Cleone is missing. Their father is so distressed that he is unable to help them, since the sight of his misery only increases their own. I know how fond they are of Miss Avening, and how well able she is to deal with their questions.'

'My dear Inglesham, that you should even have to ask! Poor little things, my heart quite goes out to them! Naturally Cecilia would be delighted, would you not, my dear?'

Cecilia, her hands gripped tightly together, met his enquiring look with one of painful directness.

'I hardly think that I can be considered a suitable companion for the young ladies, sir. I am surprised that you should suggest it.'

He frowned in puzzlement, and Mrs Ruspidge in annoyance.

'Really, Cecilia, that you should be so ungracious! You must forgive her, Inglesham — she is overwhelmed, I know, by the shock of it all! Of course she will not refuse to help.'

'It is only,' said Cecilia with dogged persistence, 'that I cannot believe my presence would help. Surely Lady Inglesham, or even Miss Cameron. . .?'

'Miss Cameron is not yet a member of the family. Rightly or wrongly, Edward has decided that he does not, at present, wish her to know of this. As for my mother, she is elderly and, as I believe you know, a prey to ill health—an alarming weakness in her chest. The shock of this has brought on one of her worst attacks, and she is quite prostrate. She thinks, besides, that someone young, someone to whom they may speak openly. . . It was she herself who told me to fetch you.'

'But she does not know. . .' she murmured in agonised tones.

'She knows, as I do, that Sophie and Minty need you. That we all do.'

She looked at him in wonder. His face expressed no more than a sincere reflection of his words. She could not resist his appeal.

'Then of course I will come. Give me only two minutes, my lord, and I will be ready.'

She ran from the room, leaving Mrs Ruspidge to make apologies on her behalf, to which he listened not at all. In almost less than the time she had specified she was back, her pelisse unbuttoned, her gloves in her hand, and her bonnet ribbons not even tied. With a swift word of farewell he was running down the stairs, and she after him.

Their journey, which in any other circumstances would have crippled both of them with embarrassment, passed in a murmured recital of all that he knew. The necessity to keep his voice low, for fear of the driver hearing him, lent a strange kind of intimacy to their talk, and she could almost have been happy if she had not been so worried.

'Cleone has, I gather, been very quiet for the last week—one might almost say sulky. There was, I believe, some kind of argument more than a week ago,' he said. 'I do not know what it concerned, but it seems that Cleone particularly wanted permission to go to something, and Edward would not agree to it. A concert,

or some such thing. The truth of it is, he had no idea
that she wished for it so strongly, and he cannot even
remember precisely what it was she wanted. All he
knows is that it was an unsuitable thing for her to be
doing, and that in any case it was on a day when he
expected to be going with Miss Cameron to some party
or other. Now he is in such a state that he can barely
speak at all, let alone remember what was said. He
recalls that Cleone pleaded with him, but he was
preoccupied at the time, and she left the room in tears.
Now, of course, he thinks he will never see her again,
and that his last memories of her will always have to be
remembered as unhappy ones.'

'Oh, poor man. It is a terrible burden. But I cannot
understand that he does not even remember what it was
that she wanted.'

'Nor could I. The truth is, Miss Avening, that he is
at present in a state where the only thing that he truly
sees is Miss Cameron. Hers is the only face, hers the
only voice of which he is aware, and it blinds him to
everything else, even his own daughters. He is like a
man under a spell, and, though it will not last, while it
does so he might just as well be on a desert island with
her, for all the sense the rest of us will get out of him.
And I, for one, can sympathise with that only too
easily.'

He could not help giving her an earnest look. She
thought it strange, then remembered Miss Chadworth,
and an expression of unhappy withdrawal came over
her face. At once he lowered his gaze, and they sat in
uncomfortable silence until they reached Grosvenor
Square. As soon as the cab drew up outside the house
he sprang down, turning to hold out his hand, but she

laid her fingers on the door-frame and jumped down without his assistance.

He was looked for, and the door was opened before he needed to knock. A few moments later Cecilia had both Sophie and Minty weeping in her arms, and with her own eyes full of tears was endeavouring to comfort them. She heard Sir Edward and Lord Inglesham giving orders to such trusted menservants and grooms as they thought could be sent out to search, and then they themselves were gone as well. Cecilia led the tearful children upstairs to the comforting familiarity of their schoolroom, where she sat down between them and let them, for a few minutes, cry out their worry and fear.

Abby was there also, feverishly ironing and folding already immaculate petticoats and nightgowns. Her plump face, so pink and comely before, was mottled with weeping, and her round cheeks seemed to sag with their own weight. Cecilia spoke as cheerfully to her as she could, and, feeling that the sight of their nurse in such a state could do the children no good, suggested that she should take her work to another room, glancing meaningfully as she did so at the two little girls. Abby nodded, her cheeks and chin quivering into a brave smile that was almost worse than her tears, and took herself off to the girls' bedchamber.

When the children were quieter Cecilia spoke to them, encouraging them to hope that all might yet be well, pointing out how many people were now searching for Cleone, and reminding them also that, while they were unhappy, their father was still more so.

'It is hard, I know, my dears. But if you may not go out and search for your sister, you can at least do something to help us all, by keeping brave faces on, and trying to cheer him with your love and sympathy. And your grandmama, also. Can you do that, do you think?'

They assured her, if rather doubtfully, that they could.

'That's good girls! Now, let us go and wash your faces and hands, and you will be surprised how much better you will feel!'

It was true that they did, and, with a child's ability to recover at speed from tears, they grew more cheerful while answering her questions as to their doings. Cleone's name was several times mentioned, and though their voices wobbled occasionally they made praiseworthy attempts to live up to her expectations of them. Back in the schoolroom she set them some simple work to do, in the belief that time would pass more easily for them if they were busy. Since they had already been questioned by their father and uncle, she knew that they had no idea of where Cleone might have gone, so she did not attempt to ask them again, merely encouraging them to tell her, in as much detail as possible, what they had done during the time since she last saw them.

Astley's Amphitheatre figured largely in their recital, particularly for Sophie, who described in minute detail just what the performing horses had done.

'And Cleone didn't like it. She said she was too old for such things,' she said sadly.

'What did she prefer, then? Shopping I suppose?'

'Well, we all like that. Especially when we go with Papa and Miss Cameron! And of course there were her singing lessons.'

'Singing lessons? She had started them, then?'

'Yes, it was awful. She would sing nothing but scales, up and down, up and down, until I could have screamed,' said Minty, then looked stricken. 'Oh, dear,

I didn't mean that! I'd give anything if she were here now; she might sing as many scales as she wished, if only she were!'

'It doesn't matter, Minty. I am sure she wouldn't mind you saying it.'

'Well, she did then. Though she didn't stop. And after another two lessons she did start to learn a new song, though I didn't understand it.'

'You didn't? Why was that?'

'It was all in Italian. He had explained it all to her, but she couldn't remember it properly to tell me what it meant. It was all about love, and that sort of thing.'

'Who explained it? Her singing master?'

'Yes, because he was Italian, you see, so of course he wanted her to sing Italian songs, because he thought they were the best. Do you think they're the best, Miss Avening?'

'Not necessarily. But she must do as he said, I suppose, if he was her teacher.'

'That's what she said.' Sophie, who had taken little part in this conversation, looked up from her work.

'She said it last night,' she said. 'I heard her—she was muttering to herself, you know, the way she does when she is cross. She said she must do as her teacher wanted, or he might not teach her any more.'

A little shiver went through Cecilia.

'What did she mean, do you know?'

'Not really. She said I was too young to understand, when I asked her. I think he wanted her to sing for his friends, at a concert, or something. I'm not very sure.'

'At a public concert, perhaps? And she wanted to do so?'

'Well, of course she did. She loved singing to people, and she'd learned the new song especially. And I was learning it, too—the piano part, that is. I wanted to surprise her, and Mama and Papa, by playing for her when she sang it to them. Of course, they've been too busy to listen, recently, but it was quite difficult so I needed time to practise it. I can play it well now— would you like to hear it?'

Cecilia would have demurred, only she saw that Sophie was eager to do so, seeing also that it helped her to remember that she had been making this effort of learning a difficult piece as a kind of gift to her sister. Sophie was leafing through the music on the top of the piano.

'I can't find it. Have you had it, Minty?'

'No, of course not. I can't play that; my hands are too small.'

'It must be here, then.' Fretfully, Sophie started to separate the books and sheets, dropping them on the floor beside her as she did so.

'Never mind for now, Sophie,' said Cecilia soothingly. 'Let me hear it another time, when Cleone is here to sing it with you.'

'No, I want to play it *now*,' was the querulous answer. 'Oh, why can't I find it? I know it was here last night— I heard her practising it.'

'Sophie.' Cecilia kept her voice as calm as she could. 'Listen, Sophie, would your papa have asked the music master for news of Cleone?'

'I don't know. Yes, I believe he did, for she had a lesson yesterday. He had not seen her at all, he said. You don't think he would have taken her away, do you? He's such a nice man, Cleone said, very small and round and bouncy like a ball, and quite old.'

'No, my dear, I am sure your father would not have chosen anyone unsuitable. But I think I should like to

know where the lessons took place. He did not come
here?'

'No, because he is famous, and has a great many
pupils. Cleone said it was an honour for her that he
agreed to teach her.'

'And you don't know where he lived?'

'No. But Abby does. She always went with Cleo when
she had a lesson.'

Cecilia slipped out of the room, and hurried to find
Abby.

'That singing master? Oh, yes, miss, but I do know
that Master has already asked him. She never went
there this morning, miss.'

'No, but where exactly does he live?'

The address meant nothing to Cecilia.

'What sort of a place was it? Is it far away?'

'Quite a way, miss. We always took a cab, for though
it was a nice enough place we had to go through some
nasty, low streets to get to it. Not the kind of place you'd
walk through with my young ladies.'

'Abby, can you take me there?'

'What, now, miss? I suppose I could, but why?'

'I know I am here to be with the young ladies, but
there is something I must try. . . I may know somebody
who could help.'

'Then we'll go right away, miss,' said Abby, laying
aside her work. 'I'll send one of the maids to sit in the
schoolroom. Annie's a good girl; they like her. They'll
be all right, now you've got them calmed down.'

Cecilia went back to the schoolroom.

'There is just a chance that I may be able to get news
of Cleone,' she said carefully. 'It is only a possibility,
and I do not want you to get your hopes up too much.

Will you stay here sensibly, with Annie, until I come back? I do not know how long I shall be.'

'I knew you could do it!' Minty was jubilant. 'I knew you'd find her for us! We'll be good as gold, gooder than gold, I promise!'

'I know you will be. Do not hope too much, my dears! But I shall do my best, which is all that any of us can do.' She kissed them, and was gone.

CHAPTER ELEVEN

BY GOOD fortune, Cecilia and her companion were able to get a cab almost at once, and were soon on their way to the music master's house. Neither of them spoke, for the familiar journey had brought back Abby's tears, and Cecilia was anxiously watching out of the window. At first she could not be sure that she recognised any of the streets through which they passed. In the bright sunshine of late afternoon buildings and places had so very different an aspect from their night-time selves. Then, she was sure, she saw a familiar butcher's shop, and after that the name of a public house that she certainly remembered. She rapped on the hatch, and spoke to the driver.

'Go slowly here, if you please. I may want to stop quite soon.'

It was not long before they were in a street that she knew, and when she had checked the name of it she stopped the cab. Abby looked alarmed as she saw Cecilia about to climb down.

'Here, miss? She'd never come here, Miss Cleone wouldn't. Innocent she may be, but she knows this isn't the place for a young lady like her. Or like you, miss, if you'll pardon me.'

'No, of course it is not. But she must have come this way, if she was going to her singing master, and I do think that she was. Her music is gone from the piano, the music of the song she was learning for him. I do not

183

ask you to come with me now, Abby. You can go back
to her sisters; I shall be all right.'

'What, and leave you here all alone, miss, in a place
like this? As if I would! If you think you can find
her. . .' Still disbelieving, she climbed heavily down
from the cab. All the lightness and grace was gone from
her movement, Cecilia saw, and she landed with a thud
on the roadway. Cecilia waited until the cab, its driver
complaining that his promised journey had been cut
short and only slightly comforted by the size of his
payment, had driven off, then she walked along the
street to the front door that was so much cleaner than
its neighbours, and knocked.

A neat maidservant answered, looking surprised by
the callers.

'I should like to see Mrs Elham, if you please,' said
Cecilia firmly.

'Well, I don't rightly know as she's at home,' said the
girl dubiously, looking at the young woman with a
companion who was obviously her maid. A young
woman on her own was not so uncommon — word had
spread that Mrs Elham took good care of her girls, and
was not infrequently visited by those who wished to put
themselves under her protection. But a gentlewoman,
with a maid — could it be the wife of one of the regular
gentlemen callers, come to make trouble? Mrs E.
wouldn't like that, not one bit.

Cecilia read some of this in the girl's face, and could
have been amused if her errand had not been so serious.

'If you will tell your mistress that Miss Cecilia
Avening is here, I think that she will see me if she
remembers me. I can assure you that I do not mean to
cause any disturbance.'

'Well, miss. . .if you will come in, I will enquire.'

They were allowed into the rather anonymous hall, and left to wait while the maid went on her errand. Abby looked around. She was secretly relieved to see the place so respectable; was it perhaps a private house after all, some eccentric lady who chose to live in this disreputable street, perhaps even one who was charitably inclined, devoting her life to helping fallen women? When Mrs Elham herself appeared, her age and obvious gentility made her relax even more.

'Miss Avening!' Mrs Elham was surprised. 'It is really you? I was not sure, at first, whether I had remembered the name correctly.'

'Mrs Elham, it is very good of you to see me,' said Cecilia, 'and I am so sorry to trouble you. But you were so kind as to say, when last we met, that you would help me if I should be in need of your assistance.'

'And you need my help? What is it — more sweetbreads?' The smile at her little joke died away as Mrs Elham saw that her visitor was very much in earnest. 'My dear, forgive me. I see that my help is really required. Will you not come into my sitting-room and tell me what I can do for you? Your maid may wait in the study; she will be quite undisturbed there.'

Abby seemed quite happy to do so, and Cecilia followed her hostess into the pretty peaceful room that she remembered from before. It was scented with roses and pinks massed into a bowl, and could almost have been a room in some pleasant country house. She felt her spirit ease a little, and sat down.

'I do not know if you have heard of a family called Maisemore?' she said, as if she were making conversation at a morning call. 'They are connected by marriage to the Ingleshams.'

Mrs Elham inclined her head. 'I have heard the

name, though I am not acquainted with either of the gentlemen.' Her voice was gently ironic, but Cecilia saw that she was pleased to be asked. To make a secret of the name of the family for whom she was asking help would have been an insult, but one that it would have been natural to make. It was a measure of her trust that Cecilia opened her account in such a way, and she did not do it without careful consideration.

'There are three girls, motherless for many years, who have been brought up by the Dowager Lady Inglesham since their mother, who was her daughter, died. Their father, Sir Edward, is about to marry for the second time, and I made the acquaintance of the young ladies when I was travelling up to London. They were journeying in the care of their uncle, Lord Inglesham, and I had occasion to be of service to them when Cleone, the eldest, was overcome with terror at a thunderstorm. She is fifteen.'

Mrs Elham nodded, indicating that she was paying attention to the story, and that she had understood its drift.

'Cleone is a sensitive, warm-hearted girl, very attached to her mother's memory but making a laudable effort to love her new mother, who is one of the most beautiful women I have ever seen. She also—Cleone, that is—possesses a remarkable singing voice, and now that she is in London her father has arranged some singing lessons for her. Some time about a week and a half ago she asked permission from her father to go to something—I do not know what, but I suspect it may have been to perform at some kind of concert or party given by her new singing master—and her father refused it. Unfortunately, he is so very busy at the moment. . . ' Mrs Elham nodded again, with a little smile.

'Not uncommon, of course. A man like that is ill-equipped to understand the feelings of a fifteen-year-old girl, particularly if she has been living with her grandmother. And now that he has fallen in love with this beauty, he is probably completely distracted.'

'Exactly. And now Cleone has disappeared, since early this morning. They are all out looking for her, and I discovered that her music is missing — for a song which I think she was learning for this master. It may well be that she was intending to go to see him. He has not seen her, but her journey to his house takes her down this road. Usually, of course, she goes in a carriage with the maid, who is with me. But on her own, since she could not order up one of her father's carriages, she might have tried to come on foot. It seemed to me that she might have met with some mischance in this part of London. Do you think so?'

Mrs Elham's face was sober.

'Poor child! How very unfortunate that she was not left with her grandmother, until after the wedding! At her age, the guidance of a mother. . . But still, you were very right to come to me. I have, as you doubtless realise, numerous — shall I say? — "acquaintances", and among them several who owe me a favour. If she is in this area, I hope I may find her for you. She left the house this morning?'

'Yes, but very early. No one saw her go. Her bed had been slept in, but when the maid went to waken her it was already cold. She did not take any of her clothes, other than what she was wearing, of course, and she is not in any case at all the kind of girl who would consider running away or eloping, even if there had been any opportunity for her to meet a man who would contemplate such a thing. Her singing is her passion, and is the only thing that I think would drive her into behaving so foolishly.'

'Tell me what she looks like, then, and what she was wearing too. You need have no fear of my revealing her name. If we are to do any good we must be quick. I do not need to tell you that we must find her before the evening gets under way.'

Cecilia gave a rapid sketch of Cleone's colouring and looks, and called in Abby, who was able to describe in some detail what her charge was wearing, since Sir Edward and Lord Inglesham had already needed to know. The sight of the sitting-room obviously gave her yet more reassurance, and she treated Mrs Elham with the respect due to an eccentric but doubtless most charitable gentlewoman.

'I shall send out as many of my people as I can spare, and go myself to see one or two of those who might need rather more persuasion,' said Mrs Elham briskly. 'It might be several hours before we find her, if indeed she is here to find. Perhaps you had both better go back to her house. I will send a message as soon as there is anything to be known.'

'If you do not mind, I should prefer to stay here,' said Cecilia. 'Abby, I think, had better go back to the other girls, but I cannot bear to leave! If. . .when. . .she is found, she may well be in great distress, and the sight of a familiar face, you know. . .'

'I'd like to stay, but I think you're right, miss. I've not got your self-control, and I'd not be able to help her as you could,' admitted Abby. 'I'll do my best with the younger ones, miss.'

'Well done, Abby. Tell them I am looking for Cleone, and keep them as cheerful as you can.'

'Very well. I shall leave you here for a while, Miss Avening. I do not know that you are right to stay here, but if you insist I cannot prevent you.' Mrs Elham gave Cecilia a serious look, and left the room. To spend several hours in what was no more nor less than a brothel could, she knew, be ruinous to Cecilia if it should ever become known. Such a thing was bad enough for a girl who had the protection of family and wealth, but for a young woman needing to find employment in a gentleman's houshold it would spell the end of all her hopes.

Cecilia knew it, and was glad to see Abby leave. It would not be possible, she thought, to conceal the nature of her friend's occupation for very long, but at least for the time being Abby was happy in her belief in Mrs Elham's respectability. If it proved impossible to find Cleone then Cecilia must go back to Harley Street with no more than a message to the Maisemore household to that effect, and she must in future count them as dead to her. If they should be successful, but too late, then it was doubtful that they could be pleased, relieved though they might be to have Cleone back. If she should still be unharmed then there was hope that Cecilia might be able to keep their friendship, although her knowledge of what must necessarily be kept a secret from the world must tinge their feelings about her with a kind of resentment, she thought. However careful she might be, they would always have the knowledge and fear that she could, with a word, destroy any chance of Cleone having a happy and settled future. Such secrets did not lead to pleasant relationships, and Cecilia still thought that it would be better if she should remove herself from their lives altogether.

The time passed impossibly slowly. The house was quiet, and all that was to be heard was an occasional distant, calling voice, a little snatch of song or laughter, all going to prove that Mrs Elham's claims about the girls in her charge were correct. In the room itself, the only sound was the ticking of the clock, for in June of course the fireplace was cold, filled with an arrangement of fresh leaves, so that there was not even the companionable murmur of flames to brighten the atmosphere. From outside came voices, wheels, the sound of feet, but they seemed somehow distanced by this silent room, and lacking in reality, as if they came from some other world.

Unused as she was to sitting idle, Cecilia had to fight to prevent herself from anxiously pacing the room. There were books on a table near her, obviously being read at present, and more on a pretty set of shelves in an alcove. Well bound and tooled in gold, they were mute testimony to the taste and intelligence of the room's owner, and there was no question that they were merely for show, for they had the worn, friendly look of books that had been enjoyed and loved. Cecilia took up a book of poems, but the words seemed trite and meaningless. She tried a novel, one which she had been wanting to read and had heard was much admired. After two chapters she was aware that it was amusing, that it was well written, and that in any other circumstances she would have enjoyed it, but had she been asked she could not have named any of the characters, nor said what they had been doing. She laid the book aside.

Outside it was still light, bright day. The inexorable march of the clock, however, told her what she did not

want to know — that the afternoon was all but over, the
evening almost begun. Though the summer sun shone
and was warm, the shadows were lengthening and the
light enriching itself to the warm gold that preceded
sunset. The maid who had admitted her came in with a
tray, and offered little sandwiches, and cakes, and tea.

'Madam said you must eat, miss. She always says
that young ladies need to eat properly, particularly this
time of day.' Mrs Elham's young ladies would, of course,
have a strenuous evening and night ahead of them.
Cecilia felt the mouthful of sandwich turn to sawdust in
her mouth. She choked it down with a mouthful of tea,
and doggedly took another bite. She could do Cleone no
good by starving herself, and she had eaten almost
nothing since breakfast, a meal which she now found it
impossible to recall. The tea, however, revived her, and
she drank several cups gratefully. She could almost have
wished that she were a man and could have recourse to
stronger beverages. The thought brought back memories of Augustus and his brandy glass, and she
shuddered.

And always, at the back of her mind, was the thought
of Marcus Inglesham. Of his arrival, that morning. Of
his request, and his mother's, that she should go to be
with his nieces. Of their journey, their murmured conversation, in the cab. Most of all, of the way her heart
had leaped at the sight of him, her whole self had
vibrated to the sound of his voice. She had thought she
would never see him again; now that she had, she did
not know whether she could bear not to be with him
one more time, at least. A few more memories to store
away, like those puzzling words he had spoken that
morning, to cherish and mull over when she was alone.
He was like a drug that once it had been tried became

necessary to the taker. He was in her mind, her blood, her heart, and she did not think she could ever be rid of him.

The clock struck, and she did not need to count the chimes or to look at it to know that it was seven o'clock. All over London the fashionable and wealthy would be preparing for an evening of gaiety. There were footsteps upstairs, more hurried now, and a buzz of conversation. As if the sound of the clock had been a signal, the door opened and Mrs Elham came in. A man behind her, discreet in the dark uniform of an upper servant, carried the drooping body of a girl. Cleone. Cecilia gave a little sob, and started forward.

The girl lay limp in his arms. She was entirely wrapped in a dark cloak, her pale hair and even her face hidden by the hood that was pulled so low that no more than an angle of cheekbone was to be seen. Her head was pillowed on his shoulder, and as Cecilia drew nearer he shifted his burden, preparatory to laying it on a convenient sofa. Cleone's head shifted from its support and fell back, the hood dropping away so that her hair, which had been fastened up in a would-be adult style, fell in pin-speared coils almost to the floor. Her eyes were closed, her mouth a little open, her skin waxen-pale and dewed with moisture. Cecilia made a little sound of distress, and reached up helpless hands as if to take hold of her.

'It is all right.' Mrs Elham's voice was low and calm. 'Let Joe put her down. Strong as an ox he might be, but he has carried her for more than a mile, and she is not precisely a feather, you know.'

'She's not. . .not dead, is she?' Obediently Cecilia withdrew her hands, putting them behind her back like a chidden schoolgirl. The man gave a grunt of relief and laughter as he bent and, with surprising gentleness, laid his burden down.

'Dead, miss? Not her. Taken a drop too much, that's all. Be right as rain, come morning, she will. Half seas under, and then some.'

Cecilia stared at him, unable in her shaken state to comprehend him.

'Half seas. . .you do not mean she tried to drown herself?'

He looked helplessly at Mrs Elham, as if doubting his own powers of communication. With a little smile, she translated.

'The child has been given too much to drink, that is all. Have you never seen anyone in an inebriated sleep before?'

'In an. . .good heavens, not a girl of her age, anyway!' The servant moved towards the door, Cecilia hurrying after him distractedly. 'Oh, thank you, thank you so much! I beg you will accept this; I only wish it were more, but I am sure her friends will wish to reward you. . .' She pressed a gold coin into his not unwilling hand. 'You will not — will not mention this to anyone, will you? The young lady, I mean?'

'Not me, miss,' he said cheerfully. 'Don't know who she is, do I? Thank you kindly, miss. No call for anything more, miss.' He left the room, shaking his head.

'You need not worry; he is an old servant of mine, and very loyal. He will not reveal anything that I have asked him to keep secret, which is why I took him with me.'

Cecilia sat down suddenly into the nearest chair. A nasty grey fog, unpleasantly patterned with sick flashes of light, seemed to be wreathing through her head and before her eyes. She took a deep breath, and, remembering Miss Herring's sensible training, leaned forward, and put her head on to her knees. She felt Mrs Elham's gentle touch on her shoulder.

'That is right, my dear. You have had an anxious afternoon. Just listen, and sit quiet, while I tell you that the child has not been harmed. Indeed, it is very likely that she will have only the most indistinct of memories of the whole thing.'

Cecilia breathed slowly and carefully, as if it were a lesson in breathing. A few tears fell from her eyes, and dropped on to the muslin of her skirt. She sniffed.

'Thank you,' she said huskily. 'Oh, thank you so very much. How did you find her?'

Mrs Elham did not answer immediately, but rang the bell and asked for wine.

'With such an example before you, it would not be surprising if you should refuse it,' she said, pouring a glass and holding it out to Cecilia, who was now upright again, but still pale. 'Nevertheless, it will do you good to drink it.' Cecilia looked at Cleone, who lay without moving, a little snore issuing from time to time between those pink lips, which were softly parted like the mouth of a sleeping baby. 'Not until you have drunk it. Then you may go and see her.' Obediently Cecilia drank, feeling the warmth spreading from her stomach and reviving her.

'Good girl. Now I will tell you. She came, as you guessed, this way, and was certainly intending to visit her singing master, who equally certainly had no knowledge of her intention, and would have been horrified by her disobedience had he known. I suspect, from what I found out, that she was accosted by some man. It may well be that he was quite innocent, and intended only to warn her away from these streets, but she was frightened, and ran from him. I expect she lost her way, as you did not so long ago.'

Cecilia went to kneel by the sofa. She stroked the dishevelled hair away from the damp forehead, and pulled aside the cloak that had enveloped the girl from head to foot. Her gown was creased and stained, her hands grubby as Minty's might have been, the nails childishly bitten and ragged. A sour smell rose from her dress, and the effluvium of gin was on her breath. Cecilia took one of the hands in her own, and held it.

'Poor little girl,' she said softly. 'She had never, probably, been out on her own, even in the country.'

'Very likely. In any event, she was then spoken to by a woman. If she had but known it, she would probably have been safer with the first man whom she met, but this woman appears respectable, and kind. She, no doubt, would have offered her help, and I do not think it would have occurred to this child to suspect her.'

'She is someone that you know?'

'Someone of whom I know. Our paths have crossed, more than once, and I know more about her than she might wish. Things that might, even, be dangerous to her. When one of my girls heard that this woman had been seen with a young, blonde, well-spoken girl, I went to see her.' She gave a grim smile. 'She did not love me before, and she loves me less now. She tried to deny it, but when she saw I was not to be fobbed off she gave the girl to me. I fancy, in the end, she was relieved to be rid of her. By the greatest good fortune the child, by goodness knows what instinct for discretion, refused to tell her her name, and insisted that she was the Signorina Angelica, a well-known singer!'

Cecilia gave a slightly hysterical giggle.

'Good heavens, how melodramatic! She did not believe her, of course? Why did she not let her go at once?'

'Well, she could see that it was no such thing, of course, but still, having persuaded her back into her house, she thought at least to get some profit from her. You know, of course, that there is a great deal of money to be made from a young virgin?'

'It is not something I have thought about a great deal,' admitted Cecilia, blushing.

'No, I don't suppose you have. But in my line of business, my dear — forgive me, but it is the main reason why she was in so much danger — such girls are something of a rarity, as you may imagine. Particularly if they are as pretty as this little one.'

'But — but it would mean the gallows, surely, if it were to be discovered that she had sold the child into debauchery? How could she hope to get away with it?'

Mrs Elham sighed, and shook her head.

'My dear, have you any idea how many girls, and children too, disappear every year in this city? And how very few of them ever are seen again? Oh, not girls of birth, like this one, but still! And this child, if she had been subjected to the whim of the kind of men who would buy her, do you think she would ever return to her father, to her innocent sisters, to her grandmother?'

'No. No, I suppose you are right. She would have been too ashamed to face them. What saved her, then?'

'Her very innocence, I believe.' Mrs Elham smiled. 'She would not, of course, have agreed willingly to what was to happen to her, and the woman who took her in must have intended to get her drunk, and so ensure her co-operation. She gave her gin and hot water, with plenty of sugar and lemons, and the child liked the taste and was happy to drink. So much so that, before either of them knew it, she was so drunk that she scarcely knew what she was doing. I don't suppose she has ever taken more than a glass of weak negus in her life?'

Cecilia laughed, remembering how firmly their uncle had made his nieces drink lemonade on their journey.

'Probably not even that! I should imagine the nearest she has ever been to strong drink is the brandy in the hard sauce at Christmas! She would have had no idea what had come over her. But surely, if she was so incapable, she would have been an easy prey to the kind of man who. . .'

'She might have been. But a constitution so unused to such excess is inclined to reject it, and that is what happened.'

'You mean. . .?'

'Precisely. The gentleman — so called — who had been offered, no doubt at great expense, the privilege of enjoying her had no sooner put his arms around her than she was extremely unwell. All over him. He was not, I think, best pleased. In fact, he is claiming the cost of a suit of clothes from the woman concerned.'

Cecilia laughed.

'Well, of all the ways to protect one's virtue, to be sick all over one's seducer has to be said to be original, and very effective. If one could but do so at will, one would not need such tricks as those you told me of the other week.'

'They have their place, too.'

'They certainly do.' The reminder clouded her face, but she put the thought resolutely from her. 'Her family should be told that she is safe. They are so very anxious.'

'I sent Johnny — do you remember Johnny? — with a message to them the moment that I had her away from that house. I told him to ask for the maid who came with you, and to speak only to her, saying that the child was found safely and should be brought back as soon as possible.'

'You are so very good. I do not know why you should go to so much trouble for her, and for me.'

Mrs Elham's voice was sad but controlled.

'I was once a girl very like her, so innocent that I was in truth a danger to myself. I was not very much older than this when I fancied myself in love, and in one foolish hour lost my honour, my family and my future. Oh, you need not sympathise too much,' she said, seeing Cecilia's face, 'for I must admit, though it may shock you, that I ended up enjoying my life a great deal. I am as happy now, with my house and my friends, as I think I would have been had I lived the life my parents intended for me. Happier, perhaps, for they were set on marrying me to a man I could neither respect nor like, and who I have reason to believe would have made me very miserable. No, I am content with my life, but in spite of that I would not see another forced into going the same way. My fault was, at least, committed voluntarily, however little I understood what I was doing.'

Cleone stirred, her eyes opened for a moment, she winced, and closed them again. Cecilia bent over her.

'Cleone! Cleone, my dear, can you hear me?'

She gave a little moan.

'Miss Avening? Is that you? Oh, where am I, have I been ill? My head hurts, and my eyes, and I feel dreadful!'

'Yes, my dear, you were taken ill, and this lady has kindly cared for you. Now I will take you home, and you will soon be better.'

Cleone's eyes opened again. She looked blearily at Cecilia, and then past her at the room.

'I don't remember this room, do I? And this is a different lady. She gave me a drink, I remember, and I liked it. And then a man wanted to hug me, and. . .oh, Miss Avening, I was so sick! And he was cross, and shouted! Oh, Miss Avening, it was horrid! Take me home, please take me home!'

'I shall, my dear. We shall go home directly.'

There was a little pause. Cleone frowned.

'I was naughty, wasn't I?' Cecilia nodded gravely. 'And Papa will be so cross with me! He wouldn't let me go, and it wasn't fair! Grandmama would have permitted it, but he just said no, and didn't even listen when I told him what it was. He doesn't love me any more, now he has Miss Cameron.'

'My dear,' Cecilia spoke gravely, 'you are quite mistaken. Your papa loves you very dearly, and he has been frantic with worry over you. If he is angry with you, as he may be, then I am afraid that you have deserved it. You were very wrong to do what you did, very wrong and very foolish. I think that now you see just how foolish and dangerous it was, to go off alone like that. You owed obedience to him in this, even if it did not please you. But you must always remember that his anger is a measure of his love for you. If he did not care, he would not be angry. In any case, I think that he will be so relieved to have you safely back that he will not scold you just yet.'

Cleone sniffed, her eyes filling with tears.

'Poor Papa, I must tell him I am sorry. Please, Miss Avening, may we go home now?'

'There is a carriage at the door,' said Mrs Elham. 'It

has come from your house, I believe. I sent a message to say that you are safe.'

Cleone swung her feet down to the floor and sat up.

'Oh, dear, I don't think I can walk. I feel so strange, and everything is going up and down.' The door opened. 'Uncle Marcus! Oh, Uncle Marcus, I am so glad it is you! Take me home, please, Uncle Marcus! I want to go home!'

'That is why I am here,' he said, a little grimly. Turning to Mrs Elham, he bowed over her hand. 'Madam, I have heard your name though I have never met you. I do not quite understand how it is that you have become involved in this, but I cannot thank you enough for your help. We — all her family — are more grateful than I can express.' He did not, Cecilia noticed, ask for her promise of silence, and she thought sadly how truly the gentleman he was. Mrs Elham smiled at him approvingly.

'Lord Inglesham, I am glad to have been able to help. You may be sure that the child came to no actual harm, and, though she has had a fright, I believe that in the end she will gain wisdom from this experience.'

'You may be right.' He bowed again. 'Miss Avening, you will come back with us, of course.' She did not look at him, hearing the controlled anger in his voice but missing the look in his eyes that was warmer than he might have wished.

'No, thank you. I must go back to my. . .to Harley Street.'

'As you wish.'

Cleone cried out at this, but Cecilia soothed her. 'You must go home to your family, and I to mine. You do not need me now, my dear.'

'But I do! I do!' She began to cry. 'Uncle Marcus, tell

Miss Avening that she must come with us! Papa will want to speak to her, at least!' Her sobs became violent, hysterical, and Cecilia took hold of her. The slight body was shaking convulsively.

'Very well, then.' His voice was angry, unwilling. 'It is true that your father must speak to her. And so shall I. But now we must take you home, where they are waiting for you.' Cleone, now that she had started, found that she could not stop. Cecilia administered a small, sharp slap on her cheek, and she gave one more sob, then breathed deeply with relief. 'Obviously we still cannot do without you, Miss Avening.' He sounded almost as if he hated her, Cecilia thought, as he picked up his niece and carried her, with a word of thanks and farewell to Mrs Elham, out of the door.

'Well, I don't know what call he has to be so angry,' she said in a voice that tried to be cheerful.

'Do you not, my dear? But I fancy he will soon tell you all about it,' said Mrs Elham, hiding her amusement.

CHAPTER TWELVE

IT WAS not a pleasant journey. Lord Inglesham sat in grim silence, a prey to so many conflicting emotions that he hardly knew what was uppermost in his mind. Fear for Cleone, fear for Cecilia, worry about his mother, all jostled for attention. The relief from all three anxieties did little to calm him. It had been one of the most hideous days of his life, and he was churning inside with the residue of all its passions.

When Sir Edward had realised that Cleone had actually disappeared, and had sent for Marcus, he had been with his mother when the note had arrived. His exclamation had alerted her so that it was impossible for him to conceal from her what had happened, as he would have preferred to do. He had inherited from his father the impulse to protect her from all unpleasantness, and though she found this very touching she sometimes thought that his care of her was a little restricting, and she was glad that on this occasion he could not keep the news from her.

He had hurried off at once, leaving her to follow him to Grosvenor Square since she could not bear to stay at home while her granddaughters were in trouble. He knew that she would try not to allow herself to be affected, but, as so often before, her body's weakness had betrayed her, and scarcely had she arrived before the familiar tightness in her chest had started. Her maid, who had been with her for so many years, had had the forethought to bring with her all the remedies that usually helped her, but this time neither the burning pastilles, nor the cordial, nor even the drops availed her. She was forced to lie on a sofa in a seldom used back sitting-room — she had refused utterly to go to bed — and fought to drag the air into her through the narrowed airways that seemed to grow tighter by the minute.

Marcus, with Edward, had been occupied with questioning the little girls, who tearfully denied any knowledge of their sister's plans. None of the servants was able to enlighten them either, and Edward could do nothing but blame himself. Marcus had tried to encourage them all, to persuade them that all would be well, but he was alarmed when he saw the blue tinge round his mother's lips and saw how she laboured to breathe. He knew that she was bitterly aware of her own uselessness and was distressed at her inability to help and comfort Sophronia and Araminta. It was as much for her sake as for the children's that he had gone to fetch Cecilia. Although his mother had been peculiarly reticent on the subject of Cecilia, he was aware that she had been much struck by that young woman's good sense and knew that she could be relied upon to do everything for the little girls that she would have done herself, if she had been able.

Her mind eased, the familiar remedies had had a chance to do their work, and she knew that the attack, which had been an unusually severe one, was retreating. She had rested for a while, then was able to rise from the sofa and return to the drawing-room. There was no news, she was told; neither Sir Edward nor his lordship had returned, and the young ladies were up in their schoolroom with Annie.

'Is Miss Avening not with them? I had understood she was to come and be with them.'

'No, my lady. Miss Avening went out, with Abby, my lady.'

It seemed strange, but Lady Inglesham had enough faith in Cecilia to assume that she knew what she was doing, so she asked no more, merely ascertaining that her granddaughters were not fretting. When told that they seemed to be occupying themselves quite contentedly she decided to leave them alone. It was impossible for her to climb all the stairs to the schoolroom, and to send for them to come down to her would only unsettle them. She set herself to wait.

Marcus came back not long after, and she needed only to hear the tone of his voice in the hall to know that he had not been successful. He came wearily through to her, brushing back with a careless hand the dark hair that was usually brushed to artful disarray.

'Mother, you are better? I was told that you had had a severe attack. I should have forbidden you to come here at all, if I had had any expectation of being listened to.'

'I am perfectly all right; you must not worry about me.' She dismissed her own health with a wave of her hand, and though he studied the shadows under her eyes and the greyish tinge to her lips he did no more than tighten his lips, aware that she disliked more than anything to be fussed over. 'There is no news? You have found nothing?'

'Nothing. I came back merely to check that no message had been received, but I understand that there has been nothing.'

'Nothing. And no word from Edward.'

'Then he has found nothing either.'

'Oh, listen! Something is happening!' Lady Inglesham strained anxious ears to the sounds of bustle from without. Marcus strode to the door, and flung it open just in time to admit Miss Cameron, very becomingly attired in a pelisse and bonnet of celestial blue that looked dim compared with her eyes. She looked at them in dismay.

'Something has happened to Edward! Oh, I knew it, I knew it!'

The wild rose-pink faded from her cheeks, and she lifted her hands to her breast in a gesture that the Dowager thought at first was melodramatic. Then she saw that the girl was acting quite unconsciously, and felt guilty.

'My dear, he is perfectly well! At least, there is some trouble, but he is quite safe, I can assure you!' She held out her hand to the younger woman, who clutched at it and sank gracefully into a chair.

'Forgive me,' she said, more rationally, 'but I have been so worried! He was to have come for me, nearly three hours ago, to take me to visit my godmother. At first I thought he was merely delayed, but when I waited, and waited, and he did not come, I thought. . .' Her eyes filled with tears, and she choked.

'You began to imagine all sorts of dreadful things and think that he had met with some terrible accident and was lying somewhere *in extremis*, did you not?' Lord Inglesham turned away with a little snort of irritation, but his mother patted the hand she still held.

'I know just how it is, my dear. It is one of the penalties of being in love, I am afraid, that one fears more than anything else that one's beloved will come to harm! But you need have no fear. Edward is gone out just now, on an errand of the first importance. That he

should have forgotten to send word to *you* will be
enough, I think, to show you how very important it is.'

'But there is trouble! You said that there is trouble!
And surely you would not be here ma'am, if it were not
so, for you have scarcely visited this house more than
three or four times since you came to London! Indeed, I
have been quite in a worry about it, and feared that you
did not wish to come here because of me!'

'No such thing, my dear, or, if it is, it is only that I
do not want to intrude upon your happiness. I am only
too well aware of the problems that you face.'

'Problems? Whatever can you mean?' The Dowager
could scarcely believe that Miss Cameron could be so
naïve, and merely shook her head at her, smiling. 'You
cannot mean the girls, can you? But how can they
possibly be problems? I love them dearly already, and I
believe they are learning to love me, also.'

Lord Inglesham cast up his eyes. He had said from
the first that Edward was wrong to try to conceal
Cleone's behaviour from his betrothed. But had he been
right in so doing? If this beautiful young woman was
really unable to imagine that the acquisition of three
half-grown girls into her household was not going to
cause any kind of problem then the shock of learning
what had happened might well be enough to make her
reconsider her wedding. Lady Inglesham looked helplessly at him, and continued mechanically to pat the
hand.

Miss Cameron, however, while not particularly intel-
ligent, was still sensitive to atmosphere. She looked
closely from one to the other.

'The trouble is in connection with the girls, is it not?
And Edward did not wish me to be told?'

Lady Inglesham nodded guiltily at her.

'Are they ill? Which of them is it?'

'None of them is ill,' said the Dowager, thinking that Edward would scarcely be out of the house if it were not so.

'I think she must be told, Mother,' broke in Marcus abruptly. 'It is scarcely going to be possible to keep it a secret from her, in any case, now that she is here. My niece Cleone, Miss Cameron, is missing from the house, and has been since early this morning. No word has been received from her, or of her, and her father and I have been out searching for several hours. I have this minute returned, to find whether anything has been heard, and will be going out again directly. Now that you are here, I should be grateful if you would bear my mother company. She is, as you may see, far from well, and I do not wish her to be here on her own.'

'Of course I will. But what of the younger girls? Should I go and see them?'

'They will like to see you, naturally, but for the moment there is no pressing need. Miss Avening is here, at my request, and is caring for them.'

'Oh, but she has. . .' began Lady Inglesham, faltering to a halt at her son's look.

'She has what? Miss Avening is not here?' He looked thunderstruck. 'I would not have believed that she would have left them,' he added sadly.

'One of the maids is with them. And she did not go alone, for she took Abby with her.'

'Abby? Their maid? She did not go home, then? It must be that she has learned something.' He rang the bell vigorously, bringing a footman running. 'Is Miss Avening returned yet? Does anyone know where she went?' he asked.

'No, my lord. But Abby might know, my lord.'

'Abby? But they were together, were they not?'

'I wouldn't like to say, my lord. But Abby came back more than two hours since, and is up in the schoolroom, my lord.'

'Then send her down here, at once!'

When Abby arrived, looking nervous, she was accompanied by the two little girls, who crept into the room unnoticed by anyone but their grandmother. Marcus questioned Abby closely, his face darkening as he spoke, then dismissed her tersely. Sophie and Minty went quietly to the corner behind their grandmother, and settled themselves out of sight. As Abby almost ran from the room she nearly collided with Sir Edward, who, with a drawn and weary face, was just coming in.

'Marcus! Is there any news? Oh, Fiona, you are here!'

'Yes, Edward, I am here. And I am quite inclined to be hurt that you did not send for me at once. Surely you know that my place is with you and your family, when trouble comes?'

He looked gratified, and would have answered, but was interrupted by Lord Inglesham.

'For heaven's sake, Edward, now is not the time for making pretty speeches! I have just learned that Miss Avening left the house with Abby, and took herself off to one of the most dangerous parts of London, and is still not returned!'

'With Abby? The maid? Why should she do that?'

'Because, forsooth, she thinks she may be able to find Cleone. She has gone to visit some woman, said by the maid to be perfectly respectable, but I ask you, Edward, do you know of any respectable woman who would live in that sink of iniquity?'

'Oh, God!' Sir Edward groaned, and buried his face in his hands.

'And now it seems that Abby left her there, more than two hours since, and there has been no word from her! Two hours! Her life may be in danger, or worse!'

'But Inglesham, we already know that Cleone must be in danger of some kind! This changes nothing!'

'I am not speaking of Cleone, you dolt!' said Marcus with fury gleaming in his eyes. 'I am speaking of Cecilia! On account of that foolish chit, who was surely old enough to have known better, she has taken herself to heaven knows what den of iniquity! It is not to be borne!'

They looked at him in astonishment. The two little girls, alarmed by his raised voice, clung together. Sir Edward was inclined to be angry at such a description of his daughter, but a growing suspicion that his brother-in-law was speaking under the influence of strong emotion kept him silent. Lady Inglesham was the only one who dared to say anything.

'If Miss Avening did such a thing, you may be quite sure, Marcus, that she acted for the best.'

'The best for whom?' he snarled, and would have flung out of the room but was brought up short by the reappearance of Abby.

'Begging your pardon, my lady,' she said, instinctively addressing herself to the least threatening person in the room, 'but there's a boy come with a message. Oh, my lady, she's safe! He says she's safe, and we're to send a carriage for her!' She burst into tears.

'Who is safe?' It was Lord Inglesham who spoke.

'Why, Miss Cleone, of course, my lord!'

'Miss Cleone, Miss Cleone! What of Cecilia? Oh, never mind, I shall go for myself.'

Before anyone could draw breath he was gone, leaving the rest of them to eye one another with growing speculation that their relief from worry made all the more interesting. Lord Inglesham had no thought for the suspicions he had planted in his relatives' minds. All his thoughts were on Cecilia. At the sight of her, pale and dishevelled, he had to fight back a powerful urge to take her in his arms and carry her away forthwith, leaving Cleone to fend for herself. The thought of the danger Cecilia might have been in made him furiously angry, both with her and with himself. He hardly dared look at her, let alone speak to her, in case she saw his feelings and was frightened of him again.

Cecilia was thankful that Cleone's condition made it impossible for there to be any speech between them during the journey. Lord Inglesham bundled his niece once again in the all enveloping cloak, hiding her face from any chance passer-by. He had also, Cecilia noticed, come in an old closed carriage that bore no distinguishing mark to show its owner. Cleone was dumped unceremoniously into the corner of the seat, and the horses were moving almost before the door had been closed on them. Cecilia unwrapped the girl, who was close to fainting or vomiting again after the sudden sensation of movement, since her head was still reeling from the remains of the drink she had been given. Cecilia brought out her smelling-salts, and used them to good effect, which was fortunate since there was no kind of container that could have been used in an extremity except, she thought without humour, his lordship's hat.

Cleone, though obviously feeling very unwell, was making a great effort to control herself, and neither cried nor complained, though when the view through the windows showed that they were nearly home she clutched at Cecilia in an agony of apprehension. When the coach came to a halt, she drew herself up with pathetic dignity.

'It's all right, Uncle Marcus, you need not carry me. I can walk.'

'Very well. But at least pull the hood of the cloak up so that you are not seen. You scarcely look as one would expect a young lady to appear.' She blushed with mortification, but did as he said, and managed to enter the house without falling, though leaning into Cecilia's embrace.

The hall seemed to be crowded with people. As soon as the front door closed, they all broke into exclamations so that the clamour was almost deafening. Among them all Sir Edward, looking pale and drawn, was the first.

'Cleone! My child! Thank God, thank God!' He strode forward and caught her in his arms, holding her close. 'How could you do it? Are you all right? Say that you are all right!'

'Oh, Papa, I am so sorry, so very sorry. I did not mean to worry you all; I never thought it would be like that!' She shed tears of relief into his chest.

'But are you all right?' He held her away from him, to look at her better. She hung her head.

'Yes, Papa. No one has harmed me. But I do not feel very well.'

It was true that she was very pale, but, with the first rapture of finding her safe now dying away, he had time to recall the anguish he had felt.

'Not very well! I should think not, indeed! And how do you think your sisters have been, and your poor grandmother, who has been prostrate with the shock? Not to mention myself, and your uncle, running hither and yon trying to find you, fearing that we would never see you alive again! How could you do this to us?'

'I'm sorry, Papa, I'm sorry,' was all that Cleone could say through her tears. Her two sisters, who had run to embrace her, wept also, their voices rising in childish sobs, while from a chair by the wall the Dowager raised her hand as if to prevent him, and wheezed a protest that went unheard.

'Running off in this way! Is this how you repay all our care of you? Merely because you could not have your own way, you must take it into your head to run off! Let me tell you, my girl, it will be a long time before we shall trust you again, aye, or your sisters! If this is what happens when I allow you to have singing lessons, because you begged so hard for them, then you must not expect for that to be continued! If you cannot be wise, then I must be wise for you. You shall not leave the house without my express permission. There will be no shopping, no visits, no concerts. . .'

His daughter, drooping before him, did not protest, and nor did Lord Inglesham, though he stirred uneasily. It was another person, who had not been in the hall but had waited, discreetly, in the small sitting-room nearby, feeling that she had not as yet any place in this family affair, who came running forward to confront Sir Edward.

'No, no! You shall not punish her so!' cried out Miss Cameron. Exquisitely gowned, perfectly turned out as ever, she stood in the dimness of the hall and shone as if she generated her own source of light. She attracted all eyes like a single candle in a darkened room, every golden hair gleaming like metal wire, the fine silk of her gown still fluttering from the movement of her running. Regardless of its delicate colour and fabric, she took Cleone into her arms, clasping the dirty, malodorous little form protectively to her. 'You must not be so hard on her, Edward! Surely she has been punished enough, can you not see that? We have all been so afraid; now that we have her safely returned, it is a time for rejoicing, not for punishments! I will not let you!'

The Dowager breathed a little sigh, feeling the air slip into lungs that were no longer straining for oxygen, and let her hand drop. Marcus nodded, thinking that he had never liked Miss Cameron so well, and that he had misjudged her character, and Cecilia dropped unobtrusively into a little chair, and took out her handkerchief to wipe her eyes. As for Cleone, she clung to her mother-to-be, and could do no more than to whisper her thanks.

'Well.' Sir Edward was dumbfounded. He had done his best to keep the unhappy state of affairs from his betrothed, and it was only because she had herself arrived at the house, and demanded to be told what was happening, that he had reluctantly informed her. She had seemed, to him, a being so exquisite, so ethereal that she must necessarily be so shocked by such a thing that she might, he feared, withdraw from their marriage. That it was not always an easy thing for a young woman to take on the care of three growing, almost grown girls was something of which he was all too uneasily aware. He had discussed Cleone's disappearance with her, because it was obvious that he would not be able to hide it from her, and she had paled, and burst into tears. That her distress might actually be for the child herself had not altogether occurred to him.

Now he gazed on the radiant vision before him as if the gates of Paradise had opened and an angel had appeared. All his anger and distress were forgotten in the joy of seeing that his future wife was able not merely to do her duty by his daughters but to love them also.

He smiled, a little sheepishly, and with the greatest care put his arms around both of them.

'You are quite right, dearest,' he said humbly. 'It was my anger and unhappiness speaking, Cleone, not my heart. How could I wish to hurt you, when you have had such a frightening time?'

'Thank you, Papa. Thank you, Mama,' said Cleone, and did not even seem aware of the words she had used.

'Now you shall come upstairs, and have a nice bath, and go to bed,' said Miss Cameron, taking charge in the most surprising way. 'You may tell me all about it, if you want, but no one shall make you speak of it until you are ready. Miss Avening will tell Papa all that he wants to know, will you not, Miss Avening?'

She turned to smile brilliantly at Cecilia, who blinked.

'Oh—yes, of course, Miss Cameron.'

'There you are! Come, now, my dear. Up we go.' She led the trembling girl up the stairs, and all their eyes followed her as she went, as if she carried some of the light of the room away with her. They turned the corner of the staircase, and were gone.

Suddenly, all the eyes that had been fixed on them were turned towards Cecilia. Nervously she rose from her chair. Sir Edward strode forward, and seized her hands in his own.

'Miss Avening! What can I say? You have all our gratitude, as you must know. Are you able now to tell us how you came to find her?'

She smiled faintly up at him.

'Yes, of course,' she said as firmly as she could, with lips that could not help trembling.

'But not here, I think,' said Lord Inglesham. 'Come, Edward, we cannot be spending the rest of the evening in the hall! Let us at least go somewhere a little more comfortable!'

'Of course, of course.' Sir Edward was flustered. 'Miss Avening, what must you be thinking of us? And Sophie and Minty, should you not be upstairs? Surely this is no place for you?'

'It is a little late for that now,' said Marcus with ill-concealed irritation. Sir Edward looked at the girls helplessly, as if he no longer dared to use any authority over them without Miss Cameron's permission.

'If I may, Sir Edward,' said Cecilia quietly, 'I will take Miss Sophie and Miss Minty upstairs. It is partly thanks to them, after all, that I was able to find their sister. I will tell them what they need to know, and settle them down. After so much excitement, a little supper and an early night will do them all the good in the world. Then, if you like, I will come down and tell you what happened, before I go home.'

'Good girl,' said Lord Inglesham quietly. Cecilia ignored him. She could not understand his earlier anger, and feared his present praise. Sir Edward looked relieved.

'It is so very good of you. . . I am sure I should not allow it, in the circumstances, that you should do the work of a governess, but if you do not mind. . .'

'Of course I do not.' Cecilia could only think that he did not consider her, after all that had happened, a suitable person to act as governess for his daughters, but she kept her hurt to herself, and took the little girls to say goodnight to their grandmother.

Lady Inglesham kissed them. There was still a little tinge of blue round her lips, and the sound of her breathing was a soft whistling. She smiled at Cecilia, but did not speak.

The children were soon settled. Cecilia told them that
their sister had been frightened, had run away and
become lost, and had been rescued by a lady who had
helped her. She thought it better, in the circumstances,
to say nothing about her drunken state, which they were
too young and inexperienced to have noticed. They
accepted without surprise that Cecilia had happened to
know the lady who had helped their sister, and did not
question that, by taking the route towards the singing
master's house, she had managed to find her.

Sophie's eyelids were drooping even before she had
finished her supper, but Minty was still almost feverishly bright-eyed. The worry and excitement of the day,
which had exhausted her sister, seemed to have had the
opposite effect on her, and she was stimulated to the
point of frenzy. It was with great difficulty that Cecilia
persuaded her to get into bed beside her sister.

'I can't sleep! I just can't, I'm too wide awake. Oh,
please, Miss Avening, don't go away yet!'

Cecilia sat down beside her. Sophie lay curled up in a
little ball, her eyelashes soft crescents on her cheeks and
her breath coming evenly and deeply. Minty wriggled
away from her to take hold of Cecilia's hand.

'You must try to be calm, my dear.' Cecilia kept her
voice low and even. 'I know you do not feel tired just at
present, but it has been a difficult day for everyone. You
want to be well tomorrow, don't you? I think that
Cleone will need both of you to comfort her tomorrow.
She was a very silly girl, and she will be feeling very
sorry about it in the morning. I was hoping that you
would be able to cheer her up, if she should feel at all
unhappy. But you won't be able to do that if you are
tired and irritable yourself, will you?'

Minty sighed.

'All right, I'll try. But it won't be easy.' Obediently she closed her eyes, screwing them up tight. Cecilia stroked the hand that held hers, and sat quietly until she felt the grip relax a little. When she stood up, however, a glint of light beneath the lowered lids showed her that Minty was still awake. Abby came back from bathing Cleone and reported that she was sound asleep in her bed, with her new mama sitting beside her like an angel out of heaven.

'You should go downstairs now, miss. They'll be wanting to talk to you, I'm sure.'

'I suppose so.' Perhaps, she thought, Lord Inglesham would be gone by now? He obviously despised and disliked her, and the effort of having to be grateful to her must be more than he could bear. She glanced at the bed. 'You'll stay here with them, will you Abby? I think they're both asleep.'

Minty spoke without opening her eyes.

'No, I'm, not. Must you go now, Miss Avening?'

'Well, I should do. Abby is right.'

'Then will you come back upstairs, before you go? Just to say goodbye to me, if I'm still awake?'

'Not if you stay awake on purpose.'

Minty's eyes flew open, and fixed themselves earnestly on Cecilia.

'No, I promise I will go to sleep if I can. But if I can't, I'll feel better if I know you're coming back.'

Cecilia bent and kissed her softly.

'Very well. I promise to come up, just for a moment.'

Reluctantly, she went downstairs.

CHAPTER THIRTEEN

CECILIA opened the door to the drawing-room. Out of
consideration for his former mother-in-law's health, Sir
Edward had caused a screen to be placed before it, in
case of treacherous draughts. Now it blocked Cecilia's
vision of the room, and she hesitated for a moment in
its comforting shelter. She could hear them talking, and
Lord Inglesham's voice was not among the others. She
told herself that he had gone, and that she was extremely
pleased, and at that moment he appeared before her.
He gave her a glass.

'Champagne,' he said. 'It seemed appropriately festive, after such a day.' Flustered, Cecilia took a large
sip, and at once the bubbles went up her nose so that
she choked. She had never tasted champagne before,
and thought it remarkably nasty. He took the glass from
her until she had recovered her breath. 'Perhaps it
wasn't such a good idea after all. Should you prefer
something else, my dear?'

'No, thank you,' she said, with an attempt at dignity.
'I am quite happy with it. It was only the bubbles.'

'Of course.'

Sir Edward came forward, and took her hand.

'I expect that the last thing you want is to be
answering questions from me, and from Cleone's grandmother. Can you bear to do it this evening? Or shall we
leave you with Marcus, and you can tell us about it
later — tomorrow, perhaps?'

'Leave me with. . .? Certainly not, Sir Edward. I am

218

only too happy to answer all your questions.' She found herself blushing, her skin hot and cold as she considered the implications of his remark. Lady Inglesham looked better; she stretched out her hand and Cecilia put her own in it, so that for a moment she was linked to both of them. Then Sir Edward let her go, and pulled a chair forward for her so that she could sit next to the Dowager. He himself sat on her other side, but his lordship took himself back to the champagne bottle, and replenished his glass.

'You said something about the younger girls helping you to find Cleone, my dear,' said the Dowager. 'Surely they did not know where she had gone?'

'No, ma'am, they did not. Cleone did not tell them what she intended. But they told me of her singing lessons, and the song she was learning that she had worked so hard on. Did she not ask you, Sir Edward, whether she might sing it at a concert, or party?'

'Something of the kind.' He looked rather shamefaced. 'I own I did not listen very hard. To me, she is still so much a child, you see. It never occurred to me that she might mind so very much. Whatever it was, I remember thinking that it was most unsuitable, at her age. I do not like to see young girls performing in public, however good they might be. One does not, after all, wish to make her into an infant prodigy, or some kind of peep-show for the masses!'

'Of course. I agree that it was probably quite unsuitable for her to do it. But she felt very strongly about it, and she seems to have feared that her master would no longer teach her if she did not do what he wished.'

'He'll teach her, all right,' murmured Inglesham cynically. 'His fees are high enough, from what I hear.'

Cecilia decided not to hear his interruption.

'In any case, by the greatest good luck Sophie had been learning the piano part for the song, to surprise her sister. She decided she wanted to play it for me, and was surprised and upset when she could not find the music. That was what gave me the idea that Cleone must have gone there. And when I saw the streets through which she had passed. . .' She paused. This, after all, was the most difficult part of her recital. She put down her glass, and folded her hands in her lap like a child reciting a lesson.

'A few weeks ago, I became lost myself when Mrs Ruspidge sent me out on an errand. Like Cleone, I was frightened by some men, and was fortunate enough to be rescued by Mrs Elham, the lady to whom I went today. She is a lady of. . .of easy virtue, I suppose I should say, but she is very kind. She made no attempt to. . .to persuade me to. . .to join her girls, but sent one of her servants to guide me home, and told me that if ever I was in need of help I might ask her.'

Her face was flaming, her eyes fixed on the floor. She could not look up at any of them.

'She was the only person I could think of who might be able to help find Cleone. Living where she did, and as she did, I thought that she must know several people who. . .who might be interested in young girls. And so it proved to be.'

She fell silent, exhausted, almost numbed by the effort of explaining. All that remained, now, was for her to assure them that she would never speak of this, and then she might go. Back to Mrs Ruspidge, who would value her all the more for a little while, because she thought she had useful connections. When she found that she would not break into the charmed circle that was Society with Cecilia's help, things must be very

different, but at least she would have a little time of
peace to recover her equilibrium. And then she would
take a place, any place, even that of a servant, as far
away as possible, and never have to see any of them
again.

Sir Edward was speaking, and she had not been
attending. His gratitude, of course. His joy at the safe
recovery of his daughter. His pleasure in welcoming her
into the family.

Into the family? She looked up at him blankly.

'Sir Edward, you cannot mean that you wish me to
stay as the girls' governess? Forgive me; I am so fond of
them, but I cannot do it. Nor would it be right. Miss
Cameron is the person they need now.'

It was his turn to be puzzled.

'The girls' governess? What can you be thinking of,
Miss Avening? Nothing could be further from my mind!'

The Dowager looked at her confused expression, and
leaned forward to pat her hand.

'My dear, you are exhausted, and no wonder, after
the day that you have had. Indeed, we are all very tired.
It seems to me that while you have been admirably
lucid in your explanations other things have not been
said to you that should have been expressed.' She did
not look at her son, who stood up and strode to the
door, opening and holding it with a compelling glare at
Sir Edward.

'Oh! Yes, quite so! Of course!' said he, rising and
preparing to leave the room. 'Miss Avening, I shall see
you later, I hope?'

'I do not think so, sir. I really must go home. Mrs
Ruspidge will be worrying about me.'

'Oh, I do not think so, when she knows you are here,'
soothed the Dowager, rising in her turn. 'Stay here, dear

child. I believe my son has something very particular that he wishes to say to you.'

'To say to me? Do not leave, ma'am, I beg of you. His lordship can have nothing to say to me that may not be heard by you. In fact, I do not think his lordship has anything to say to me at all. Anything that I want to hear.'

'Well, I hope that you are wrong,' said the Dowager, 'but that must of course be as you think best.' She walked from the room, acknowledging Lord Inglesham's half-mocking bow as she passed. He pushed the door shut, and came back to stand before the fireplace. Unnoticed by either of them, the door opened a fraction, and a small figure in a white nightgown slipped into the room. Abby, believing both the little girls to be asleep, had gone to sit with Cleone so that Miss Cameron might rejoin Sir Edward. Minty, however, could not sleep. She had heard the small bustle as the rest of the family left the drawing-room, and, fearing that Cecilia might leave the house without saying goodbye, she slipped quietly downstairs.

Peeping round the corner of the screen, she saw that Cecilia was alone with Uncle Marcus. She would have crept out again, but a footstep outside the door reminded her that she was behaving naughtily in leaving her bed. Without stopping to think, she slipped out of the far side of the screen, through a gap that no adult could have passed, and scuttled to hide herself in the deep window-seat where the curtains would conceal her.

Cecilia stood up, glancing helplessly around her for some means of escape, and then sat down again. Lord Inglesham was between her and the door, and something in his face told her that she would not be allowed to pass him.

'My lord!' Her voice came out as a squeak. She cleared her throat, and tried again.

'My lord. I beg that you will allow me to go home now. I am very tired. If you have something to say, can it not wait until tomorrow?'

'No,' he said brusquely. 'I do wish that you would not keep calling me "my lord" as if I were a bishop, or a judge,' he added irritably. 'It's not as if I haven't mentioned it before.'

'I beg your pardon, my — sir. I cannot see in what way it is incorrect. You are, after all, a lord.'

'And you are a. . .' He paused.

'And I am a governess,' she continued for him.

'For heaven's sake, will you cease this eternal harping on about your profession?'

'You are determined to be angry with me,' she said bitterly. 'I cannot think why you keep me here, if I vex you so much. And I quite understand that I do, after what has happened. . .'

'Quite. How dare you, how *dare* you do such a thing?' he asked. 'When I think of the danger, the risk. . .' He flung his hand in the air, unable adequately to express his feelings. Pale but controlled, Cecilia faced him.

'I know. I beg your pardon. But it was a risk I had to take. And I think that no great harm has been done. At least she managed to reach Cleone in time, and the dear girl had enough sense, at least, not to admit her name to anyone.' She tightened her lips for a moment. 'Perhaps you feel, Lord Inglesham, that I should have exercised a similar restraint. I did consider it. But I felt, rightly or wrongly, that to do so while asking Mrs Elham for her help would be such an insult to her that she would be far from inclined to give it. If I was wrong, I ask your forgiveness, but I do not think she will ever reveal what she knows. And nor, of course, will I. Now, if you please, may I go home?'

He looked at her as if she were mad.

'I don't know what on earth you think you are talking about. Of course you did no harm in revealing Cleone's name, if in so doing you managed to get her back. Mrs Elham struck me as a perfectly respectable woman — for one in her line of business.'

'Then I do not understand why you are so angry with me!' She almost shouted the words.

'Because you risked your own safety, you stupid girl!' he snapped back. 'Why on earth you could not send for me, or Edward, or even one of the servants when you found the music was missing, I do not know! But what good would it have done Cleone if you yourself had been carried off in that hell-hole? Did you not think of that?'

'Of course I did; that is why I took Abby with me. In any case,' she added bitterly, 'you have already seen how well able I am to protect myself from attack! And as for sending for you, or Sir Edward, or one of the servants, I had no idea where to find you, and besides, were either of you acquainted with Mrs Elham? Or another like her, who might have been able to do as she did?'

'I could have gone to her myself. Asked her. On your behalf.'

'Yes, you could, but it was me she knew, it was to me she said that she would help me, if she could. I could do no less than go to her myself. *Now* may I go home?'

'No. I have something else to ask you. Will you marry me?'

'Marry you? *Marry* you?' Cecilia stared at him in horror. 'There is no need for such a sacrifice.'

'A sacrifice? What are you talking about, Cecilia?'

She scarcely heard him.

'I have never been so insulted. Never! Oh, why must you stand near that door like that? Why will you not let me go?'

His voice was quieter now.

'I will let you go. You said to me once before that you never wanted to see me again. Is that true? Am I truly so hateful to you?'

'No! Yes! Oh, I don't know!' She struggled to contain her tears.

'But you are insulted by my offer of marriage?'

She raised her chin proudly.

'Yes.'

'Then I can say no more.' He stood away from the door and opened it. 'One of the carriages will take you home, Miss Avening. I wish you a very good evening.' He strode from the room. Cecilia looked after him, her feelings in a turmoil. The temptation to run after him, to throw herself at his feet and say that she would do anything, be his wife, his mistress, even, if he would say that he loved her, made her body actually ache with the strain of keeping still. But to do so, to see the revulsion in his face at her touch, the resignation in his eyes when he knew he must buy her silence with his name. . .it was not to be borne. She heard his voice in the hall, snarling an order at one of the servants. Well, as he had insulted her, so she had him. Now she might go back to Harley Street, and enjoy her victory. The front door closed with a slam, and he was gone.

Cecilia sat on in frozen stillness. A few tears ran down her face, but she did not notice them until her breath caught in a sob. Then, unable for once to control herself, she put her face down on the sofa cushions and wept as though her heart would break. A small, cold hand was laid on her neck, and she started up to see Minty, round-eyed, looking down at her.

'Oh, Minty, how you startled me,' she said, with a pitiful attempt at a smile. 'Did you come down to find me?'

'Yes. Oh, Miss Avening, why are you crying? Has Uncle Marcus made you cry?'

'Yes — I mean no. Oh, Minty. . .' Cecilia gathered the little girl into her arms, and they clung together.

'Don't you like Uncle Marcus?'

'Oh, hush, Minty. You must not ask me questions like that.'

'But you do, don't you?'

'Oh, Minty!' It was as near to a confession as Cecilia was likely to come. Wiser than her years, Minty hugged Cecilia in silence while she struggled to control herself. Presently she sat up and wiped her eyes.

'Well, we are a silly pair and no mistake! Now you must go back to bed, my dear. It was naughty of you to come down like this.' Meekly, Minty allowed herself to be led back upstairs. In bed, she closed her eyes obediently, but she was still revolving many thoughts long after Cecilia had kissed her and gone.

Wearily Cecilia walked to the hall. Her bonnet and pelisse were lying on a chair where she had left them earlier. She put them on, absorbing her attention with the mundane details of buttons and ribbons. A man-servant came, soft-footed.

'Is there a carriage for me?' she asked. She owed that much, at least, to Mrs Ruspidge, to come back respectably and in style, rather than do what she would have preferred and walk slowly back.

'Yes, miss. Just coming now, miss.' He spoke to her respectfully. Her mind was on Marcus. It had all been planned, of course, while she was upstairs with the girls. He had told them of her presence at Mrs Elham's, and they had probably agreed it together. It said much for his family loyalty, of course, that he was prepared to sacrifice himself for his niece, but it would have been a marriage in name only, she supposed. For all Lady Inglesham's apparent kindness, she could not have been pleased at the idea of welcoming such a daughter-in-law.

The carriage came, and she found the effort of climbing into it almost beyond her. Once inside it she leaned back against the cushions, dry-eyed. It was dusk now. Dusk on a beautiful June day. The houses that she passed were lit up, candles and lamps glowed in windows and doors — all the marks of preparation for another night of gaiety. She closed her eyes, and forced the tears back.

Sir Edward and his former mother-in-law, coming downstairs later on and looking discreetly into the drawing-room, found it empty. A servant, questioned, said that my lord had left, and miss also just after. Lady Inglesham frowned and shook her head, but Sir Edward was more sanguine.

'Perhaps he has gone to speak to that woman — what is her name, the one Miss Avening lives with? Does she not stand as her mother now? Perhaps he wishes to ask her sanction.'

The Dowager doubted it, but did not say so. She knew that if Marcus were now engaged the first person he would have come to find would have been herself. She sighed. It was decided that she would not return that evening, and she allowed herself to be put to bed quite early. She kept her candles burning and her door ajar, however, and some while later her son came quietly into the room. She waited in silence, unwilling to mention Cecilia's name but feeling it between them as if it were written on the carpet in letters of fire a foot high. 'I think I shall go abroad again soon, Mother,' he said at last. She bowed her head, still not speaking. 'She will not have me, Mother!' he burst out at last. 'She will not have me,' he repeated dully.

'You asked her, then?' She kept her voice non-committal.

'This evening. Oh, God, I never realised, Mother! I might have married Miss Chadworth, and never have realised what I was doing, what I was missing! Perhaps it would have been better had I done so,' he added bitterly.

'I cannot believe that. Forgive me, Marcus, but are you quite sure? I had thought. . .but perhaps I was mistaken. Yet I did not think her altogther indifferent to you.'

'Indifferent? That she is not! But she hates me, Mother. She has said that my offer of marriage was an insult to her.'

'An insult? Few women would think it so.'

'But she is not like other women, Mother.' For a moment he spoke almost with pride. 'Titles and money mean nothing to her.'

'But love, Marcus? No woman can be unmoved to learn that she is loved.'

'She does not value it. Do not look like that, Mother! It is not merely *my* love that she rejects, I believe, but that of any man. She cannot bear me to be near her. I fear that her experiences in the past have given her a distaste for the company of men.'

She looked a question, and he told her of the scene he had found at Harley Street when he called there.

'You should have seen her, Mother; she was magnificent!' he said, almost animated in his description. 'She protected herself from him in the bravest way, and stood there so still, so proudly, when I came in, that she might have been a queen, and he a vanquished prisoner! But she shrank from me, Mother, as I believe she would have shrunk from any man.'

She was silent for a moment. It seemed to her that he might well be right, and that there was no help for him. And yet what she had seen in Cecilia's face, when she had thought herself unobserved, was not at all the virginal shrinking that he had described, nor the disgust he thought.

'If that is so,' she said slowly, 'then you must allow her to do as she wishes. Naturally, we will wish to help her in whatever way we can.'

'That damned school!' he grumbled. 'I would buy her fifty schools, if it would make her happy.'

'My dear, you must give her time,' she said, powerless to comfort him. He left her, and she lay for a long time sleepless, grieving for him.

Cecilia, too, was sleepless. Mrs Ruspidge had greeted her with a kiss, on her return, and had actually dismissed her daughters to their room, so that she might the better question Cecilia about the events of the day. Wearily, Cecilia gave her the story that had been agreed for general consumption: Cleone had foolishly gone out alone, had become lost, and had at last been helped by a kindly woman who had cared for her until her friends had come to fetch her. Cecilia herself had been with the younger children, and had gone to bring Cleone back. It was all disappointingly dull, but Mrs Ruspidge was easily contented by the descripion of the house, its furnishings, the Dowager's and Miss Cameron's clothes, and even went so far as to shed a sentimental tear at the touching scene Cecilia painted of the reunion between the missing girl and her family.

'And to think it was you that they sent for. Do you not think that I should call, tomorrow, with you? To present my felicitations, as it were?'

'Not tomorrow, ma'am.' Cecilia felt that she could do no more, at present, than confront each day as it came. If necessary she must lie, and say that she had quarrelled with the young people, or with Miss Cameron, or with anyone rather than allow Mrs Ruspidge to encroach her way into their acquaintance.

'No, maybe it would be a little soon. But a note, perhaps? And a visit the next day?'

'Perhaps,' said Cecilia wearily, and her hostess went off into a happy dream where her daughters were presented at Court by the Dowager Lady Inglesham, who was such a good friend, the dear thing!

In spite of her late night, Minty woke at her usual time. She was unusually silent as she ate nursery breakfast with her sister and Abby, though the maid was pleased to see that her appetite was in no way impaired.

'You shall see Miss Cleone later, my dearie. She's still asleep, and likely to stay that way for a while! But she's quite well, you know.' Abby watched the two little faces, but could see no particular anxiety or relief in them.

'Is Grandmama coming here today?' Minty asked abruptly.

'Lady Inglesham? Bless you, she never went home! Didn't you know she stayed the night here, in the end? It didn't seem worthwhile to carry her back, when she knew she would want to be here today. You shall see her presently.'

Minty went to put her arms round Abby's comfortable form.

'I really need to see her, Abby, darling. Mayn't I just peep round her door, and see if she's awake yet? I promise I won't disturb her if she's not. Please, Abby?'

Abby looked down at the pale face and shadowed eyes.

'Very well, my love,' she said gently. Sophie looked on in surprise.

'What's the matter, Minty? Shall I come too?'

'Oh, just something I need to talk to her about. I'll tell you later,' she said airily, and whisked out of the door.

Lady Inglesham was sitting up in bed, sipping a cup of chocolate.

'Who is that? Araminta, darling, come and give me a kiss.'

Minty climbed on to the bed, and offered lips still sticky from bread and honey. Lady Inglesham sipped at her chocolate, and waited.

'Do you like Miss Avening, Grandmama?'

Whatever her grandmother had expected, it was not this.

'Yes, my dear, very much,' she answered cautiously. 'Why do you ask?'

'So do I. I love her. And she loves me too,' said Minty with the cheerful certainty of a child who had never encountered dislike from an adult.

'Of course she does, dear. She certainly proved herself a good friend to our family yesterday.'

'Uncle Marcus likes her too, doesn't he? Although he was so cross with her.'

'Yes, I believe he does.' Unconsciously, Lady Inglesham sighed.

'I thought so. But he didn't tell her that he likes her.' She shook her head wisely. 'And she likes him, too.'

Her grandmother's attention was attracted. She looked at Minty.

'You are too young to be thinking of your elders in this way, let alone speaking of it,' she said firmly.

'Yes, Grandmama.' Minty's gaze was limpid, so innocent that her grandmother was immediately suspicious.

'Araminta,' she said seriously, 'I think that we should have a little talk, you and I, don't you?'

Minty considered. The wish for independence was strong within her, but she was aware that she had trespassed over the boundaries of an adult world where she was not at home, and where the signs and signals were in a language she had not yet learned to read. She nodded.

'Yes, Grandmama. I think so too.'

Cecilia was sitting with Mrs Ruspidge. She ached all over as though she had been beaten, her head was throbbing and her eyes sore and gritty, but she forced her back to stay straight and drove her needle grimly in and out of a large darn in Amelia's stocking, having chosen this work masochistically as the most boring she could find. She was not quite sure why she should feel the need to punish herself this way, but since she was going to be miserable in any case she might as well do unpleasant work as not. Mrs Ruspidge was being unusually sympathetic, and had even ordered the girls back to their schoolroom when they would have joined her in the drawing-room. She was longing to talk over the events of the previous day, and was sensible enough to know that they could hardly be spoken of in front of her indiscreet daughters.

She had already assured Cecilia, several times, that she would not speak of it to a soul. Cecilia hoped very much that it was true, and knew that she must make herself as pleasant to her hostess as possible, since it was only the possibility of being accepted by the Maisemores and, perhaps, the Ingleshams that would keep Mrs Ruspidge from making capital out of this delicious little scandal. She was therefore obliged to repeat the story several times, giving as many trivial details as she could think of while keeping the most serious things to herself. It was hard work, the hardest she thought she had ever done, but she schooled her mouth to smile and speak, and her eyes to remain dry.

The entry of the footman gave her a few moments' respite.

'What is it, Henry? Surely I told you that I am not at home this morning?'

'A letter, ma'am, for miss.'

'A letter? However many times have I told you, Henry, that letters are to be brought up on the silver tray, not in your hand?'

'Beg your pardon, ma'am. Shall I take it away again?'

'For heaven's sake, not now! Only remember for the future, if you please.'

He bowed, his politeness just brushing the edges of insolence, and Cecilia took the note. It was, she saw at a glance, in a child's hand. She would have given anything to have been able to take it, and herself, away to the privacy of her room before opening it, but Mrs Ruspidge was watching her with avid interest, and she knew she could not. With trembling fingers and assumed nonchalance she opened it. The words danced up and down like drops of water on a hot griddle, and she could make no sense of them. She blinked hard, and forced herself to read it through. She had to read it twice before she could make sense of the words. She read in the round, childish script,

> Dear Miss Avening, Please come back and see me today. I need you very badly and so does Sophie, and I ecspect Cleone does too. Please please come, dear Miss Avening, I must talk to you. I promise you sha'n't be bothered by anyone else, if you will only come. Grandmama wants you to come, and says she will send her carriage for you.

It was signed, with a flourish, Araminta Maisemore.

Cecilia looked up from her third reading of the letter to find Mrs Ruspidge's eyes fixed avidly upon her.

'My dear child! What does it say?' No considerations of the privacy of others' correspondence had ever bothered Mrs Ruspidge, and it did not occur to her that she should not ask.

'It is from one of the little girls,' admitted Cecilia.

'And she says?' prompted the other.

'She asks me to visit her, but I do not know. . .'

'Now, my dear, you are not going to give me any more of that nonsense you began yesteday, are you? Because if so, I must tell you that it will not do, it really will not do! Even without the events of yesterday, it would have been unthinkable to refuse, and now — I do not know what you can be thinking of.'

'I am very tired, ma'am,' pleaded Cecilia.

'Tired! *Tired*! And a young girl like you is going to tell me that she has not the strength to visit a poor, motherless little girl, when all she has to do is to put on her bonnet, and take a cab! And I will pay for it myself, what is more!'

'No need, ma'am,' said Cecilia, bowing to the inevitable. 'Lady Inglesham's carriage is waiting for me, if I decide to go.'

'If you decide to go!' Mrs Ruspidge's voice rose to a shriek of anguish. 'How you can behave so. . .for goodness' sake, girl, go and put on your pelisse, and your bonnet and gloves, and let us have no more of this foolishness! Keeping her ladyship's carriage waiting like this! I never heard the like!'

She chivvied Cecilia up the stairs, standing over her while she put on a fresh gown — 'That one will not do, it might as well be a dish-rag,' — and tidied her hair — 'No need to take it down again, my dear! Let me smooth it for you,' — then actually kissed her before watching her climb into the carriage and waving to her until it turned the corner and was out of sight.

CHAPTER FOURTEEN

IF CECILIA had been in a state to think more clearly, she might have found it odd that Lady Inglesham should be giving her small granddaughter the use of her carriage. As it was, she thought little more than that the Dowager, an indulgent grandparent, had given in to Minty's importunities, and allowed her to send for Cecilia to gain a little tranquillity for the family. It was flattering, of course, that the little girl should set such store by Cecilia's presence, but it was an honour that Cecilia could well have done without, just then. All she could hope for was that she could stay in the nursery, and see no one else but the little girls and Abby.

It was to the nursery that she was taken, but when she went in she found not Sophie but her ladyship herself sitting with Minty. The little girl ran forward and clasped her arms round Cecilia's waist. Cecilia bent to kiss her, thankful for that moment of respite to subdue her dismayed embarrassment. Of course the Dowager must wish to express her gratitude, however much she might deplore the necessity to see Cecilia again.

Minty's cheek was velvet-soft against her lips.

'Don't be cross with me, Miss Avening,' she whispered. 'I told Grandmama about last night. You must listen to her, really you must, dear Miss Avening!'

Cecilia was too flustered to understand her. The Dowager was greeting her with the most unnerving kindness, actually rising to her feet and coming forward. Cecilia bobbed a deferential curtsy, and was astonished to have her hand taken, and to find her ladyship leaning forward to give her a kiss.

'My dear, you are so cold! Your cheek is like ice! I shall have the fire lit at once!'

'Oh, no, my lady,' exclaimed Cecilia in some distress. 'I beg that you will not bother. It is only that I am a little tired.'

'I think we are all that,' said the Dowager with a smile. 'I assure you that it is not uncommon for me to have a fire, even in August!' She rang, and the servant came. A few minutes later the fire was lit, the flames crackling cheerfully as they licked at the logs. Lady Inglesham sighed with pleasure. 'There, now. Is that not better? Now you will take off your bonnet and pelisse, and be comfortable with me, will you not?'

The thought of being comfortable with one who bore so close a resemblance to her son was not one which came easily to Cecilia's imagination, but she murmured her assent. Minty, very much the hostess in what was her own domain, helpfully undid the bonnet ribbons and laid the sadly battered headgear on a nearby cushion with as much reverence as if it had been a crown. When Cecilia had sat down she climbed on to her knee.

'Now you cannot escape,' she said smugly. 'We shall drink some chocolate, and I shall be very careful not to spill any on your gown, and you shall talk to Grandmama.'

Her tone was admonitory, and she gave a look at the Dowager that clearly implied that she thought that time was being wasted. Lady Inglesham's lips twitched, but she meekly rang for chocolate, and began to talk to Cecilia.

She spoke of Cleone, and Cecilia's tongue was loosened until she was surprised to hear herself almost chattering. Her opinion was sought with the most flattering attention, and she was encouraged to speak of her time with Miss Herring and her experiences with the girls at the school. She relaxed, and was even able to talk about her intentions for the future, before the recollection of where she was, and to whom she spoke, came back to her, and she fell silent.

'I was aware,' Lady Inglesham said easily as if she noticed nothing of her guest's discomfiture, 'that you intended to open a school of your own, if the opportunity should ever present itelf. It is of course a most laudable ambition. Do you still wish to do so?'

For once, Minty was silent, but she twined her arms round Cecilia's neck as if she feared that her friend was about to go and start a school that very instant. Agonised, Cecilia whispered an assent. She was, she thought, about to be given a reward for her help and, though it might not be so expressed, a bribe for her silence. For a moment her pride told her that she could not, would not accept it. But could she really refuse? What other future could possibly be open to her? And if she turned down this opportunity she might regret it for the rest of her life. She should, she told herself, be overjoyed that she was to have the chance to fulfil what had been her ambition.

'If it is really what you wish for,' the Dowager continued, 'then I can only say that I will help and encourage you in every way that I can. But I should be disappointed, none the less.'

'Disappointed, my lady?'

'You are so very young, my dear. Are you sure, so very sure that this is the life you wish to lead? I am not saying that married life is unmitigated bliss, nor are you so foolish that you would believe such a fairy-tale if I did. But a husband, a home, children of your own. . . these are all things that are not given up lightly.' She paused. Cecilia's cheeks flamed, she fixed her eyes with painful intensity on those other eyes that looked at her questioningly. A log shifted in the fire, attracting both their eyes for a moment. The Dowager smiled slightly.

'My son, were he here,' she said deliberately, 'would certainly be kicking at that log, and very likely putting out the fire in the process. It is a habit that he has, and his father before him, when he is worried or distressed. And just now, my dear, he is both.'

'I am sorry to hear that, my lady.' Cecilia spoke through lips that trembled.

'He thinks that you dislike and fear him, that his presence is repugnant to you. He has told me that it is the fault of a young man who attacked you and gave you a disgust of men in general. He said that although you protected yourself with the greatest courage you were now unable to accept or to return his love. My dear, I am a mother, with all a mother's natural partiality to her only son, but I am also a woman. If it is true, if what he has told me is how you truly feel, then I cannot blame you, much though I may regret it. Something that Araminta told me, this morning, has made me hope that he might be wrong. If you can find within you any possibility, any hope that you may one day conquer your fear, will you not tell me? My son's happiness is more to me than anything. If you had been the most unsuitable woman in the world, I must still have begged you to reconsider. But as you are someone whom I, and all my family, would welcome with so much joy, must I not beg still harder?'

Cecilia looked down at Minty.

'Oh, Minty, what have you been doing?' Her voice trembled. Minty hid her face in Cecilia's neck.

'I'm sorry, I didn't mean to listen. I was there, behind the curtain. I heard you, and Uncle Marcus. And I heard you crying. And I don't believe you hate him, so I told Grandmama that you like him. . . Don't be vexed with me. I love you, too, and so does Uncle Marcus.'

'Oh, Minty. . .'

Cecilia stared at Lady Inglesham. Her face was answer enough, but she struggled to speak.

'I did not know. . .he never said. . . I thought. . .'

'It is just as I feared. He never thought to tell you that he loved you, did he, my dear. How like a man!'

Cecilia laughed shakily, wiping the tears from her eyes. The Dowager held out her hand, and Cecilia gently lifted Minty off her knee so that she could go to that loving embrace.

'I should have known better. And to think that I actually persuaded myself that he asked me to marry him merely to ensure that I would keep my silence about Cleone!'

'You thought that? Really, my dear child, I could almost be angry with you. Do you really suppose that he would do such a thing, or that I should not have done my utmost to prevent him from making so ill-starred a match? For a clever girl, my dear, you will forgive me for saying that you are quite a simpleton!'

'I know it. But he looked so angry with me!'

'He had been badly frightened for your safety. He made it clear to us all then that you mattered more to him than a hundred Cleones. You may imagine poor Edward's expression.'

'Oh, dear. I do not know how he will ever forgive me. I have been so very foolish. What can I say to him?'

'I do not think you will find it so difficult, you know. You have only to tell him the truth.'

'You would not. . .no. I must do it myself.'

'You are as brave as he said you were. I have never heard him speak with such admiration as he did when describing how you vanquished that poor wretched young man.'

'Admiration? I thought that he despised me. I was so ashamed of myself.'

'Ashamed of yourself, why ever was that? You succeeded in protecting yourself from a man who was set on raping you. Most girls would simply have fainted, or fallen into hysterics, yet he said you stood as proudly as a queen.'

'And I was so embarrassed! I had used a trick told me by. . .by the lady who helped me yesterday. I had told her that Augustus — Mrs Ruspidge's son — had been pestering me, and she told me what to do. I had not thought I would ever need to do it, and, when I did, and he came in just after, I thought he would despise me for doing such a thing. "A whorehouse trick", Augustus called it, and so it was. Oh, I beg your pardon. I should not have said. . .'

'My dear, I am far too old to be shocked by such things, and Araminta is still too young to understand what you are saying. Besides, one must call them something, after all, and, if it is good enough for the Bible, so it should be for us. Pray tell me, though at my age I hardly need to know it, what was it that you did?'

Blushing and laughing, Cecilia whispered to her. The Dowager shook her head.

'Is that all? My dear, I saw one of my father's grooms do that to a footpad, when I was no more than six years old.'

'Well, I am not a groom. But I suppose that I have led rather a sheltered life.'

'And are none the worse for that, I am sure. And now, my dear Cecilia, it is time that I said goodbye to you.'

'Oh, I beg your pardon. You have been ill, and are tired. I should have thought.'

'Not tired at all. But there is one who is tired, very tired. Tired of waiting. Will you not see him, and put him out of his misery? He is not very far away. I can send Araminta for him, and he will come. May I do so?'

'But what shall I say to him? How shall I begin?'

'My dear child, how can I tell you that? She shall tell him that I wish to speak to him, and no more. Do not look at me like that! Your heart, and your clever head, will find the words.' Minty was hovering eagerly, and when she saw Cecilia give a little nod she ran from the room.

Cecilia went to the looking-glass over the fireplace, and anxiously inspected herself. Her hair, as usual, was escaping in wild tendrils all round her face, and she brushed them back automatically, knowing that it would do no good. Her face had quite lost the pallor of the last week, and there was a glow of pink in her cheeks, while her eyes, for all the tears she had shed, were bright. The Dowager watched her with amusement. The sound of footsteps sent her flying back to her chair, in which she sat bolt upright with her hands primly in her lap. When the door opened she started, and a tide of colour flowed over her face. Minty led him in proudly, like a captive in an ancient victory parade. He made a formal bow in her direction, but did not look at her.

'You wanted me, Mother?'

'Yes, Marcus. Miss Avening is here, as you see, and I believe she has something that she wishes to say to you. My dear child, I shall see you later, I hope. Come, Araminta.' The little girl ran to give Cecilia one last kiss, looked sternly at her uncle, and went obediently to put her hand in the one her grandmother was holding out to her. Cecilia looked at them imploringly, but the Dowager merely smiled and left the room, closing the door firmly behind her.

There was a short, charged pause.

'I should like to. . .' began Cecilia in a breathless voice.

'I believe that I should. . .' He spoke in the same instant. Each stopped at once.

'I beg your pardon,' he said stiffly. 'Please continue.'

'No, no, it was of no moment,' she said. 'Pray finish what you were saying.'

'Merely that I wished to thank you, as perhaps I failed to do yesterday, for the service you did Cleone, and all my family. I am well aware that if it were not for you she might have been lost to us forever. I would not like you to think that we are ungrateful.'

He spoke in a distant, hard voice, and had not stirred from his place near the door. In this house, she scarcely knew how to beg him to sit down, and, since he would not look at her, she could not even gesture towards a chair. She wondered whether to stand up, but feared that her knees would buckle if she did, so stayed where she was. He was waiting, obviously, for her to speak.

'Please do not thank me any more. It was the merest luck that I was able to help Cleone, and my reward is in knowing that she is safe.' She bit her lip. 'Your mother — Lady Inglesham — has told me of your generous offer to help me start a school. I am, of course, very grateful. . .'

'But?' he prompted when she paused. The nursery, furnished as it was for children, and his own stillness made him look huge; she had the impression even at that distance that he towered over her, and she shivered.

'You are cold?' Though he had not appeared to be looking in her direction at all, he was instantly aware of the movement. He crossed to the fireplace and stood, one hand gripping the mantel shelf. The fire was burning merrily, scenting the room with its incense. 'Shall I put more wood on the fire?'

He stooped as if to perform the action himself.

'Oh, no! I am perfectly warm, and I have never been used to a fire in summer-time.'

'One of Miss Herring's maxims, I suppose,' he said sourly.

'No — common sense and good management,' she snapped, nettled. His eyebrows drew together in a black bar. 'Oh, I beg your pardon! I did not mean to imply . . .of course, Lady Inglesham has been so unwell, and the case is quite different. . .'

There was another pause, which neither of them knew how to break. It seemed to Cecilia that, whatever his mother had said, Lord Inglesham felt nothing but dislike for her, and that he was there only because Minty had fetched him, and because he did not know how to leave. Perhaps the best thing would be for her to go. As she pondered this, he lifted one booted foot, and kicked at the flaming logs. She remembered what the Dowager had said, and gave a little gasp of laughter, which he did not hear. He kicked again, harder, and one of the burning logs, dislodged from its careful placing, rolled from the fire basket in a flurry of sparks.

The fender at the edge of the fireplace stopped it, but, in doing so, a lump of flaming bark was jerked loose and flew to land near her feet.

With a little exclamation she jumped to her feet and drew back her skirts, vulnerable as they were to the glowing ember. He moved faster, however, and almost before she had reacted he was across the room, and had scooped up the burning fragment in his bare hands and flung it back into the hearth.

A little blackened patch in the carpet and a strong smell of singed wool was all that remained of the incident. She stood beside her chair, looking down at the place and then at him.

'Are you all right?' he asked, almost angrily.

'Yes, of course! I was scarcely even in danger. But your hands, are they not burned?'

He looked at them as if he had never noticed that he had such appendages.

'My hands? No, I do not think so. Nothing to signify. It was in them only for a moment, and the skin is hard, from driving and riding.'

'Nevertheless, it was a brave act, and I must thank you again.'

'For saving you from danger that I myself had put you in? Again?'

'You, put me in danger? I do not know what you can mean.'

'I knew that all was not right with Cleone. I should have been more careful of her.'

'Cleone is not your responsibility. What could you have done? Besides, I was never in danger.' He looked as though he was ready to argue the point, but she was desperately conscious of the seconds ticking away. At any minute he might decide he had no more time to waste on her, and she would have missed her chance. She could not believe, still, that he loved her, but she clung stubbornly to the wish to explain away some of the misunderstandings between them.

'That is in the past now, and beside the point,' she said in a rush. 'But yesterday, when you were so kind as to ask me to. . .to marry you. . .and I said that I was insulted. . . I did not precisely mean it the way you thought.'

'There are different ways of being insulted, then? Does it really matter which of them was yours, while the result is the same? Or do you mean that you did not, after all, feel insulted?'

His sarcasm cut her, but she saw in it the hurt that he had felt and that, perversely, gave her encouragement.

'I thought it an insult, but that was because I quite misunderstood your motives. I thought that you — that you were trying to buy my silence, about Cleone.'

'But of course. Only now I find that I may buy it more cheaply, by giving you a school instead. It is a bargain, is it not?'

'Now it is your turn to feel insulted, and yet I did not mean that.'

'Then we are quits, and the game is over. But let me assure you, Miss Avening, that I, for one, would not consider making an offer of marriage for such a reason, not even for the sake of my own daughter if I had one, let alone for a niece. And if you think that I would you are as much mistaken in my character as I believe I was in yours.'

It was, she thought, as close to a declaration of love as he would come, believing himself rejected. Her heart melted within her, and she burst into speech.

'I was mistaken, and I ask your pardon. Indeed, we were both mistaken, but perhaps not in the way that you think. There is something else — something I must explain to you.'

'There is no need. I understand how you must feel, and do not blame you.'

'But you don't understand!' She was becoming exasperated. 'There is a misapprehension; you are quite mistaken in some of your ideas, my l——'

'For heaven's sake!' For the first time he turned to her, with a look of blazing fury on his face that dimmed the flames of the fire. '*Will* you once and for all cease this servile rubbish and stop calling me my lord?'

'I wasn't going to call you my lord!' she flung back. 'I was going to call you. . .'

She looked at him, and he at her. The anger died out of his face, and there was an arrested look in his expression.

'You were going to call me. . .what?'

Again she felt her face glow, but she did not drop her eyes from his.

'My love,' she said, quite simply.

He did not answer, or move. It was as though he was transfixed by her words, and as yet had scarcely understood their meaning. His face, however, spoke for him, and she had no fear of being repulsed when she walked forward, reaching up to lay her hands on his shoulders. His own hands came up as if to grasp her but hesitated, as if reluctant to touch her. This time she understood his diffidence, and leaned forward to press her body against his until his arms closed around her with a strength that she gloried in.

'You see, I am quite shameless,' she murmured, 'and so far from finding your touch repugnant that I should

not object if you were to. . .' She was silenced by his
kiss. His arms were like bars of iron round her, a cage
she thought she could never want to leave even if he
should permit it. Her hands were locked behind his
neck, and she returned his kisses with an enthusiasm
which should have set all his doubts at rest. And yet,
she noticed, his hands did not actually touch her. She
leaned a little way from him, against the support of his
arms, and looked up at his face, which was transformed
as she had never seen it.

'What is it, my darling?'

'Your hands, Marcus. Is something wrong with your
hands? Did you burn them more than you admitted?'

He smiled.

'Perhaps a little, but I can assure you that I no longer
feel it.'

'Then why do you not touch me?'

He laughed, and, taking one hand from behind her,
held it up for her to see. It was true that there were a
few reddening blisters, but they were almost hidden by
the black of charcoal from the ember.

'They are so dirty, you see!' he said lovingly. 'I cannot
let you be seen with a pattern of black hand prints all
over your gown, can I?'

She laughed.

'Who knows, I might set a new fashion!' Nevertheless
she took out her handkerchief, moistened it in a little
jug of hot water that stood on a tray that had not been
removed, and carefully wiped both his palms, dabbing
gently at the burns and, finally, kissing them.

'There. Is that better?'

'Much better. Would that I had burned myself in
more places.' He drew her to sit on the sofa beside him,
his arm around her and her head resting on his shoulder.

His newly cleaned hand wandered, caressing and exploring the contours of her face, stroking her neck, and twisting the springing curls between his fingers. He felt with wonder how the pulse throbbed in the hollow at the base of her neck, and lowered his head to kiss the place while his hand strayed lower yet, and hesitated. She took it in her own, and kissed it again before placing it on her breast.

'That is what I wanted to do. . .that day,' he murmured. 'I was ashamed that I should think of taking advantage of your weakened state. I could almost have died of longing to hold and kiss you then, and I dared scarcely come near you. I thought you must sense it, and be still more frightened.'

'Frightened? Of Augustus, perhaps, though there was scarcely time for fear, but of you? Never! If I had not been so embarrassed I could almost have thrown myself into your arms there and then! But you looked at me so strangely, and I thought you were disgusted by me.'

'So far from being disgusted that I could scarcely prevent myself from continuing what the wretched Hatherley had started. Perhaps it is just as well that you did not throw yourself into my arms, after all! That is not the way I want things to be for you, my darling. But I warn you, I shall not be patient for long. Thank heavens you have no covey of female relatives to fuss around and say that you must have at least six months to prepare your bride-clothes.'

'No. Only Mrs Ruspidge. Oh, Marcus, I am very sorry, but I am afraid she will be a dreadful nuisance! She will be sure to want us to invite her, and the girls, to your house, and before we know where we are she will be expecting us to give balls for their come-outs,

and I know not what! I am afraid we shall never be rid
of her!'

He looked a little daunted by the prospect.

'Then there is nothing for it but to go abroad at once.
Now that the war is over, there is nothing to stop us
from travelling, and our honeymoon may well be
stretched to several months. By the time we come
back, she will have forgotten all about us, with any
luck.'

She doubted it, but reflected that, though she could
not altogether cast off her stepfather's wife, she should
be in a position to dictate, to a certain extent, the terms
of their relationship.

'And what about my school, my lord?' she teased
him. 'Do not forget that you promised me a school.'

'Well, by the time you have helped Miss Cameron to
care for Cleone, Sophie and Minty, and Mrs Ruspidge
to instil some manners into her three, I hope you will
have little time to miss your teaching too much. There
is a school on the estate, of course, which you will be
able to oversee to your heart's content, and then,
naturally, there will be our own nursery and schoolroom. Will that not suffice?'

'I suppose it will have to.' She gave a pout of
pretended disappointment, which was an invitation to
be kissed again that he did not refuse. 'Of course,' she
said when she could, 'I am really only marrying you to
save myself from having to travel in the stage-coach.
Never have I known such a contrast! That, you know,
was my first taste of luxury, to be travelling in your
carriage, and naturally I made up my mind there and
then that I should live like that always.'

'Of course you did. There is nothing more delightful,
to my way of thinking, than to be shut up in a moving

coach for several hours with three great, restless girls, one of whom is forever in hysterics, another who is a positive gabble-monger, and a third who threatens to be sick every time you go round a bend. No wonder you could not resist me, when I could offer such delights.'

'Well, it seemed very wonderful to me. I expect I shall shame you, for the first few years, by displaying far too much enthusiasm for everything, like a true country miss.'

'*That*, of course, is why I mean to take you abroad,' he informed her with great seriousness. 'And, naturally, to cure you of this habit of trying to look after every young girl who crosses your path. I want to look after you, for a change, even if it means I must put up with you giving me little lessons all the time.'

'Lessons? When have I ever done so?'

'Well, not lessons, precisely. But you are so extremely well educated, my dear, that it is quite alarming. You will have to be careful you are not taken for a bluestocking.'

She laughed.

'But it was you who quoted poetry, not me! I own I was very impressed, for while naturally I am acquainted with the poem that contains my name I scarcely expect others to be so familiar with it.'

'Ah, yes, poor Addison.'

'Poor? Why so?'

'He had no idea, did he? He confused the thing with the person.'

'I do not understand you, Marcus.'

'In my inept way, I am trying to pay you a compliment, my dear. It is not — though do not tell Cleone I said so — music that is "*the greatest good that mortals know*",

' but Cecilia, of course. "*All of heaven we have below*", and I have found it.'

'We have found it,' she corrected him, raising her face once more for his kiss.

HERITAGE OF LOVE
Sarah Westleigh

Life was hard in the Devon fishing village where
Charlotte Falconer tried to keep her vulnerable family
afloat, but it was her mother's death that caused a real
catalyst, when Charlotte discovered she was not the
child of the man she had always called father!

Victorian social mores were strict, and she had no
expectation that her real father would ever acknowledge
her. What she couldn't guess was that the secret
relationship would cause untold damage between her
and Francis Longford, an intriguing American
businessman, who found Charlotte's warmth and
sincerity charming, her attitudes so different to those in
his own circles . . . until he overstepped the mark and
alienated Charlotte!

An irresistible offer for you

We'd love you to become a regular reader of Masquerade. And we will send you 2 books, a cuddly teddy bear and a mystery gift absolutely FREE.

You can then look forward to receiving 2 brand new Masquerade historical romances every two months for just £1.70 each. Delivered to your door, along with our regular Newsletter featuring authors, competitions, special offers and lots more. Postage and packing is FREE!

This offer comes with no strings attached. You may cancel or suspend your subscription at any time and still keep your FREE books and gifts. It's so easy. Send no money now but simply complete the coupon below and return it today to:-

**Mills & Boon Reader Service, FREEPOST,
PO Box 236, Croydon, Surrey CR9 9EL.**

— — — — — **NO STAMP REQUIRED** — — — ✂—

YES! Please rush me 2 FREE Masquerade historical romances and 2 FREE gifts Please also reserve me a Reader Service subscription. If I decide to subscribe, I ca look forward to receiving 4 brand new Masquerades every two months for only £9.00 - postage and packing FREE. If I choose not to subscribe, I shall write to yo within 10 days and still keep the FREE books and gifts. I may cancel or suspend my subscription at any time simply by writing to you. I am over 18 years of age.

Ms/Mrs/Miss/Mr _____ EP50M

Address _____

_____

_____ Postcode _____

Signature _____

mps
MAILING
PREFERENCE
SERVICE